Pyrrhic Victoria

STICKY
NOVELS
BOOKS TOO GOOD TO PUT DOWN

Pyrrhic Victoria

THE COST OF VICTORY IN LOVE'S WAR

Jade Green

Pyrrhic Victoria

Contemporary Fiction - Fiction.
Erotic Drama - Fiction.
LGBTQIA - Fiction.
BISAC Codes
FIC049030 FICTION / African American & Black / Erotica
FIC056020 FICTION / Hispanic & Latino / Erotica
FIC005070 FICTION / Erotica / LGBTQ+ / General
FIC005010 FICTION / Erotica / BDSM
FIC031080 FICTION / Thrillers / Psychological

Pyrrhic Victoria
Story Created By: Jade Green
Book Cover Concept: Jade Green
Book Cover Design: CapriAGE
www.instagram.com/capriage
https://www.facebook.com/capriage

Printed in the United States of America

First Edition: June 2024

10 9 8 7 6 5 4 3 2 1

READER ADVISORY

This novel is dedicated to the little girl who was not medically diagnosed or properly treated. The under-dog who beat the odds and became responsible for everyone's happiness except her own. The dream maker, who deferred her own dreams. Who sings for the songbird? Me, and this book is my song to you, my sweet girl. XOXO

-Jade

CHAPTER
One

VICTORIA'S TURNING POINT

The ice-tinged air and the ringing of the distant hand-held bell provided a backdrop of holiday serenity, while Santé's penis, nestled in my throat, made it difficult for me to breathe.

My heart may have been full of hope, but my mouth was full of dick. Fortunately, I had years of experience attempting to swallow Santé Sabatino's eleven-inch Puerto Rican Pinga. By contrast, I had only recently dared hope to win his love.

Who would have imagined me, Victoria Robbins, ass-up, hunched over the gear shift of a Toyota Camry? Christmas shoppers traversed the parking area of the popular retailer while, just feet away, my tongue traced the head of Santé's dick for the tenth time. I sincerely hoped the customers and store employees of the Audubon, New Jersey, 'Bigstore' would remain oblivious to the unassuming, blue Toyota at rest in the desolate rear parking lot, steeped in the emerging evening darkness.

My spirit gushed with pure joy as I witnessed the scant, warm light of dusk reflected in Santé's amber eyes. The illuminated yellow overtones, coupled with his green undertones and red hue near the center, provided a hypnotic visual. His eyelids slowly lowered, half-masked from the succulent delight I offered. Unadulterated validation rushed through my heart as I heard him utter a deep, gratified moan, sounding like a cat's purr.

Santé's head was cradled by the beige leather headrest. My green eyes surveilled his every facial motion. Though he had become skillful at masking his more demonstrative signs of pleasure, his involuntary facial tics and muscle contractions unintentionally disclosed his euphoric bliss.

The natural flavor of Santé's dick was reminiscent of butterscotch and a hint of caramel. Despite the stiffness of his shaft, his flesh was tender as a fine delicacy. I was fully intoxicated. Pumping my mouth with increasing fervency, I was barely aware that my dominating Papi had destroyed one of my last personal boundaries… public shame.

All of my conscious energy focused on satisfying his manhood. I slurped and sucked on the dick I had studied for a decade. I was a woman of better-than-average intellect. Nevertheless, I was only tacitly aware of how far I had fallen. As he partially watched for strangers, I fully increased my suction, and I rotated my lips in circles around his dick, just as Papi preferred.

"Yeah, like dat. Suck that dick bitch." His light Spanish accent softened his language's coarseness, but not too much. I was with a bad boy, and I knew it. Temporarily, at least, I also knew that he had chosen me. My pleasure sensors were on overdrive, matching or exceeding his, despite the fact he was the only one receiving oral service.

Sucking dick in a random parking lot wasn't much gratification for most girls and woefully less for most women. However, for me, giving Santé Sabatino pleasure and having him with me, even for a fleeting moment of lust, meant everything to me. In December of 2018, I was naively unaware of the toll such encounters had taken on my self-esteem. I was even less aware of the impending, life-altering crossroads ahead.

CHAPTER
Two

LUNCH, LAUGHTER, AND LINGERING PAIN

My long auburn curls, lightly streaked with blonde, caught the wind, lifting like a cape behind me. An unseasonably cool breeze for August in Philadelphia enveloped me.

"Is that Miss Ross?" Patricia called from across the street, pulling me from my thoughts. I smiled as my bestie crossed to where I stood on the corner of Seventh and Chestnut.

Patricia looked effortlessly chic in a black Versace sweatshirt paired with baby-blue leggings. Her crimson lipstick was as bold as her attitude, always turning heads. Her whole look screamed confidence.

Embracing, Patricia teased, "I'm sorry, I thought you were Diana Ross with all that hair blowing in the wind. Too tall to be Miss Ross, though."

I laughed, loving the comparison to my lifelong paragon, and brushed a lock of hair behind my ear. "Oh, stop it. If I'm Miss Ross, you must be Monica's long-lost twin," I shot back, referencing her resemblance to the R&B singer, though Patricia was two shades lighter.

Patricia stepped back, giving me an exaggerated once-over. "Those gray leggings and that chenille sweater? Girl, you're slaying it. Only Victoria Robbins would be this coordinated mid-day."

I grinned, smoothing my sweater with a touch of drama. "Well, you know I had to step it up for lunch. It's been weeks since we caught up."

"I know, right?" she replied, linking her arm through mine. "Let's get inside before we turn into fashion statues."

Inside Lorenzo's, the restaurant buzzed with quiet elegance. Diana Ross's "Do You Know Where You're Going To" played softly in the background, adding both irony and a cinematic touch—not lost on Patricia.

"They're playing your soundtrack," Patricia mused as we followed the maître d' to a private, elevated table where sunlight spilled through oversized windows.

For the hundredth time, my life does not play out like a movie, but I'll take the compliment," I said, chuckling.

Settling into our seats, we scanned the menus as Vito, our waiter, approached to take our drink orders.

"I'll have a Lemon Perrier, please," I said.

"And I'll take a Diet Coke," Patricia added, flashing him a charming smile.

As we waited, our conversation flowed easily, ranging from her latest fashion finds to my whirlwind first month at Nybor Productions, punctuated by laughter and knowing glances.

Minutes later, Vito returned with our meals, the rich aromas swirling around us. Patricia took a bite of her risotto, her face lighting up.

"Worth every calorie," she declared, pointing her fork at me. "And your salmon?"

I smiled, lifting a forkful. "Crusted to perfection, as always."

As we ate, Patricia's playful smirk faded, her tone shifting. "So, you're a rich bitch now, huh? They had to pay you big, didn't they?"

I paused, setting down my fork. "No, Pat. I upgraded my condo and cleared debts. I'm not exactly rolling in it."

Patricia raised an eyebrow. "I'm not hitting you up for a loan. I just want to know if my best friend is filthy rich."

I shook my head, smiling. "Nope, not rich and not broke either. Trust me on that one. If I were broke, you'd know—we wouldn't be eating here. We'd be yelling our order into a clown's mouth at a drive-thru."

Patricia laughed but pressed on. "But really, you beat FexorMedia. Not many people can say that."

I sighed, recalling the stress of the lawsuit. "Yeah, improbable as it was, I spanked that ass. They thought they could steal from my small production company and get away with it. But after months of court battles, they settled." I tilted my head. "I miss being my own boss, but at least I can breathe easier now."

I sipped my Perrier, letting the tartness linger. "But trust me, Pat, I didn't win 'buy a yacht' money."

The conversation shifted. Patricia leaned back, her face growing serious. "Three dates in four months, and none went anywhere. I'm running out of time, Vicky. I want a family, a husband… and it feels like the chance is slipping away."

I reached for her hand. "You still have time. We're not that old."

"Bitch, speak for yourself, I'm older than you," she countered, her voice heavy. "And I've had three miscarriages. Do you know what that feels like? Every year, the chances get smaller."

Her words hung in the air, heavy with pain she hadn't shared before. A twinge stirred inside me. *Should I tell her?* I opened my mouth but stopped myself. *Not now.*

"I'm so sorry, Pat. I didn't know," I said softly.

"I didn't want to talk about it. But it's been eating at me," she continued.

"When the time is right, I believe it'll work out," I said gently.

Patricia gave a faint smile, though it didn't reach her eyes. "Maybe. Or maybe not."

A familiar tune playing softly on the restaurant's sound system caught my ear. "*Ooh na-na… ooh na-na-nev'r let go.*" The melody tingled down my spine, and I knew tears were not far behind.

Though the volume was low, the tune was instantly recognizable. My stomach churned as if doing somersaults. Memories of early mornings filled with anticipation and lonely nights steeped in longing flooded my mind.

Patricia noticed the change in my expression. "So, we're not going to talk about him, are we?"

"There's nothing to say," I replied, keeping my eyes on the table. "It's just a song."

But Patricia wasn't fooled. "Girl please, It's not just a song for you. If it were, you wouldn't still react like this every time you hear it."

I sighed, pushing the memories back down where they belonged. "It didn't work out, Pat. That's all there is to it."

Patricia shook her head, her voice firm. "He left you. You gave him everything, and he walked away."

"I don't need a man," I said, more to convince myself than her.

Patricia arched an eyebrow."Uh-huh. And I don't need these truffle fries, and you know how much we both love truffles." I smiled as Patricia continued, "Besides, as long as men carry the dick, we'll always need men…"

I joined her, and we finished in unison, "…because we both love dick!"

We dissolved into laughter, the tension breaking as we leaned on each other, both physically and emotionally. The heaviness lifted, if only for a moment.

We finished our meal, toasting with our non-alcoholic drinks—two independent women navigating life's messy terrain.

As we left Lorenzo's, the city's noise wrapped around us once again. But that song—"Never Let You Go," by the pop star who'd once seemed to soundtrack an entire generation—and all the feelings it stirred, stayed with me.

A bittersweet reminder of what I'd lost, and maybe, what I still wanted.

CHAPTER
Three

COMMAND AND CONFLICT

The floating elevator gently landed on the fifth floor, and as the mirrored doors slid open, they revealed my workspace within the television production juggernaut, Nybor Productions Inc. The black, beveled granite underfoot gleamed, and my heels clicked against its sleek opulence.

The cascade of water greeted me as I passed the twenty-foot marble slab in the waiting area—a steady stream falling before Nybor's signature logo. Cool bluish-white lighting added to the grandeur, a reminder that Nybor was no ordinary production company. I allowed the space to settle my nerves, momentarily appreciating the elegance of my new workplace.

The moment's peace shattered as I neared my office and saw Beth Kerrigan, my secretary, standing in front of it—fidgeting with her hands, her dark brown hair a mess, pale skin even paler under the cold lighting. At just 5'4, she seemed even smaller than usual, her posture tense as though bracing for bad news.

"There you are, boss," she said, her voice tight. "I was hoping you'd come back soon."

I didn't know what the fuck she was talking about. However, one thing was clear: I couldn't allow her incoherent freakout to continue outside my office. Glancing to ensure no bystanders were nearby, I grabbed Beth by the elbow and instructed firmly, "Get in here," before opening my office door.

The glass-and-steel walls gleamed in the late afternoon light. Once inside, Beth collapsed into nervous rambling. "You haven't been here long, but you've done more than he has in four years..."

I closed the door lightly, aiming to calm her and keep the matter private. I silently prayed, "Lord, please don't let me have a psycho for an assistant."

Positioning myself near my transparent desk, I asked, "What's going on with you?"

Beth stepped forward, words tumbling out.

"It's Ken. He's been...

"Ken's been... what?" I prompted, my tone steady but coaxing.

Ken Rutherford—or Ken-Doll, as I privately called him—was a man who could charm any room, but his ambition was sharp as a knife. Beneath the polished smile lurked biases he let loose when management wasn't around.

Beth hesitated, then stammered, "He's been undermining you—making himself look good at your expense. He's making sure Mr. Murray knows whenever you're out of the office. Implying you're always gone, that he's the one doing the real work."

I folded my arms. "Thank you for telling me."

"I didn't want him to succeed," she said. "You deserve this job. Not him."

Behind my composed exterior, calculations were already forming. Reacting rashly would only feed into Ken's plan.

Before I could dismiss her, Beth hesitated, shuffling nervously. "I... need to ask you something."

I folded my arms. "Go ahead."

"My car broke down, and I have to take the bus to pick up my son, Timmy, from school. Can I leave an hour early?"

"I wouldn't ask, but my mom's in a nursing home, and Timmy's only seven," she added.

For a moment, I noted the parallels—both of us managing aging mothers. I shut the thought down. My role wasn't to sympathize; it was to get the job done.

"Fine, but this is a one-time offer. If you ever ask me to leave early again, I will tell you to pack your personal items and never return."

Beth's relief was palpable. "Thank you, boss. I'll make sure everything's ready before I leave."

"Good. And get me the final numbers for the pilot by the end of the day."

"They're already on your desk," she said, pointing to neatly stacked folders.

I gave a quick nod. Beth took it as her cue to leave. The door clicked softly behind her.

I sank into my chair, fingers tapping rhythmically against the glass desk. Ken Rutherford was already on my radar, and now his petty games had my full attention.

THE FOLLOWING MORNING, I ARRIVED EARLY, TENSION COILING tight beneath the polished surface of Nybor's gleaming floors. Paul Glick's retirement wasn't just news—it was ammunition, ricocheting through the office, splitting alliances with every whispered word and sideways glance.

Ken had been preparing for this moment since the day I stepped into this place. His polished exterior might fool some, but I'd seen the knife beneath it. He'd been undermining me with precision, his every move designed to paint himself as the only contender.

As I approached the conference room, my heart was a steady drumbeat, my thoughts laser-focused. Ken wouldn't waste a second. The rumors about Paul's health had emboldened him, and I could feel his confidence bleeding through the walls.

Inside, there he was, the smug asshole. Lounging like a king on his throne. His crisp white shirt and tailored blazer screamed effort, his calculated casualness designed to needle. His eyes locked on me the moment I stepped through the door.

"Good morning, Victoria," he said, his voice slick with faux cordiality. "Big changes coming. Heard about Paul?"

I didn't give him the satisfaction of a reaction. Sliding into my chair, I felt his gaze linger, an almost physical pressure. The air between us crackled—tension, competition, and a mutual understanding that only one of us could win.

Then Mr. Murray entered, shutting the door with a finality that cut through the unspoken war in the room.

"We'll get straight to it," he said, his tone all business. "Paul Glick is retiring at the end of the month. That means we need to decide who will take over as Vice President of Production."

Ken leaned forward, every inch of him exuding smug anticipation. He was a predator circling prey, practically vibrating with the opportunity.

"This will be a thorough process," Murray continued, his gaze flicking between us. "You're both contenders, but we're also considering Grace Ambrose."

Grace. I kept my face neutral, but inside, my thoughts shifted gears. She was competent, sure, but her skills didn't measure up to either of ours. She was the third wheel in a two-person race.

Ken didn't hesitate. "With all due respect, Terrence," he said, leaning back in his chair like he already owned the room, "I've been preparing for this. I've got the experience and the vision to take Nybor to the next level."

Murray didn't so much as blink. "Experience is one thing, Ken, but leadership is another. This isn't just about the damn numbers. It's about who can bring out the best in their team."

Ken's smirk deepened, his eyes sliding to me with just enough edge to make his intentions clear. "Of course. We'll see how everything plays out."

His voice dripped condescension, but I let it roll off me. If he thought his little games would unnerve me, he didn't know who the hell he was up against. My grip tightened on

the armrest, my resolve a steel wire pulled taut. If Ken wanted a fight, I was more than ready to bring it.

CHAPTER

Four

THE WOUNDS BETWEEN US

The stench of urine wasn't as prominent as it had been in the past. Nevertheless, it was a nursing home, and it seemed all such facilities had something in the handbook requiring the smell of urine to linger, even if only latently adrift in the air.

The decision to let Beth leave work early to visit her mother's nursing home weighed on my mind, refusing to dissipate. An entire week had passed, and yesterday, it struck me like a sudden gust of wind: it had been nearly two years since I last set foot in my own mother's nursing home. That morning, I finally accepted the uncomfortable truth. My avoidance was unsustainable, and so, there I was.

My relationship with Sarah Gardener Robbins, my mother, transcended convention. It wove a delicate web of complexities that frequently pierced me with searing pain. Contemplating our bond brought forth a swirl of emotions—an intricate tangle that was unpredictable, paradoxical, and as personal as my own signature.

Making my way past the bustling nurses' station, a twinge of resentment simmered within me, aimed at Beth and her devotion to her mother. Undeniably admirable. But if not for her shining example, I wouldn't find myself in this place. "Damn that goody-two-shoes, Beth," I muttered, my steps carrying me toward Room 505.

In the dimly lit room, my mother lay in the first bed nearest to the door. I paused in the doorway, silently observing her for a few fleeting moments before she registered my presence. Her voice croaked with inquiry. "Is that you, Vick?"

I forced a plastic smile and responded, "It's Vicky, your daughter, Mother."

With a flicker of recognition, she whispered, "Of course. I would know my baby anywhere, no matter how long it's been since I've seen my precious child."

The room crackled with unspoken conflict. My mother's voice trembled. "My eyes aren't what they used to be. Baby, don't be distant. Come closer."

Alarm bells rang in my mind, urging me, *Run, bitch, run.* But my mother's soft encouragement drew me forward, and, defying reason, I inched closer to her hospital bed. Machines surrounded her, their presence imposing, though none were connected to her during my visit

I was tempted to offer empathy, but the scars of our shared history acted as barriers, leaving me suspended in a state of conflicted emotions.

"So, what brings you to these parts?" my mother questioned.

I answered truthfully, "You crossed my mind, and I wanted to check in with you, that's all." I observed her struggle to sit up in bed.

She smiled, saying, "No matter what brought you here, I'm glad you'll spend time with me."

A pit formed in my stomach. "Mother, I won't stay long," I declared.

My mother strained her neck to look at me. "You don't have to rush off. There's no line of visitors waiting," she sighed.

I dragged the wooden chair from the corner, placing it by her bed. Taking a seat, I braced myself for the inevitable flood of emotions that would accompany our time together.

The hospital blanket rustled as she shifted. "Have you signed those power-of-attorney papers yet?" she asked. "It's been years since I asked you, and now I need someone to handle the medical stuff, you know."

I winced at her nerve. "Isn't it something? Me being responsible for your medical decisions, when you never were too concerned about mine."

My mother flinched but quickly recovered, offering a dismissive shrug. "It is what it is. Someone's got to do it."

I leaned back, exhaling through my nose. "I'll take care of it, but…" I stammered before the truth leapt from my mouth. "This was a bad idea."

My mother's face crunched into a harsh frown. "What'cha just say?" she asked daringly.

"Bad timing. I've got work," I said curtly, trying to cut the conversation short. "Deadlines to meet, people counting on me."

She sighed—a deep, tired sound. "You're always working, always too damn busy. Funny how, with all your changes, that's still the same."

I stayed silent, unwilling to take the bait. The last thing I wanted was a full-blown blowout in the nursing home, but I could feel the tension building, as it always did between us.

She shot me a knowing look, one that dripped with bitterness.

Without another word, I rose and turned toward the door. Pausing just long enough, I said, "We'll speak again, Mother, but for today, I'm done."

My mother's voice spilled from her room. "Bye, baby. You come back soon, ya hear?"

I moved briskly into the cold hallway, which felt like a sweet release—though the tension between us followed me like a bitter aftertaste that refused to fade.

CHAPTER
Five

FOUNDATIONS AND FUTURES

The muffled sound of bouncing clothes from my dryer filled the background as I folded laundry, phone pressed to my ear. Patricia's voice came through light with a hint of curiosity.

"So, you're really thinking of moving to New Jersey, huh?" she asked.

I sighed, folding a towel. "Well, if I get the VP of Productions job, I'll finally be making enough to consider it."

Patricia's teasing tone crackled. "You've had enough money to move for a while, Vicky. Why are you still in North Philly when you could be living it up in Jersey—or at least the suburbs?"

My eyes drifted to the image in my mind of the kitchen I'd worked hard to renovate—gray cabinets, quartz countertops, everything tailored to my vision. "I like it here. My condo's paid off. I didn't want to bite off more than I could chew."

"Okay, your place is great, but it's still North Philly," Patricia quipped, her laughter popping like popcorn. "You've got enough to move to a safer area, and we both know it."

I leaned on the folding table, the faint lavender of the softener drifting in the air. "It's not about the money, Pat. I used the settlement to make this place mine. It's small, sure, but I'm not paying a mortgage every month. Moving's a big decision."

"I get it. You want security," Patricia said, her tone softening. "But don't you think it's time to aim higher? You've basically turned that place into a mini-penthouse. You should be living in the real thing by now."

I smoothed a wrinkle from the towel in my hands, a faint smile touching my lips. "Maybe. But I want to make sure everything's stable before making any big moves. You know how I am about planning."

Patricia chuckled. "Yeah, yeah. But admit it—you're thinking about Jersey because of someone who works over there."

I rolled my eyes. "Oh, stop, Pat. I'm not moving just for Santé."

She laughed. "Key word: 'Just.'"

I let the subject drop, though my thoughts lingered. Moving had always been a dream, but I couldn't shake the need for more certainty before making a major change.

Before I could dwell, Patricia shifted abruptly. "Speaking of changes, I have a confession."

"Okay, what now?"

"I joined a dating site," she admitted.

That caught me off guard. "Since when?"

"A month ago. I've been needing some dick," she said boldly before adding. "It's been… interesting, but there's this one guy, Jagger. He's not my type, but I think he'd be perfect for you."

I raised an eyebrow. "For me? How?"

"He's cute, funny, a pretty boy—right up your alley. You've always loved pretty boys."

I paused, an old pain tugging at me as I folded another towel. "I loved one pretty boy, and look where that got me."

"Vicky, that was the wrong one. Don't let Santé ruin all pretty boys for you."

"I don't know," I replied, trying to envision a new chapter in my life but feeling hesitant.

Patricia's tone lightened again. "Just think about it. I'll give him your number."

A knock at the door interrupted us. "I've got to go. Mr. Livingston's here for the final kitchen adjustments."

Patricia snickered. "Go handle your handyman. Just don't reach for his wrench and grab his dick instead."

CHAPTER

Six

SUNKEN SENSATIONS

The day had been long, and the week even longer, with work keeping me on edge as the battle for the VP position loomed like a dark cloud. Visiting my mother in the hospital added another layer of stress. Though I hated to admit it, her health weighed on me, complicating my already tangled emotions.

I needed an escape—some kind of release from the tension that had been building for weeks. As I walked into my bathroom, the luxury of the space felt like a reprieve from everything outside. The room was my sanctuary, the one place where I could let go, even if just for a while.

I unwrapped the towel from around my body, letting it fall to the marble floor. The cool air kissed my skin as I stood there for a moment, taking in the peace of the room—the soft scent of fresh tulips in the vase by the tub, the gentle flicker of light from the chandelier above.

The soft glow of the glass-block window let just enough light filter in, adding to the atmosphere I had carefully curated. This was my space, where my investment had paid off in spades. The unique environment where I could push away everything—work, loneliness, memories—and just be. Or at least, try to.

I climbed into the tub, sinking into the warm water as the scent of lavender oil filled the air. My long legs disappeared into the liquid oasis. Very quickly, I felt more than relaxed; I became amorous.

I reached for the remote, and the ceiling-mounted television flickered to life. I flipped past the usual channels. I knew what I wanted. It was time to reunite with porn star Alex Jones.

The porn superstar, Alex Jones was the kind of man who knew what he wanted. He had exactly the type of energy I craved. The water jets hummed quietly, and I let myself sink deeper into the tub, allowing the imagery on the screen to blend with the steady warmth of the water.

As Alex's massive dick swung across my screen, my mouth watered like a leaky faucet. I watched as his tall, masculine, and agile body laid dick to his female sex partners with the precision of a carpenter and the energy of an athlete. In an instant, a spark of envy ignited a flame of lust, warming me deep inside.

I allowed my fingers to gently explore my tender opening. Increasingly warm inside, I closed my eyes, letting the sounds of Alex's powerful voice fill my head.

Intermittently, I peeked at Mr. Jones' naughty performance. Curiosity and longing transfixed me to Alex's every motion. Tingles rushed throughout my body, but so did frustration. I tried to imagine what it would feel like. I allowed my mind to drift with visions of Alex—at least, that's what I wanted.

But, when I closed my eyes the sixth time, flashes of Santé crept into my vision. His face, his beautiful dick, but most of all, his stunning eyes. The way he used to look at me, that maddening mix of lust and distance. It was frustrating how he still had this hold over me, even in the quiet of my own mind.

I sighed, shaking my head as I realized the video wasn't working. My disconnection from my body and my attachment to Santé was an unfortunate reality. He was still there, lingering in the corners of my thoughts, no matter how hard I tried to forget him.

As the water jets softly sent bubbles rippling through the tub, I sank deeper beneath the surface. Alex was fucking feverishly toward his finale. My eyes widened as Alex manhandled his co-star moving her into the doggy-style position and pumping her pussy from behind.

After a few intense moments, Alex pulled out for his cum shot. His beige sex rocket throbbed just as he erupted in grand, fluid glory.

Cum burst forward and both he and his female co-star were elated. I longed for the lustful passion and the rawness of such a sexual experience.

I turned off the television but stayed in the warm tub for a while, just floating, trying to push away my lack of sexual satisfaction. But when I finally pulled myself out of the water, grabbing the towel and wrapping it tightly around me, I knew something had to give.

Maybe Patricia was right. Maybe I did need to stop hiding behind work and allow myself to experience something, even if it was just a distraction.

The idea of going out with Jagger still didn't sit well with me—Patricia's sloppy seconds, really? But at this point, I wasn't looking for love. Just a night out—and maybe a little more.

Leaning closer to the mirror, I muttered to myself, "Desperate times, right?" With a new sense of resolve, I decided I'd go on that date with Jagger. After the past few weeks, maybe that's exactly what I needed.

ENTER JAGGER

Before arriving at the restaurant, I exchanged a few text messages with Jagger, the enigmatic man I was about to meet. His description of himself—wearing a casual blue shirt and denim jeans—eased some of my pre-date jitters, but only slightly.

Dressed in denim-colored leggings and a sweater that hinted at just enough cleavage, I carefully applied evening-style makeup to accentuate my pale green eyes. Dating felt foreign to me—far removed from the boardroom, where I thrived.

I arrived at the upscale steakhouse, heart pounding from a mix of excitement and nerves. Timing my arrival ten minutes late felt like a delicate balance—interested, but not too eager.

A handsome young man with a thin mustache greeted me warmly at the entrance. "Will anyone be joining you tonight?"

"Yes, my guest is already here," I replied, scanning the restaurant for Jagger. "His first name is Jagger, but I must admit, I don't know his last name." My face flushed slightly at the admission.

The host chuckled softly, checking the reservation list. "Ah, here it is—Mr. Jagger... Latham." I smiled at his subtle release of information and followed him through the restaurant.

As we weaved through the tables, the anticipation grew. When we reached a secluded circular table, even before he rose, I knew the man in front of me was Jagger. Patricia's description had been remarkably accurate.

Seated, Jagger still gave the impression of being tall, just over six feet. His olive skin and wavy black hair added a touch of exotic allure. His deep brown eyes held an intensity that hinted at layers beneath the surface.

Rising to greet me, he smiled, his blue cotton shirt fitting perfectly, accented by a bold red tie. A gold link bracelet caught my eye—left wrist, no ring, no tan lines. Finally, my eyes wandered, lingering briefly—decent size bulge... not bad.

"Victoria?" he asked.

I smiled. "Yes, but you may call me Vicky. Nice to meet you." I extended my hand, expecting a handshake, but Jagger took it and gently kissed it. His lips lingered longer than expected.

"Nice to meet you, Vicky," he said, pulling out my chair with chivalrous grace.

Once seated, the courteous waiter approached with menus, adding to the softly lit restaurant's enchanting atmosphere. I studied the choices carefully—ribeye steak or pork chops? Ultimately, I opted for a grilled chicken salad, though the allure of the steak was hard to resist.

As we savored our meals, I found myself surprisingly at ease. Jagger spoke about his work at a security company, sharing stories of chasing down would-be thieves. His eyes lit up as he talked about the adrenaline of it all, and his dream of starting his own security firm.

"I've been thinking about it for a while," he said, excitement in his voice. "But with regulations, insurance, and all that, it's not as easy as just hanging up a neon sign."

"I imagine," I said, intrigued by his ambition but staying quiet enough to keep some mystery.

Dessert arrived, and Jagger inquired about my past relationships, a question I swiftly dodged. "Mmmm," I purred, dragging out the sound as I raised a forkful of caramel-coated cheesecake to my mouth. "This... this is amazing!"

Jagger appeared to get the message, posing a more interesting question. "So, Vicky," he asked, leaning back slightly, "what's your idea of a perfect day?"

I smiled, letting my imagination take over. "A perfect day for me would start under pink satin sheets on a California king-size bed, gently waking up to the sound of waves just outside a Malibu beach house. I see myself looking at the pale blue Pacific Ocean through a sliding glass wall, fully open to let in the tranquil breeze."

His eyes stayed fixed on me as I continued, "I'd take my morning orange juice on the balcony just outside the bedroom, maybe reading a good television script, and sipping on a glass of Domaine Blain-Gagnard Le Montrachet Grand Cru."

Jagger's eyes widened, his expression amused and baffled. "What—The—Fuck—Is that?"

I laughed, delighted. "It's the best white wine France has to offer."

He grinned, shaking his head. "Oh, you're fancy, huh?"

We both laughed, and the tension dissolved. I realized how different we were, yet the conversation flowed naturally.

His version of a perfect day was far simpler—waffles and strawberries for breakfast, a long, relaxing shower, basketball, and a candlelight dinner, ending with a romantic walk on the beach.

Then he asked, "I noticed in your perfect day, there's no man involved. Any particular reason?"

The question gave me pause. I glanced down, gathering my thoughts. Slowly, I met his gaze. "That's because, despite my strong desire for companionship, the man who would share that day with me... hasn't arrived yet."

A shift in the atmosphere signaled that my words had landed. A silence settled—not uncomfortable, but thoughtful.

Jagger eventually broke it with a soft confession. "Love's tricky, huh? I was married once... had a daughter." His voice took on a bittersweet tone. "Haven't seen her in two years—things got ugly. Court didn't go in my favor."

The pain in his voice was palpable, and I felt a pang of empathy. I reached across the table and placed my hand on his. "I'm sorry, Jagger. That must be incredibly difficult."

He nodded, eyes distant. "There's not a day that goes by that I don't think of her. I just want to be in her life, you know?"

I offered a gentle smile. "I hope things change for you one day. It's clear how much you care."

As the evening drew to a close, Jagger paid the bill, and we stepped outside. The cool night air wrapped around us as we walked to the parking lot. There was something easy about the way we moved side by side, yet underneath, I sensed that elusive spark was missing.

When we reached my car, a chirping sound drew my attention to a blue Charger parked beside my 300C—both Chrysler products. I hadn't even noticed it when I arrived, but now it was clear—it had been there the whole time. For a fleeting moment, I wondered if it was some kind of sign, a subtle connection waiting to be acknowledged. But as Jagger pulled me into a warm, lingering hug, I couldn't ignore the truth. He was kind, good-looking, and driven—everything a woman should want. And yet, deep down, the spark just wasn't there.

Driving home, I replayed the evening in my mind. Jagger was a great man, no doubt. But no one had managed to replace the shadow of my past love left behind.

As the traffic light flicked to green, I couldn't shake the thought. Could anyone fill the void left by Santé?

CHAPTER
Eight

CRISIS AND CARE

A stroke? My keys fell somewhere between the couch cushions, and I frantically searched for them, trying to process the news. Life could change so quickly, moving toward disaster with alarming speed. Finally, my fingers wrapped around the metal, and I sprinted to the door, barely remembering to lock it behind me before rushing to my car. The evening with Jagger had been pleasant, almost perfect, but now it felt like a distant memory as panic took over.

Just a few blocks more, and I'd be at the hospital. The red lights I'd managed to avoid were finally catching up to me. The woman on the other end of the phone wasn't much help, though. Her robotic tone didn't match the gravity of what she'd just told me. "Miss Robbins?"

I remembered my hand trembling as I asked, "Yes, this is Miss Robbins. To whom am I speaking?"

"This is Miss Cayuga. I'm a nurse at your mother's nursing facility. I regret to inform you that your mother had a stroke this evening."

Another red light. The last thing I needed. My mind swirled with fragmented memories of my mother's first stroke, how she was found on the apartment floor, helpless and alone. And now, this. She had nurses now. How could this happen again?

Finally, the light turned green, and I sped forward, my hands tightening on the wheel. Chestnut Hill Hospital loomed ahead. The TD Bank sign to my left showed the date and time: 11:47 PM, Friday, September 14, 2018.

THE HOSPITAL SMELLED OF JANITORIAL SUPPLIES AND OLD CARpet. As I approached the front desk, a plump woman looked through the patient records, her brow furrowed.

"I can't find your mother," she said.

I sighed, trying to stay patient. "She had a stroke earlier. They said she'd be here."

"Oh! There she is. Your mother's in our step-down unit," she finally confirmed.

I glanced at her name tag. "And where is your step-down unit, Carol-Ann?"

She paused, then chuckled, "Girl, don't get me lying. Oh, wait, I remember now. Go down the hall, walk to the end, and make a left. You'll see a phone on the wall—just lift it, and they'll let you in."

I nodded, exhaling, and followed her directions. The hallways seemed to stretch longer than they should have, the sterile smell clinging to my senses. At the end of the hall, I picked up the phone, and a voice answered immediately.

"Who are you here to see?"

"Sarah Robbins."

The doors swung open after a mechanical click, and I was greeted by Nurse Turner, a heavyset woman with a no-nonsense demeanor. She led me down another corridor, the beep of machines growing louder.

MY MOTHER'S GAZE MET MINE AS SOON AS I ENTERED HER room. "You're finally here," she said, her speech slightly slurred but still sharp enough to cut.

I swallowed the mixture of concern and anger rising in my chest. "What are you babbling about? I came here as soon as I got the call."

She didn't miss a beat. "I've been here since three this afternoon. Numb arm, tingling lip—it passed. Not that it matters."

My irritation bubbled over. "That's it? That's all? I rushed through the streets—" I stopped, realizing I'd said too much, but the words were already out there.

She scoffed, her face hardening. "I'm sorry to have inconvenienced you with my 'small stroke.' The next time I stroke-out, I'll have a massive one so it'll feel worth your time."

I stood there, speechless for a moment, anger clashing with guilt. "I didn't mean it like that," I muttered, the words hollow even to me.

"You never mean it like that," she said, her tone icy. "You always find a way to make everything about you, anything to push me away."

I couldn't hold back the venom in my response. "I'm here, aren't I? If I took longer than you expected, maybe I learned how to delay medical necessities from you."

She closed her eyes, as if trying to collect herself. When she opened them again, she said, "I want to go home."

"Home?" I asked, my mind racing.

"The nursing home is my home. I have friends there. Melvin—he's my boyfriend."

I raised an eyebrow. "Boyfriend, really? Well, at least you have a boyfriend. Thanks to you, my options are limited."

She didn't even flinch. "Have you signed the power of attorney papers yet?" she asked, brushing off my bitterness.

"I'll sign them when I get back to the nurse's station," I replied, my voice cold.

I leaned down, my eyes locked on hers, and said with a calm but cutting edge, "You should hope I do a better job being the guardian of your medical care than you ever were for mine."

My mother's expression was blank beyond the contemptuous eye roll and thick, lingering silence.

Nurse Turner returned, breaking the tension. "It's after midnight. Visiting hours for the ICU are over."

I nodded, turning to my mother. "I have to go, but we'll talk again. Trust me on that."

She gave a slight nod, her expression unreadable. Without waiting for more, I turned and left the room, the sound of medical equipment fading as I walked down the long hallway. The echo of my footsteps matched the thoughts swirling in my head—conflicting emotions tangled with resentment and guilt.

AT THE NURSE'S STATION, I LEANED AGAINST THE COUNTER, gathering my breath. "My mother mentioned something about a power of attorney," I said, my voice feeling distant, even to me.

The nurse on duty looked puzzled. "Let me check with the supervisor," she said, disappearing briefly before returning with another nurse—her name tag read Indira Martin, Supervising Nurse.

"Miss Robbins?" Indira confirmed, her voice calm but professional. I nodded.

"Your mother wants you to sign a power of attorney?"

"Yes," I replied.

Indira smiled kindly. "We don't handle that paperwork here. I recommend contacting a family lawyer. Once it's signed and notarized, we can add it to her medical file."

I nodded. "Thanks. Do you know when she might be discharged back to the nursing home?"

Indira gestured to another nurse, Judith, who was typing at a nearby computer. "Judith can check her chart."

Judith scanned the details. "Your mother's stroke was mild, thankfully. But we'll need to monitor her for a few more days. Once she's stable, we'll arrange for her transfer back to her facility."

"Alright. Please keep me informed," I said, my impatience barely hidden.

As I left the nurse's station, the hospital's sterile environment seemed to suffocate me. My mind raced with thoughts of my mother and the power of attorney hanging over my head like an unspoken promise.

The night outside felt just as heavy, and as I pulled away from the hospital, the memory of the flashing TD Bank sign came back to me as a timestamp: 11:47 PM, Friday, September 14, 2018, forever memorializing the turn in my mother's health and the countdown to our inevitable confrontation.

CHAPTER
Nine

A SEAT AT THE TABLE

"Good morning, boss. How was your weekend?"

I glanced up from my desk to find Beth standing in the doorway, her smile bright and eager. It was 7:40 AM—too early for pleasantries. I preferred to warm up by 10 AM. But Beth's morning cheer was endearing, so I forced a half-smile.

"It was okay," I replied.

Beth, always perceptive, seemed to sense my lack of enthusiasm. "I'll get your cinnamon tea and the focus group results for The Chantel Sisters," our newest pilot.

"Thank you," I murmured as she left the room.

Today was Monday, and there was no time for weekend reflections. I had work to do, and more importantly, the VP announcement looming in the back of my mind.

Just as I turned to the pilot budget for our Queens New York shoot, Beth knocked again, this time with a look of urgency that piqued my curiosity. She didn't buzz the intercom as she normally would.

"Come in," I called.

Beth stepped inside, breathless. "It's time."

"Time for what?"

"The announcement. They're naming the new Vice President of Production in twenty minutes."

My pulse quickened. So, it was happening. After a week of silence, the decision had been made. I stood, trying to calm the excitement bubbling beneath the surface. I confirmed, "Twenty minutes, boardroom?"

Beth nodded. "Twenty minutes. Boardroom.

THE BOARDROOM FELT ELECTRIC, THE AIR THICK WITH ANTICI-pation. I took a seat near the end of the polished mahogany table, discreetly rubbing my lavender-scented wrists to calm my nerves.

Robyn Jade Green, chairwoman of the board and the face of Nybor Productions, entered last. She wore a striking Richard Tyler velvet pantsuit; her sea-foam green eyes swept the room with a model's gaze. Her ice-blue diamond necklace caught the light, casting a glint of brilliance that seemed to amplify her presence. Robyn wasn't just a figurehead—she was the embodiment of power and success in an industry dominated by men. Every time our eyes met, I felt both humbled and empowered.

To my left, Grace Ambrose sat poised, her cool demeanor a mask for uncertainty. She was the other candidate for the Vice President of Production role, though her lack of confidence was evident.

Across the table sat Ken Rutherford, wearing his arrogance like a second skin, leaning back as if the decision was already in his favor. Rumors on the elevator suggested Mr. Murray himself had said Ken had all the experience for the role.

Ken's smug grin deepened as he caught my eye, radiating a silent challenge. He'd always believed he was the natural choice.

The tension in the room mounted as the board settled in. Dale Cassen, the oldest member, reeked faintly of brandy, his red face and disheveled appearance providing brief levity in the charged atmosphere.

Sharon Bolen adjusted her glasses, her wrinkled face a symbol of her decades of climbing the corporate ladder. She nodded at me briefly, a small but meaningful acknowledgment.

Earl Thomas, a tall, imposing African-American man, exuded quiet authority. His focused gaze betrayed no emotion. Then there was my boss, Terrence Murray, who thumbed through his notes briefly.

Finally, the room quieted as Mr. Murray cleared his throat. "After much deliberation, the board has come to a decision."

My heart raced, the anticipation unbearable. I glanced at Ken, who straightened in his seat, his cocky smile, boldly displayed. Grace remained rigid, her eyes fixed ahead.

Mr. Murray looked directly at me. "Victoria, it is my pleasure to announce that you will be taking on the role of Vice President of Production."

Time seemed to stop. The words sank in: I had done it.

Ken's face twisted in disbelief. "What? You said—" His voice sputtered, but Mr. Murray raised a hand.

"Ken, you are an asset to this company, no doubt. But Victoria has demonstrated the vision and leadership we need. It's her time."

Across the table, Grace's stoic expression flickered with frustration.

The board members murmured amongst themselves while the announcement sank in. My head spun.

This was more than a title—it was validation. Everything I'd fought for. All the late nights spent on budget reviews, sacrificing the autonomy of my own small operation to join Nybor, and the silent battles fought behind the scenes to ensure shows ran smoothly—it had all led to this moment.

The position of Vice President of Production was mine, in a little over a month. It was only up from there—or so I thought.

AS THE ROOM SLOWLY EMPTIED, I FOUND MYSELF FACE-TO-FACE with Robyn Jade Green. Her necklace sparkled under the lights, casting reflections around the room.

"Robyn, your necklace is stunning," I said, unable to help myself.

Robyn smiled, touching the diamond lightly. "Thank you, Victoria. It was a special gift to myself," she shared, her eyes reflecting a deep, personal journey. "A reminder that it's okay to love others, but ultimately, my heart belongs to me."

Her words struck a chord, leaving me momentarily lost in thought. It was a simple statement, yet it carried a world of meaning. I found myself pondering the powerful statement. The depth of her self-assurance was something I admired; it was a powerful example of strength and independence.

Robyn's perspective, so elegantly expressed, unsettled me, a puzzle my mind wasn't yet capable of solving. Why did her declaration, so simple yet profound, leave me feeling this way? The question lingered, a soft murmur in the back of my mind.

Shaking off the introspection, Robyn and I gracefully parted ways. Robyn's last words were, "I have my eye on you. Keep on your path."

I nodded and said, "Okay," not understanding the significance of her comment.

I stood, ready to embrace the challenges and opportunities of my new role. The path ahead was illuminated by the examples of those who had paved the way, like Robyn, whose legacy of strength and self-love would inspire me at every step.

This was my moment, a chance to leave my mark on Nybor Productions and prove that I was worthy of this position and ready to redefine it.

With a heart full of excitement and determination, I stepped out of the boardroom, the door closing behind me on one chapter and opening to another.

CHAPTER

Ten

THE RETURN OF TEMPTATION

The intoxicating warm water flowed over my head, a soothing cascade that celebrated my week's professional victory while simultaneously washing away the stress caused by the drought of men in my personal life. As the water enveloped me, I let out a contented sigh.

Haircare was next on the agenda, so I reached for my favorite product: OptiMoist Shampoo from Ellin LaVar Textures. Savoring its familiar, sumptuous scent, I applied it generously to my long curls. Running my fingers through my hair, I worked up a rich lather, relishing the soothing sensation on my scalp.

Practicing self-care amidst the chaos of life was essential.

Five minutes later, I felt the unmistakable squeak of my hair between my fingers—authentically squeaky clean. Next in the routine: Ellin LaVar Textures SatinSoft Conditioner. I saturated my hair with it, popped on a plastic cap, and headed for my computer.

I settled in front of my laptop, ready to unwind and prepare for a restful Sunday evening fast approaching. But just as I was about to dive into the digital world, the doorbell rang, shattering the tranquility. An unscheduled intrusion annoyed me, forcing me to abandon my desk and return to my bedroom, where I could monitor the front door through security cameras.

I had no particular expectations about who might be at the door—most likely someone with the wrong address, as I rarely entertained drop-in visitors. My guests always had prearranged visits, and everyone knew it.

As my eyes locked on the security monitor, a rush of sensations coursed through me. Panic surged momentarily as I questioned whether my eyes were deceiving me. But there he was, unmistakable. Santé Sabatino, standing at my front door after two long years.

Euphoria mixed with adrenaline surged through me, a joy I hadn't felt in years, coupled with an unexpected sense of relief. Santé's absence had left a void in my heart, and now, in an instant, hope of fulfillment.

I quickly grabbed my pink Versace robe—the companion to the one I'd bought Santé for his birthday a few years back. Heart racing, I sprinted to the front door. I knocked lightly to signal him to wait a moment, fumbling with the locks in my eagerness to see him again.

Finally, the door swung open, and there he was—Santé Sabatino, in the flesh, as vivid as ever.

Wearing a yellow-and-black number six jersey and ball shorts, Santé effortlessly palmed a basketball. His signature grin spread across his face, his amber eyes sparkled, and for a fleeting moment, all the time apart seemed to melt away.

"Hey," he said, his voice stirring emotions within me as it always had.

I managed to utter a single, breathless word in response. "Hi."

But even as elation flooded through me, I couldn't ignore the pain he had caused.

I murmured, "It's been two years, Papi." The words felt heavy on my tongue, even heavier in the lonely chambers of my aching heart. In that instant, I wasn't the strong business executive who had just been promoted to Vice President of Production. She had vanished, leaving behind a younger, more fragile version of me—the one still struggling to process the sting of abandonment.

"You left me, Papi," I said, the burn in my chest threatening to consume me. "And you broke my heart." My voice cracked as I recited the words from his cold email, the ones that had never stopped replaying in my mind: *Don't email me anymore.*

Santé stepped across the threshold of my door, and in doing so, walked back into my life. My eyes tingled as I listened to his explanation, thin but grounded in practical reality.

"She found your email," he said softly. "I had no choice."

My glassy eyes lowered as I struggled to determine if his return was genuine. Was this real?

The soft click of the door closing behind him offered no answers—just a clue, and an echo.

FIVE MINUTES LATER, WE WERE TALKING INTERMITTENTLY, OUR conversation punctuated by long gaps of tender silence. I told him about my new job, and I learned he had officially moved to New Jersey—a move that made sense, given he had worked there for years.

I considered mentioning my plans to move there too, but second thoughts held me back. I didn't want him to think I was stalking him. Instead, I simply congratulated him.

Silence returned, and as I considered the distance between us, I found myself wondering if some twist of fate had brought him here to give me the closure I needed but dared not seek.

Then I realized Santé was still standing just inside my door.

"I'm sorry. I'm being rude. Do you have a minute to sit?"

Santé nodded. "Yeah, I got a minute."

We walked over to my couch and sat down.

"Sorry, I was conditioning my hair. I must look a mess," I said.

Santé looked at me with those piercing, x-ray eyes that seemed to read my soul. "It's new—when'd you get it?"

Confusion scrambled my brain, and I felt my face tighten. "My hair?"

"The couch," he clarified, tapping lightly on the gray suede. "You had a peach leather couch before. This one's new."

"Oh, yeah. I got it last year."

"Nice," he said, nodding appreciatively.

"Thank you," I replied, a small degree of awkwardness creeping in. Santé and I rarely made small talk, and the unfamiliarity of it unsettled me.

"Why'd you give up your own company to work for someone else?" he asked.

"Expenses," I explained. "I was making money on paper, but I had a lot of overhead. The media market has changed. Unless you've got a Netflix deal or an in with a network, independent productions are tough."

Santé appeared to understand—or did a very good job faking it.

The conversation shifted to what he had been doing during our time apart.

"Basketball, kids, and work," he said simply, adding, "I also swim now. It's relaxing."

Santé's swimming was new information—a reminder of how little I had really gotten to know about him over the decade. We generally shared brief conversations and glimpses of our lives after moments of intimacy—moments I still cherished.

"Would you mind if I rinsed the conditioner out of my hair?" I asked, adding, "I feel awkward."

"I don't mind, but you look great." he said, flashing me a 100-watt smile.

My cheeks warmed at his compliment.

"Thank you, Papi," I said softly, lowering my head shyly.

Santé waited patiently until I lifted my head. Then he caught my eye and asked softly, "Did you miss me?"

The understatement in his question was jarring. How could he not realize the emotional and mental fracture his abrupt end to our affair had caused me?

Then it occurred to me—it wasn't Santé who found me crying in the Whole Foods Market, surrounded by produce I had dragged down with me as I slid to the floor. It was Patricia.

So, I dared not tell him how missing him had consumed my thoughts to the point where I hit rock bottom—or how much effort it took to rebuild myself, to focus on even the simplest tasks, like earning a living.

Uncertain whether he would offer comfort or simply revel in a boost to his ego, I chose not to reveal the heartbreaking details. Yet lying to Santé was also not an option.

So, I nodded and simply replied, "Yes, Papi, I missed you." Once more, my eyes fell involuntarily, again revealing the vulnerability I tried to suppress.

OVER THE DECADE OF OUR CONNECTION, SANTÉ AND I RARELY spent much time together, despite my constant craving to do so. He was always on the run—basketball practice, his job, and a few years into our relationship… her.

So, when he offered to sit on my couch while I rinsed and dried my hair, the experience felt almost surreal.

When I stepped out of the bathroom—hair clean and silky, towel in hand—and approached my living room, I hoped I hadn't merely conjured Santé's return.

To my sheer delight, the man who had been my sole romantic interest for over a decade was sitting on my couch, wide-legged and ready to talk.

A joy bubbled up from a deep space within me, one I had almost forgotten existed. My love-filled, shimmering green eyes met his amber-and-sea-foam beauties, and, as if on cue, we both giggled.

I sat beside him, and silence returned. Vulnerable but tempted to trust, I felt my eyes caught in a battle—shifting between downward demureness and careful contact, moving up and down with each of our words.

"I've thought about you... a lot," he said, his voice slow and deliberate. I wanted to believe him, but I was confused by the contradictions.

"It felt like... like you threw me away," I protested gently.

Santé shook his head, a kernel of annoyance flickering across his face. "I told you—she caught us. I had no choice. I didn't wanna break up with you; I had to. But now I'm back. The past is the past, so what's up?"

I had forgotten how focused and intense Santé could be when he wanted my attention. He hadn't yet asked for us to return to the familiar dance of our affair, but he seemed on that path, while I hesitated, still seeking answers to heal a broken heart.

I stammered and stuttered, unable to form a single question despite my desire for answers.

Santé, in contrast, was direct. "I was thinking we could start again," he said, his eyes lingering on my lips.

My head considered saying no—or at least not now—but my heart wanted to say yes immediately and figure out the details later. Despite all my external progress since Santé's absence, my core was still inexcusably naïve. In that space, I sought healing from the very one who had hurt me. I needed an emotional band-aid—a justification.

"So you didn't mean to break my heart?" I asked.

Santé's smirk returned, and a hint of mischief danced in his amber eyes. "No, I didn't mean to break your heart."

He edged closer, the light traces of his manly musk filling the air between us. "Like I've said, I've thought about you a lot." He lightly ran his index finger across my bottom lip, his touch soft yet unmistakably masculine.

His words and swagger were enough to make my heart warm, but the comment he made next gave me pause. "One of the things I think about the most is how you used to suck my dick." My heart fluttered as he added, "No one in this world can suck my dick like you Vicky—I miss that." His words resembled a confession.

To my surprise, a surge of longing welled up within me, and before I could stop myself, I admitted, "I miss that too."

"You think we could start again?" he asked.

Confusion and conflicting emotions engulfed me. Then Santé continued, his tone soft but insistent. "It's not too late for us, is it?" He lightly groped his dick. I saw the outline move just under his ball shorts, he appeared half hard.

My resolve weakened, and the wall I had built around my heart during his absence crumbled into pieces. My unhealed place lay bare, unable to shield my raw vulnerability with subtext or codewords.

I pushed my sexual desire down, the unhealed pain demanding attention. Unfiltered, and with a child's innocence; my voice spoke for every abandoned heart. "I thought you were never coming back, Papi." My voice was bleak and shaky.

Daring further, I confessed, "I thought I'd never get a chance to say goodbye to you."

With my emotional floodgates opened and my eyes welling, I fought hard to hold back the torrent of tears pressing against my lower lids.

Santé moved closer, his presence magnetic, and touched my hand gently, reassuringly. "No, you don't have to worry about that," he said. "It's never goodbye; it's always 'see you later.'"

His words stirred a potent blend of hope and doubt, pulling me toward him despite the risks. I wanted him as much as he wanted me—probably more. But I needed time.

"I don't think it's too late for us, Papi. But if I open up to you again, you can't leave me like before."

He didn't address my words directly, offering only a vague condition. "I don't want her to find out about us again," he warned, seeking my complicity in his deception. His words subtly confirmed what I had already suspected—he was still with her, his girlfriend Jackie.

I didn't want to lose him again. I couldn't bear the thought of enduring years without seeing him all over again. So, I made a desperate choice: I chose to embrace the fragile possibility of happiness with him, even if it meant turning a blind eye to his relationship with another woman.

As he hugged me tightly before leaving, I dreaded his departure. In his embrace, I felt whole. A flame reignited within me, and I was unwilling to extinguish it, no matter the complexities.

When he reached for his basketball and asked for my new number, I recited it with a smile. We were back together—or our version. Feeling like a schoolgirl with a crush. I craved a chance at love, at being chosen by him.

At that moment, I allowed myself to believe the improbable—that he could love me too. I committed to the dream of emerging victorious in the battle for Santé's heart.

CHAPTER
Eleven

NEW HEIGHTS, NEW CHALLENGES

All ten fingertips touched the enormous window wall as I leaned forward, almost imagining I could fly over the panoramic view of downtown Philadelphia, seven stories beneath me. The view I'd always admired from the boardroom was now mine—one floor higher.

A phenomenal vista and a corner office on the penthouse floor were some of the spoils of my victory. As Vice President of Production, I'd finally arrived. There was no time to bask in it, though—I had my first meeting with my junior vice presidents to get through.

The meeting was a success. My new team reported updates on projects in development, particularly the stages of production for three television shows and one film in pre-production. For a smaller company like ours, without the financial clout that publicly traded studios had, it was an ambitious slate.

The faces around me were familiar: Grace Ambrose, Andy Paulson, and, of course, Ken Rutherford. Ken and Andy shared a notable trait—both were legacy hires. But while Andy carried his with humility, proving himself both a creative asset and a prudent manager, Ken saw his inheritance as an entitlement.

As the meeting adjourned, Grace approached me with a quick, "I just want to congratulate you on your new position."

I said, "Thank you, Grace. I look forward to working with you in my new role."

She nodded quickly and left, a touch of sadness evident in her eyes. I wondered if she'd held on to hopes of getting the promotion despite the clear signals at the board meeting.

Next up was Andy. He stayed behind to discuss production ideas, and I mentioned my admiration for his climb up the ladder. "Writing experience," I said, "really positions a producer for television—so much relies on strong storytelling."

Andy grinned, admitting, "It wasn't easy becoming executive producer, but it didn't hurt that my brother was the star of the show." His humility and gratitude shone through, making him someone I could see as a valuable ally.

After a warm handshake, which he bypassed with a quick, genuine hug, Andy gave me a look of real excitement. "I'm really glad to be on your team, Victoria," he said, his energy infectious.

Then there was Ken. To my disappointment, but not surprise, he remained seated, radiating defiance. I refused to let him drive me out of my own office.

I walked past him, calm and measured. "Please close the door to my office when you leave."

Ken's eyes narrowed as he met my gaze. His voice dripped with contempt. "So, affirmative action wins again."

I approached him, gaze unyielding. "I'm only going to say this once. You will show me the respect I deserve, or you will be unemployed and escorted from the premises. Do I make myself clear?"

Ken's lip curled in a sneer as he rose slowly to his feet, saying, "The only thing that makes this experiment bearable is that it's temporary. You'll fail because this title was handed to you. It's meaningless—and it will be mine."

Then, with a look of triumph, Ken turned, heading for the door as if the conversation was over. But as he reached the doorway, I called after him, my tone sharp.

"Your boss has not dismissed you."

Ken stiffened, halting mid-step. He turned back, defiance in his eyes. I closed the distance between us, and within seconds we met nose to nose. Leaning into the doorframe, my voice had a steely edge. "Your entitlement and arrogance are nauseating, Ken. But your talent, I can use. That's why I'll keep you here."

His expression hardened as I leaned in, one hand firmly on the doorframe. I added, "Know this, Ken. The moment your arrogance exceeds your talent, you'll be looking up at this office from the sidewalk."

I let the silence stretch between us before saying, "Your boss is done with you—Now, you are dismissed!"

He stormed out, my office door thudding shut behind him. I turned back to the window, taking in the view—my view. I'd earned it

CHAPTER
Twelve

TWO HARD TRUTHS

I sat in my executive office suite, surrounded by the unique blend of pink and black decor, feeling the soft leather of my oversized chair against my back. The view from my seventh-floor window gave me a bird's-eye perspective of Philadelphia's cityscape. The sight usually calmed me, but today, unanswered questions buzzed in my mind.

Beth's voice broke through the intercom. "Victoria, Patricia's on line two. Do you want me to put her through?"

"Yes, thanks," I said, pressing the button to connect the call.

A moment later, Patricia's familiar voice filled the room. "Miss Vicky," she greeted. "You've been quiet lately. I'm calling to make sure you haven't fallen off the face of the Earth."

I smiled despite myself. "I've been swamped, Pat. You wouldn't believe it."

"Try me. Start with why I had to hear about your date with Jagger from him instead of you," she teased, her tone playful but pointed.

I sighed, standing and walking toward the window. "There's not much to tell. He's nice, but... it just didn't click."

"Nice?" Patricia pressed. "He checks all the boxes!"

"And yet, there was no spark," I said, steering the conversation deliberately.

Beth's voice interrupted over the intercom again. "Victoria, Roger Wilcox is on line three. He says there's an issue with Megan refusing to leave her trailer over script changes."

I pressed the hold button to pause Patricia's call. "Tell him I'll handle it in a minute. I delegated that issue to Ken Doll, and either he dropped the ball, or he's trying to make me look bad. I'll take care of it."

"Got it," Beth said before the line went silent.

Switching back to Patricia, I said, "Now, where were we?"

"I was waiting on an explanation of what you have against Jagger," she quipped.

"What? Nothing, girl, you're not going to let this go, are you?"

"Nope," Patricia said, her tone shifting. "Especially not since I'm going out with him on Friday."

I stopped mid-step, caught off guard. "You're taking him back already? I thought you didn't want him."

Patricia hesitated for a beat. "He asked, and I figured, why not? I wasn't sure how you'd feel about it, though."

"I'm surprised, but maybe he was right for you from the beginning," I said, just as an unexplained chill ran down my arm.

"Thanks, girl. I just didn't want it to be weird."

"It's not weird," I replied quickly. "I want you to be happy."

Sensing an opening, I hesitated only briefly before saying, "There's something I *do* need to tell you."

"What is it?"

"Santé... he's back."

The line went quiet for a moment, then Pat's voice rang out,"That motherfucka? Vicky No. You're serious? After everything he put you through?"

I sighed and returned to my chair, wrapping my hands around the still-warm cinnamon tea mug. "I know. But seeing him brought back so many feelings."

"But Vicky, don't you remember what happened in the supermarket?"

I paused, meeting the memory head-on. "We don't need to revisit that. Trust me—I remember."

Patricia's voice carried a note of hesitation. "I just don't want you to get hurt again. You deserve someone who sees your worth."

"I know, Pat. I'll be careful," I promised, taking a sip of tea, the heat brushing against my lips.

Patricia's tone softened. "And thanks for not flipping out about Jagger. I wasn't sure how you'd react."

"It's fine," I said quietly. Then, before switching over to Roger's call, I glanced out the window at the city below, my thoughts lingering.

Pat deserved happiness, and maybe Jagger could give her that. But if they really hit it off, what would happen to us?

The chill returned, creeping up my arm as I pressed the button to switch lines. "Roger," I said evenly, "tell me exactly what's going on."

CHAPTER
Thirteen

A LOVER'S TASTE

The moon's soft glow bathed the parking lot below as I sat by my kitchen window, my plans of sleeping in late long forgotten. It had been just a little more than a week since Santé reappeared in my life, and already, he was exerting his influence over my decisions. I was joyful waiting for my forbidden lover despite the fear that one day he might not return.

The scent of lavender filled my condo while the pulsating beat of Jeremih's "Don't Tell 'Em" played through my speakers. The music seemed to mirror my emotions, and I could feel my dopamine levels rising as anticipation built.

As his familiar truck pulled into the parking lot, my heart quickened. I noticed that I had set the song to repeat, inadvertently emphasizing its significance in this moment. It felt like a soundtrack to this pivotal scene in my life.

With my gaze fixed on Santé's truck, memories of our encounters through the years flooded back. It was a cycle I had repeated for years—the anticipation, the temporary reward, and the inevitable loneliness that followed. But this time, as Santé stepped out of his 2005 Chevrolet Suburban, I couldn't help but wonder if things could be different. Could I finally win him over?

Showtime had arrived, and I knew that my choices over the next few moments would shape the course of this rekindled connection. I steeled myself for whatever lay ahead as the moon's light continued to cast its ethereal glow on the unfolding drama below.

I HAD TAKEN MY ASSIGNED POSITION, ON MY KNEES, IN FRONT OF my unlocked front door, anticipating the man I loved. I knew he would be walking through the door horny as ever and in only a matter of moments. It had been two years since I had the delight of his taste.

As the sound of footsteps approached, my heart quickened. Seconds later, Santé, my Papi, entered with a confident stride. The sight of me, submissive and eager to please, seemed to delight him.

Santé shed his lime green sweatshirt without a word, captivating me with every move. My breath hitched as he tugged at his belt buckle, and I couldn't tear my green eyes away as he approached. Clutching the pale gray fluffy rug , I felt a mix of excitement and anticipation. When his shoes reached my hands, he halted, and my heart raced, watching him loosen his belt.

Santé stepped out of his pants and casually strolled over to my couch, discarding his socks haphazardly on the floor. Once he reached the center of the sofa, he had already removed his underwear with one swift move. Seeing him toss his boxers on the floor and watching his huge eleven-inch dick jump up like it was spring-loaded left my mouth involuntarily watering.

Soon, the back of his calves grazed the gray suede of my couch—he was bare and uninhibited. Suddenly, those legs were on the move—towards me. Once I was between his legs, I felt an overwhelming and inexplicable sense of belonging—I had finally returned home. I allowed my nose to graze his balls, inhaling slightly. I was intoxicated by a hint of his male musk.

My heart raced, my palms sweaty, and my breath hitched as my love and obsession gazed down at me. His mesmerizing amber eyes held me captive, adorned with a seafoam green outer ring and accents of light red around the pupils, leaving me spellbound.

I licked his balls gently, my tongue circling clockwise, always clockwise first. After a few tantalizing moments, I took his nuts into my mouth, and a low-pitched purr escaped him as he took a deep, intoxicating breath. Locking my gaze with his, I felt an overwhelming blend of love and lust surge through me. At that moment, I belonged to him, and I imagined he belonged to me, if only for that fleeting, passionate moment.

His familiar fleshy taste invigorated my pallet and enveloped my mouth. With the area wet and sloppy, I used my tongue to outline the rim of his dick's head. Then, I flickered my velvet pleasure pillow down the base of his Puerto Rican pinga. When I felt his leg twitch, I took that as my cue to devour his manhood whole.

I felt Santé pulsating in my mouth and noticed his hands trembling. In our shared ecstasy, possible consequences were forgotten, and time seemed to bend to our will, allowing our magical moment to stretch out, unhurried and unbridled.

Fifteen minutes had passed as I dutifully bobbed and slobbed upon Santé's dick. I loved altering my speed, suction, and technique on the man I loved. Santé Sabatino became the center of my universe, consuming my focus and existence. I could tell from his parted lips and slightly masked eyes that he, too, was immersed in ecstasy.

A sense of gratification washed over me, filling me with inspiration. Santé attempted to muffle his moans, but some still slipped past his lips. His eyes, once half-masked, were now fully closed in the blissful abandon of the moment. He was lost in the overwhelming pleasure.

My pussy was wet, but remained concealed by my pink satin pajama bottoms. I dare not reach inside them to touch myself. This moment, like so many before, was about Santé and his pleasure. I was also carrying a secret that had remained unspoken for years. So my attention returned to sucking Santé with ferocity.

As certain as the rhythm of my own heartbeat, I was sure Santé was close to his climax. The countdown had begun. Within a few seconds, his fountain of manhood would flow. The only question remaining was whether to prepare for a geyser or a leaky faucet.

Approaching the finality of our session and after deep-throating Santé to my maximum capacity, I slowly lifted, allowing a coat of drool to glisten over the head of his pretty, pulsating penis. I gently pushed my lips together as if preparing to whistle. Instead, I blew warm air on the head of his wet dick.

I jerked off the man of my desire at increased speed. Santé's thigh muscles convulsed. His head rocked back and forth. His moan returned louder and longer in duration.

"Don't stop," he insisted. Santé's body jerked, and he announced what I already knew, "Ahh, I'm cumming!"

Heaps of white joy juice leaped from Santé's dick. One huge dollop landed on my tongue. His bitter-sweet flavor invigorated me, but the sight of Santé' spent—fully relaxed, filled me with a comforting sense of satisfaction.

For almost an additional three minutes, I would bask in the warmth of his presence before the familiar fear of his absence would return.

CHAPTER
Fourteen

DESIRE AND DUTY

I stepped off the elevator onto the seventh floor, greeted by the familiar aroma of lilies and the low buzz of office chatter. My heart was still buoyant from the morning's rendezvous with Santé.

Beth looked up from her desk, her brow lifting. "Boss, you're late, you okay?"

"Traffic," I said, brushing it off with a smile.

She smirked. "Ken stopped by twice. Then he went to see Mr. Murray."

The mention of Ken instantly deflated my mood. "Did he say why?"

"No, but you know him," she replied with a shrug.

I nodded. Ken's reputation for stirring trouble was well known, but Ken-Doll wouldn't ruin my day. "Thanks, Beth," I said before heading into my office.

Once inside, I took a breath, shutting the door behind me. Ken could wait. I wouldn't let his scheming overshadow the spark Santé had brought back into my life.

Settling at my desk, I dialed a number for one of our longer-running productions. "Ms. Robbins, Vice President of Production," I began. "Hey Leo, do you have time to pitch your ideas for season three?"

The conversation unfolded smoothly, anchoring me in work. I stayed focused, immersing myself in the production schedules and show developments. By mid-afternoon, I felt accomplished, despite the undercurrent of tension caused by Ken.

As the workday wound down, I passed Beth's desk. "Thanks for everything today. I'll deal with Ken tomorrow."

"Good luck," she replied, flashing a knowing smile.

Stepping out into the cool evening air, I let the office politics fall away. A smile crept across my lips as I thought of Santé. My personal life, finally, felt alive again.

CHAPTER
Fifteen

I KNOW YOUR SECRET

The evening of Monday, September 17, 2018, was a day unlike any other. I finally escaped the bustling office and ventured home, my spirits soaring high. Oddly enough, the usual workplace irritations that ordinarily got under my skin seemed insignificant. Even Ken's attempts to anger me failed miserably.

I managed to breeze through the day with both productivity and politeness. It was as if some unseen force had granted me a reprieve from life's annoyances.

However, my elation soon waned, replaced by an overwhelming sense of exhaustion as I dragged my weary body up to my condominium. I barely mustered the energy to check my mailbox, finding the usual pile of mundane envelopes waiting for me. Bills and advertisements mocked me, but one particular envelope caught my attention. It bore my name, written in familiar handwriting, but the sender left only one name—Santé.

An inexplicable shiver ran down my spine as I stumbled inside, collapsing into the nearest chair. The letter taunted me from the edge of the table, and without thinking, I tore it open with such haste that I nearly cut myself on the paper.

The message inside struck me like a bolt of lightning:

You've been hiding something from me. I know it. It's been ten-plus years together. Why haven't we ever fucked? You never want to get totally naked. Think I know what you're hiding. I want you to suck my dick tomorrow morning. I'll be there at 5 AM. This time, I want you to be completely naked. We don't have to have to fuck, but I do want to see your body. After all these years, you shouldn't be hiding anything from Big Dick Papi.

Panic surged through me, my heart pounding in my chest, and my hands trembled uncontrollably.

His words hinted at accusations and were demanding. Did Santé genuinely know my secret, or was he playing a sinister game meant to trap me? Was I in danger?

Unable to sleep, I knew I would be ready and waiting for him at 5 AM. A chilling ultimatum loomed before me. Be vulnerable, expose my deepest fears, or risk losing Santé forever.

Fear gripped me like a vice, and my mind was overrun with questions. How could he know? What if he intended to seek revenge for some perceived slight or lie? Was my safety in jeopardy? The uncertainty felt paralyzing, and I couldn't shake the sensation of impending exposure and vulnerability.

I had to decide whether to trust or retreat. Forging a profound connection or falling further into the shadows.

My mind raced, my heart conflicted, and the seconds ticked by relentlessly, driving me to the edge of my sanity.

As I stared at the letter, its words echoing in my head, I knew that whatever happened next, life as I knew it would change forever.

CHAPTER
Sixteen

BARE AND EXPOSED

Tuesday morning arrived with a glimmer of promise, but as the sun tiptoed over the horizon, its golden rays did little to calm the anxious storm brewing within me. Restless, I paced the narrow hallways of my condominium, feeling like a ghost haunting my own home after a sleepless night.

The promise of Santé's arrival at 5 AM weighed heavily on my thoughts, each minute dragging on like an hour. By 2 AM, I was in the kitchen, staring at the neon clock, willing time to move faster.

The fridge's soft glow spilled into the darkness, its faint light drawing my focus as I clasped and unclasped my hands.

My heartbeat pressed against the moment, every passing second a taut string on the verge of snapping.

Santé expected to see me nude. It had been ten years, and he hadn't seen me fully naked even once. It wasn't an unreasonable demand, but given my confidential complication, his ultimatum weighed on me like a ton of bricks.

I had lived thirty-six years managing to avoid revealing my secret. In a few short hours, that would all change. I had been so afraid of being judged, hated, and scorned that it was much easier to abstain from sexual intercourse.

I hadn't fully grasped how my decision to remain a technical virgin had trapped me in a state of arrested development. What I once romanticized as a symbol of virtue was, in truth, a mask for my fear.

I longed to trust Santé completely, but my secret stood as a barrier—not mere modesty, but something deeper, something I had kept hidden, even from myself at times.

Over the years, I had watched others navigate relationships and intimacy, sharing their joys and heartaches. I remained an observer, yearning for a connection I had never allowed myself to explore.

I had denied myself the tenderness of touch, the warmth of an embrace, the passion of shared desire. That denial became my shield against rejection or misunderstanding—and perhaps something worse.

In locking myself away, I had also denied the possibility of love—the chance to be seen and cherished.

My shield was not just from rejection, but from the misinterpretation of who I was. To reveal my skeleton would mean risking the distortion of my truth—a paradox, once exposed, that might never allow me to be seen for who I truly was.

Lost in these thoughts, I wondered how my exposure would change my relationship with Santé. Then, I saw Santé's Chevrolet Suburban pull up. Rising from my chair, I walked to the front door and unlocked it. As I headed to my bedroom, my leg began to shake involuntarily.

From my bedroom, I heard the soft sound of the front door opening and closing. I knew Santé was only seconds away. Sitting on my knees in front of the bed, I braced myself, every nerve throbbing with anticipation.

My heart skipped a beat as the bedroom door swung open. Santé's silhouette filled the doorway. He stepped inside with a smirk—not exactly warm, but inviting enough that half my fears began to melt away.

As Santé's eyes met mine, a burden I had carried for far too long lifted slightly. With him, there was an unexpected sense of safety—perhaps even acceptance—a novelty for me. In this intimate space, surrounded by the rawness of impending revelation, I found comfort in one simple truth: whatever happened next, I was no longer alone.

WITHIN A FEW STEPS, SANTÉ HAD CROSSED THE THRESHOLD into my bedroom and reached me at the foot of my bed. His magnetic presence filled the space. Despite his modest height of 5'9, he carried himself with a confidence that seemed to tower over me.

He looked down at me and asked, "Why are you wearing panties?"

I replied, "Because I want you to take them off me."

I thought he might be angered by my reply. Instead, he smiled.

Although he didn't strip me of my panties immediately, Santé removed his clothes quickly. Before long, he stood in front of me, beautifully naked.

My Puerto Rican Papi moved close to my face and slid his manhood down the center of my forehead just before dropping his dick across my nose, then down into my mouth. I opened wide, and he pushed his hard dick deep into my throat.

After five minutes of sucking Santé, I almost forgot about his demand for my nudity. That was until he removed his dick from my mouth and walked to the top of my bed. Santé said, "Bring that ass over here." I got up from my knees and joined him on top of my black fur blanket. "On your knees and arch your back," he instructed.

My face was securely nestled in his crotch, his balls across my nose. His dick pulsating on my forehead. Suddenly, he leaned forward, reaching over me. I felt my man's hands rub my ass, his hands were firm, yet his touch was tinder.

Pap!—An electric surge ran through my body as the sound of Santé slapping my caramel-complected ass echoed off my peach-colored bedroom walls. I reflexively called out, "Papi."

A few seconds later, the moment came. Santé slowly pulled my panties down—then completely off.

I inhaled slowly and exhaled even slower. To my relief, Santé had no visible reaction to my genitals. I wasn't sure what he could see. Most of his body still faced me.

Nevertheless, that moment was the first time in my entire life I had been fully nude in the presence of a lover. "Put my dick back in your mouth," he said. I complied eagerly.

I slurped and savored him passionately. I tried to translate my devotion through my tongue twirls, pulsating suction, and my wet, warm drool that fell gracefully from my lips down across his balls.

Before long, he placed me on my back and then sat on my chest. The head of Santé's dick consumed my vision, and behind that, upward, I glimpsed his mesmerizing eyes. Self-consciously, I cross my legs, suddenly aware of my nakedness.

Although he did not look behind himself, Santé was aware of my every move. He reached behind his back. Swiftly and forcefully, Santé pushed my legs apart. I was both surprised and turned on at the same time. Manhandled, I got the message. I was to remain just as he had placed me. I felt his power, and it encouraged my submission. It was a powerful reminder of what I missed during Santé's absence.

From my position, I had to work harder to please him. Santé slid his dick between my 38 double D breasts and titty fucked me before putting his dick back in my mouth for more of the face fucking he enjoyed delivering.

Before long, he had a rhythm and powerful strokes into my mouth, about five strokes, then fucking my tits six strokes.

Eventually, Santé focused exclusively on pushing his dick deep into my throat. He had long tamed my gag reflex not to overreact, but my lazy reflex could still be triggered whenever Santé went balls deep into my throat.

I had no room left in my mouth, and my throat had been stretched to capacity. Breathing was impossible. I would simply have to hold my breath with the determination of an Olympic swimmer. I didn't mind. I was committed to his pleasure and, thus, to mine.

Each time I felt lightheaded, he would pull his throbbing manhood from my throat long enough for me to capture a few precious breaths before repeating the process all over again.

A few tears involuntarily fell from my left eye. After several pounds to the back of my throat, he noticed my tears. "You alright?" he asked.

With no way to answer him verbally, I simply nodded my head and uttered an audible "Mm-hmm."

Satisfied, Santé continued his deep-throat-dickin.

Fifteen minutes later, I could tell Santé was about to climax. His legs tightened around my chest. The gyration of his hips increased with greater intensity. I looked into his face. He occasionally glanced down directly into my eyes, sending sensations through my body.

Finally, Santé's eyes widened, and the beautiful color palette of hazel and green shone like precious gems. His head lurched backward. He pulled his penis from my throat and out of my mouth. He stroked his manhood inches from my face.

Several licks later, Santé's body jerked, and he announced what was obvious, "Ahh, I'm cumming!"

Within a few seconds, his dick pumped cum like lava from a volcano. His warm, man milk leaped from his lust pole onto my face. A small portion entered my mouth. I could hear the pleasure in his moans and witnessed the convulsions of his body. His body tremors triggered my own mini-orgasm.

A few seconds later, Santé rolled off my chest and onto the bed and lay motionless. His bitter-sweet flavor invigorated me, but the sight of him spent and limp everywhere, except for his half-erect penis, gave me comforting satisfaction. I licked my lips, overwhelmed by his powerful bitter-sweet aftertaste.

Unaware of what the future had in store for us, I only knew that I had achieved my goal: Santé's contentment was temporarily complete, thereby rendering me complete in a manner that left me befuddled yet blissfully beguiled.

My awareness narrowed to a single, sharp focus as Santé lowered his face just inches from mine. Eye to eye, so close I could smell the mint of his toothpaste, the moment felt electric.

The warmth of his breath tickled my nose as his words reshaped my heart and pierced my soul. "Accept yourself. You're just fine."

In the presence of those simple, profound words, time seemed to stretch, giving my mind space to absorb the depth of his message.

Any lingering doubts about why I loved him dissolved into obscurity. For ten magnificent seconds, I felt truly accepted—for the first time in my life. Not only by Santé but, more astonishingly, by me.

As my fixed gaze followed Santé dressing, I couldn't ignore knowing it was the second time he'd done so that morning. Jackie's presence lingered like a shadow, her unspoken claim on him amplifying the precarious nature of our relationship.

My insecurities gnawed at me. *What did Santé really think of my genitals?* Where did I fit into his life? Would Santé truly accept me as he had implied in the moment—and as he had written in his letter?

Questions sprouted like unwanted weeds, filling my mind with curious clutter. Yet, as Santé prepared to leave, he reassured me he would reach out later. I nodded lovingly, without a single word crossing my cum flavored lips.

CHAPTER
Seventeen

SANTÉ SPEAKS

I had only told one of my friends about Victoria. Partly because of Jackie, but mainly because I didn't want complicated questions. Vicky's differences weren't immediately obvious, or offensive. In fact, Vicky was beautiful.

Her light-caramel skin was damn near flawless, and her pale-green eyes made my balls tingle every time I saw them.

One of my favorite places in the world was confidently above her, catching glimpses of her sexy eyes while watching Vicky slurp up and down on my big Puerto Rican dick.

I especially loved the times she would struggle and choke on me, it was the best, and she never stopped until my balls were empty and my dick was both sloppy and sleepy.

The sword swallowers from the best circus acts had nothing on my Victoria. Watching Victoria make my eleven-inch pinga disappear—with no teeth, always felt like having a VIP seat at the most incredible magic show—with a happy ending included.

I made it a point to get my dick sucked by plenty of bitches—on the regular, but with Victoria's sweet suction, her tongue's speed and softness, not to mention her snaking throat... let's just say—there was no place like home.

What I know for sure in this world was from the first time my soul settled back into my body after Vicky's two-hour dick sucking-séance... I was hooked. No matter how many times I left, I could never say goodbye to Victoria Robbins. At best, my absence always meant, "See you later."

I don't know if Victoria Robbins was the best dick sucker in the world. I can only say, she's the best I'd ever known, and my dick had been in more bitches mouth's than thermometers—so that's saying something.

But, don't get it twisted; the situation wasn't perfect, and I wasn't stupid. I caught the hints from the start—her height, large hands, and raspy voice. I kinda figured "she" might at least be partly a "he." So, keeping it real, I knew from Jump Street Vicky would be different from the rest of my side bitches.

But even with all that said, I wasn't prepared for what I just saw. What the fuck was that? Of all the possibilities, I never once thought my side bitch would have both a pussy and a dick. Funny thing—it was her pussy that surprised me.

Vicky put a real twist on everything with this morning's gender reveal. I decided not to make her feel some-kind-of-way about her body and I tried not to stare. But next time I got her naked, you can best believe I planned to take a better peek. The situation wasn't perfect, but it was better than I'd imagined.

I'm a straight dude who was wondering if I'd have to make some kind of exception for Vicky. Because the ladyboy thing? If that was real, I wasn't sure how I'd adjust to that long-term. Even trying would never have been a consideration before Vicky. Yeah, Victoria changed the game—prettier and more feminine than most women, of any kind.

It also helped that Victoria always tried to see me in my best light—kinda naïve, but she wasn't stupid. She was smart and strong, right from the start. She had her own money and used to be my boss. That's how we met. Victoria Robbins signed me to one of her first companies, her modeling agency—I was just eighteen.

Back then, I had a baby face, a rap sheet for fighting, and a huge dick that bitches couldn't stop licking and sitting on. My seduction game wasn't perfected at the time but fortunately, Vicky had a thing for me. I think it was my amber eyes that helped me first seal the deal with Vicky, and later many others.

Over time, I warmed up to the idea of professional chicks who could do things for me instead of attaching myself to a bunch of needy bitches always having their hands in my pockets.

Through the years, Vicky'd offer financial advice and even spot me a few dollars when I really needed it.

Bottom line? Victoria was the most loyal of all my bitches—with the possible exception of my number one... Jackie.

But Victoria's avoiding nudity, and no real fucking, eventually became a turn-off. I knew she was into me deep, so I figured her abstinence would last a few months—but a decade? That was madness. It also made me mad-suspicious.

I have to give it to the girl, though—Vicky's 'wait game' was epic. My respect for her discipline grew a few years back when I had to practice my own 'sexual wait game' or at least self-discipline, after my girlfriend found some emails.

I almost lost the woman I loved, Jackie Lopez. My Puerto Rican Princess and I were 'hot-n-heavy' at that point. She had a five-year-old son from another relationship, and we really bonded. For the first time, I felt like a real dad, not just a power figure like when my side bitches called me Daddy. A few years into the relationship, Jackie delivered our own son—two months later—she found dirty emails.

Emails between Vicky and me. Kay and me. Megan and me. Even Sheila and me, I think.

Those damn emails gave Jackie actual proof I was cheating on her for sure. I was cold-busted, and I knew it.

For the first time, I believed her when she said she'd leave me. So, I cut off all my side situations, including Vicky. To save my family, I gave in and locked down with Jackie.

Now, two years later, with the birth of our baby girl, I was ready to start fresh. So Jackie and I moved to Turnersville, New Jersey. My new house was closer to my job, amateur basketball team, and a local swim club. Plus, my kids could play in the park down the street without bullets whizzing by, which happened too often in the mean streets of Philadelphia.

But before I put Philly in my rearview, I planned to settle my suspicions about Vicky once and for all.

Days ago, I came back to Vicky as I had done many times before. But this time I had a purpose. I had to officially settle my suspicions and curiosities. I had to officially know if Vicky was one hundred percent woman or just a high fraction.

Regardless of the answer, I already made the decision to collect on that ass. After waiting a little more than a decade, Vicky owed me big time. Fuckin' her ass—at least once, was the goal.

I had fucked plenty of women up their asses, but I suspected like everything else about Victoria—it would be better. I had waited a decade to find out and now it looked like I could get the asshole and more—pussy—a bonus!

I was running behind schedule because I had hung out at Vicky's place longer than planned. Her skills did that to me sometimes. I could probably make up the time by taking a few Camden backstreets to work. After a two-year absence, Vicky deserved a few extra minutes here and there—at least for a while.

I was a few blocks away from my job when I smiled—no matter how successful Victoria had been in business she always showed me respect as her man. In fact, Vicky was a straight-up submissive with me, and I loved it.

I have to admit that sometimes, I'd find her constantly trying to please me a lil predictable and boring, but then I'd return to Jackie, with her frequent disobedience and disrespect. It made me appreciate my Victoria. Sometimes I'd wanna tell 'Jac', "You couldn't pay my bitch Vicky to speak to me like that. Respect me, whore!"

One of the reasons complicated men need a roster of side bitches, is that each of his side bitches should be best in at least one of the things he needs or loves most sexually. And within that list of things, at least one of his bitches must be super submissive. The kind of chick that will put her King first, above all else.

Over my entire adult life, Victoria Robbins was my super submissive, and that's always a comfortable place for a man to put his dick.

I knew that as long as I never gave her my heart, I'd be cool. My heart's been 'on-lock' for years; so fallin' for a side bitch wasn't a problem for me.

But if I ever fucked up and caught feelings that even rhymed with love, I'd be smart enough never to let any of them know. That went double for the bitch I'd been involved with the longest... Victoria.

Pulling onto Fairlane Road, I checked my extracurricular activities phone; 6:46 AM. I had made good time. Kay had texted:

Going out of town for work. Hope you have time for me when I get back.

I replied: *I will.*

Then I added two emojis—a smiling face and an eggplant.

Another text came through on my friends and family cell phone from Jackie:

Don't forget Junior's game.

If Jackie put as much effort into keeping a job as nagging me, we'd have some damn money.

I replied: *Got it.*

She texted: *Love you.*

Sure, she loved me. I guess that's why she couldn't be bothered to wake me up suckin' ma dick, the way Vicky would've.

That's cool. That's why I have Vicky, Kay, and the team.

But to keep my world spinning on its proper axis, I replied: *Love you too.*

Glancing in the rearview mirror, I still got it at twenty-nine. My amber eyes alone could pull the baddest bitches. God himself painted a masterpiece in my gaze.

Slamming the Suburban closed, I headed to the steel front door at the factory. I mentally prepped for the hard labor ahead, the kind of work that leaves a coat of sweat glistening on my body.

Fully aware of my love for Jackie and even more for my kids, I also had total clarity that I could feel deep in my balls. My inner truth was as obvious as oxygen, and without a hint of apology:

No matter my attachments, bonds, or amusements, my most loyal devotion was always to the man I had just glimpsed in my rearview mirror.

That self-devotion would always eclipse any love or affection I would ever have for anyone else in the rest of the world, for the rest of my life.

CHAPTER

Eighteen

MOMMY ISSUES

Enveloped in Santé's lingering musk, the thought of reaching out to my secretary Beth, revealing my intention to claim a personal day, teased my consciousness. Yet, ultimately, I chose a different course. I would dare to venture into the office late in the day and unannounced.

A curious thought gnawed at the corners of my consciousness as I luxuriated in the tender aftermath of Santé's acceptance and dick sucking delights. How might the trajectory of my life have diverged if I had tasted Santé's enchantment earlier in life? To be unburdened by the weight of judgment? Beads of perspiration formed delicate constellations upon my forehead, my skin flushed with a gentle warmth, and my abdomen muscles tightened in a bittersweet ache.

A burning desire surged within me. I suddenly had an insatiable longing to confront the bitch I occasionally called Mother. I was acutely aware that it was she who bore the responsibility for my anguish and torment and that knowledge was eating at my soul.

As the clock struck 9:00 AM, I stormed through the entrance of the nursing facility, paying no heed to the startled woman stationed at the front desk, my determination propelling me forward. The ascent to the fifth floor felt endless, tension mounting with every passing second.

At my mother's door, I paused, took a breath, and entered. Our eyes locked—a silent standoff.

I approached her bed, my words cutting through the silence. "Why did you spread the venomous lie that I was a boy?"

Her gasp was theatrical, a poor imitation of shock. Propping herself on her elbows, she replied coldly, "I thought you *were* a boy. I still don't understand what was going on with you."

Leaning in, I hissed, "Can you even fathom how badly you've fucked me up?"

Her response was a nonchalant shrug. "I suppose we never had that heartwarming mother-daughter chat, *did we*?" Her mocking tone burned in my gut.

"No! There was never any conversation," I snapped, my voice raw. "You left me lost and vulnerable. Worst of all, you burdened me with a false identity—a cruel deception, that affects my life to this day.

She turned away, her tone cold. "You don't visit me enough to complain."

"Why should I waste my time visiting you?" I shot back.

"Because I birthed you. That's why."

Her words hijacked the conversation as always. "You call yourself my mother, but what do you even know about me?"

Her expression faltered briefly. "Do you even understand the depth of your cruelty?" I pressed. "Because of your neglect and lies, I'm a thirty-six-year-old virgin."

Amusement flickered in her eyes. "Well, isn't that the most delightful news I've heard in ages?" she said, her smile cutting me deeper than words.

"Do you think I chose this?" I demanded.

"We all have choices," she replied smugly. "Staying a virgin is a wise one. Learn to accept a compliment."

Stepping back, I struggled to make sense of her callousness. "A compliment? You consider that a compliment?"

"Sex, my dear, is vastly overrated," she said, her voice dripping with condescension. "It only distracts from your true goals in life."

Her words, potentially wise, were lost on me. I was too overwhelmed by the rage and sorrow surging through me, leaving me lightheaded and trembling.

"Sex is only acceptable within marriage," she asserted.

A bitter laugh escaped me. "Marriage? I can't even get a man to take me on a date, let alone get a husband, and the man I sorta have—he's not even single."

Regret clawed at my chest as I realized what I'd revealed.

Her tone turned sharp and mocking. "Oh, well...my pride in your decision-making abilities didn't last long, did it?

Lil' Miss Virgin is whoring around with a man who already has a woman?"

My mother folded her arms, her disgust palpable. "Well... I never imagined I'd raise a daughter to become a heartless home-wrecker."

"You never truly raised a daughter at all, and I want to know why damnit!" I declared, my words laced with a bitter mix of defiance and traces of sorrow.

Just then, an older nurse with ghostly white hair standing on end appeared in my mother's room. "Okay, Miss Robbins, it's medicine time."

I glanced swiftly at her name tag, balling my fist as I yelped, "Betty—Nurse Betty, please! Could you give me a moment alone with my mother?"

The pale woman lost what little color she had, her eyes darting toward my mother as if seeking permission to leave. My mother gently nodded, then turned her head towards the cold beams of daylight streaming through the distant window, she lay silent and unmoved.

Nurse Betty hesitated. "Oookay. I'll come back later," she mumbled before retreating quietly, her shoes making a faint sticky sound against the linoleum floor with each step.

Neither my mother nor I acknowledged her comment or her departure. The sticky echo of Nurse Betty's steps faded into the hallway.

I scampered to the other side of the bed, desperate for my mother's attention and casting a shadow on her tense face. "Answer my question," I demanded.

She stubbornly turned her head back toward the doorway.

Frustrated, I crossed back to the other side of the bed. "You had to know," I pressed, my voice trembling with insistence.

The room seemed to hold its breath as my mother deliberately shut her eyes, tension thick in the air. After a lingering pause, her eyelids fluttered open, and her voice trembled with a haunting vulnerability. "We couldn't bear to lose another son," she whispered. Her admission echoed lightly through the room, leaving me stunned and entangled in a web of emotions and untold secrets.

The furrowed lines on my brow mirrored the depths of my utter confusion. "What son?" I asked, my voice quivering with perplexity. Suddenly, a long-forgotten conversation with my father surged forth from the recesses of my memory, vividly replaying in my mind.

It had been an ordinary evening, with my father and me sitting on the couch during a commercial break in a Sixers game. My mother had joined us briefly, waiting for her baked chicken to finish cooking. A cute little boy appeared on the screen. What I remembered most was my mother quietly rising and leaving the room, her sadness as transparent as glass.

My father had uttered those haunting words: "Your mother will always grieve Tony." Seeking clarity, I pressed him for an explanation, but he ignored me.

I had long concluded my mother's secret was an affair with a man named Tony. The little boy on the screen and my father's revelation about the man named Tony never seemed to correlate precisely. But now, with trepidation, I dared to consider another truth haunting our family.

I voiced the question that could no longer be avoided. "Tony? Did you and Dad have a son named Tony?" My words charged the air with gripping anticipation and complicated emotions.

In an instant, my mother's eyes snapped open, wide with disbelief and a flicker of fear. "How do you know that name? Who told you your brother's name?"

A lump grew heavy in my throat as I swallowed hard before responding. "Dad told me his name. And now, you've just confirmed that he was my brother." A solitary tear slipped from my mother's left eye, tracing a sorrowful path down her face. It had been over two decades since I last saw her cry.

In a hushed tone, my mother spoke, her voice weighted with melancholy. "He passed away long before you came into this world. That's why your father struggled to accept his newborn son, Victor, having physical traits that made him look female."

My grip on the side railing tightened, my knuckles whitening as I shot back, "I had a vagina because I am a female."

Dismissing my words with a wave of her hand, my mother pleaded, "Enough. I cannot bear this any longer. Society's judgment, our lack of understanding at the time… It was a different era."

Silence enveloped the room, but it was a silence I could no longer tolerate. I seized the moment to say the words I had longed to express all my life. "You and Daddy turned a blind eye to my need for medical intervention, stripping away any choices I could have had. That's how I ended up with a man who isn't even single."

My mother's lips hardened into a frosty line, her irises glacial as they locked onto mine. Her voice cut through the air, cold and unrelenting. "Neither your father nor I bear any responsibility for your involvement with another woman's man—that's called being a whore."

Her words pierced me like a dagger, and my hands convulsed around the hospital bed's railing, the force so great my knuckles audibly cracked under the strain.

I leaned forward, bringing my face nose to nose with hers, my voice flat and frigid. "Do you think that's the first time I've been called disgusting names? How about a freak, faggot or even a tranny?"

I rose, straightening to my full height, and proclaimed, "After all the disgusting and vile things I've been called, your venom has no power over me."

Brushing my hands against the smooth silk teal outline of my black pantsuit, I took a few steps back before continuing. My voice was steady and resolute as I said, "And as for my personal relationship? The saddest part is that despite everything I now know about Santé, despite all that has been spoken and unspoken about the other woman, I still long for him. Because of you, Mother, he's the option I have. And I yearn for him."

I felt my mother's gaze follow me as I turned to leave without uttering a farewell.

After a few sweeping footsteps, I left her room in the distance, with the finality of my departure hanging in the air.

CHAPTER *Nineteen*

THE TRUTH BETWEEN FRIENDS

The sparsely populated Lorenzo's felt unusually tranquil for a Thursday afternoon. With a plastered smile, I scanned the room, noting the few occupied tables as Patricia's words droned on, my mind elsewhere.

Her sharp voice broke my distraction. "Why aren't you paying attention?"

"I am listening," I lied softly.

Patricia's doubtful gaze lingered. "Then you must know I'm telling the truth. Do you really think Santé is boyfriend material?"

I hesitated, my thoughts spinning. "How can I know if I don't give him another chance?"

Patricia's response was swift. "Santé is back in your life after you claimed to have no interest. What changed?

I took a deep breath and acknowledged the truth, "I never fully stopped loving Santé."

The sound of Patricia's fork hitting the plate reverberated through the empty restaurant, filling the silence.

She stared at me, her expression a mix of confusion and anger. "What did you just say?" Patricia questioned, her voice flat as she tried to maintain composure.

Annoyed by her dramatic display, I defiantly declared, "I have always loved Santé. I don't know if he'll truly have me, but I never said I stopped loving him."

Patricia shook her head, her emotions in evident turmoil. I attempted to reason with her and continued, "I don't know what pretending will accomplish. Clearly, I'm not ready to let him go completely, so why should I lie to you or to myself?"

Pat looked at me sternly, her eyes searching mine as she questioned, "Why would you want someone who doesn't want you? The fact that he has another woman speaks volumes."

It was my turn to be candid with Pat and match her directness. "He accepts me, and that matters." My voice tinged with determination and vulnerability.

As Patricia took a deep swig of her lemonade, setting the glass back on the table, she looked at me perplexedly. "What is there to accept, Vicky? You're amazing," she stated, her words both reassuring and fear-inducing. I couldn't help but recall the freedom I felt being myself with Santé, so the idea of sharing my medical condition with my best friend for the first time crossed my mind.

My gaze lowered as I began to speak, the weight of my confession building in my chest. "There's something I need to tell you," I whispered. Patricia stared at me, her face blank, unresponsive. Realizing she wouldn't break the silence, I gathered my courage and continued, "A few years before I met you, I was known as Victor."

Patricia's eyes widened, and after a few seconds of watching her expressionless face and enduring the oppressive silence, she asked, "So, what are you saying? You're trans?"

"No," I replied, "I'm intersex."

Patricia's confusion was palpable as she questioned, "What the hell is intersex?" The sound of the word intersex leaving her mouth sounded strange, but I couldn't dwell on that. I had an opportunity to educate.

"Intersex is when someone has ambiguous sexual genitalia," I explained. "It can involve fully formed genitalia that exhibit characteristics of both male and female, which used to be called hermaphroditism. Or someone can have a combination of genitals from both sexes. There are even cases where the genitals may appear typical, but the person has genetic differences in other ways."

As Patricia grappled with my revelation, I mobilized the courage to persist in my candidness, desperately yearning to illuminate my truth. "Forgive me for potentially disrupting your meal, but I have suffered from the burden of ambiguous genitalia," I confessed, unleashing a thunderclap of truth. The impact was instantaneous, rendering Patricia speechless. Her face morphed into a mask of shock, her complexion ashen and her expression frozen in disbelief.

After the pregnant silence that followed, Pat's voice emerged, trembling with a mix of trepidation and curiosity.

"An-And Santé knows about this? Her question lingered but before I could respond, additional words spilled forth from Pat. "So, this is what you meant by his acceptance?"

With my tear ducts tingling, I said, "He has an idea."

Patricia's face contorted as she questioned further, "What? After all the years you've been together, how does he not know for sure?"

Tapping nervously on the table, I responded, "It's a long story, but let's just say our physical intimacy has been very limited." I licked my lips, feeling my truth hanging heavily in the air.

Gradually, color returned to Patricia's face as she sipped her lemonade. I heard the slurping sounds as her drink reached the glass's bottom. When she looked up, her face was filled with a newfound confusion.

"Wait," she said, "I'm just going to be real. You've been with this man for ten years, he's never asked for sex, and all you do is suck his dick?"

My anger simmered as I struggled to find the words to explain. Before I could respond, Pat continued her blunt, if not rude, questioning. "And you think he's accepted you?"

"That's not what I said," I retorted. "Look, he hasn't pushed me beyond my boundaries. He's asked for more but agreed to wait. And now, I think I'm ready to go further than before."

Patricia sat back in her chair, briefly putting a hand to her forehead. "Girl, no man I've ever messed with has waited longer than six months. I'll tell you one thing for sure—you must give a hell of a dick suck!"

"Be serious, Pat," I said with a nervous chuckle.

"I am serious," she shot back. "And six months was back in the day. Today's men won't wait six weeks to fuck. Hell, you're doing good if you can get them to wait six hours."

"Girl, if you don't stop it," I said, my amusement fading, replaced by annoyance.

Pat shrugged and leaned forward. "The last date I went on before Jagger? That fool didn't even want to wait six minutes. He was reaching for his zipper in the restaurant parking lot—and we hadn't even gone in yet!"

"Pat!" I yelled, trying to snap her out of her bad-dates-before-Jagger rant.

"Oh, I'm sorry. I'm back," she said, holding up her hands in mock surrender.

I shook my head but couldn't help offering a reluctant smile. Her humor, no matter how outrageous, was irresistible.

Pat tilted her head, studying me with a glimmer of curiosity. "But seriously, girl, after ten years you're ready to have sex with Santé for the first time?"

I corrected her, my frustration seeping through, "I'm ready for penetration for the first time."

Pat replied, "Yeah, that's what I meant. So it'll be your first time with Santé."

I placed my hands on my temples, attempting to maintain composure, "Pat, you're not listening to me," I said, leaning in. "I'm ready for penetrative sex for the first time—ever."

Patricia's words, escaping from her lips with more force than she had intended, reverberated through the air, echoing, "You're a virgin?" Her exclamation bore down on me, igniting an inferno of embarrassment that flooded my cheeks with a fiery hue.

With a swift and anxious glance around the sparsely populated restaurant, I sought solace in the reassurance that our private conversation had remained veiled from prying ears. Fortunately, the few scattered patrons were positioned at a distance far enough to be blissfully unaware of Patricia's piercing outburst.

"Lower your voice," I scolded, chastising her for her lack of discretion. It was Pat's turn to look around cautiously before she continued questioning me. Anticipating the inevitable repetition of her question, I offered a vulnerable admission, "Yes, I am a virgin. Hopefully, not for long. I finally have the courage to address my situation."

Patricia's right eyebrow ascended in astonishment, subtly reflecting her processing my revelation. "So, you're planning to have sex reassignment surgery?" she inquired, her voice filled with curiosity and sincere attempts at comprehension.

With a gentle sigh, I rolled my eyes, mindful of the limited binary understanding of gender she had inherited from society's indoctrination. I responded, striving to maintain an air of composure, "It's not exactly a sex change, but it is a confirmation of sorts, an acknowledgment of my true self."

Patricia slid her hand across the table, touching mine gently. "This is amazing," she said softly, her eyes filled with compassion and new understanding. "I've known you for all these years, and I never knew. Even if you never let anyone else know, you could have let me know."

I smiled shyly, grateful for her support. "Thank you," I murmured.

Pat's voice, filled with empathy, continued, "Although I firmly believe that Santé may not be the best person for you, at least now I understand why you're so devoted to him."

Patricia warned, her tone solemn, "Be careful because your devotion to him doesn't guarantee his devotion to you. You deserve someone who will be devoted to you."

Taking a few bites of my cooled truffle fries, I pondered Patricia's words.

What she said made sense on the surface but didn't change the fundamental truth: I didn't have the options most women had. I fought the temptation to debate the issue with Patricia because I knew she couldn't understand.

Pat seemed genuinely curious when she asked, "How did he find out about your situation?"

I cleared my throat, composed myself, and responded, "So, that's what we're calling it now? My situation?"

Patricia smirked and said, "I'm sorry, I didn't know what else to call it."

Sidestepping the awkwardness, I replied, "He told me that he knew I was hiding something. He insisted on seeing me naked, so I obliged. Well, kind of. I allowed him to remove my panties."

Patricia's curiosity was piqued as she leaned forward. "So, he saw you completely naked?" she probed.

I nodded slowly, my eyes blinking deliberately, before taking a cleansing breath. "Yes, to my complete astonishment, he didn't make a big deal out of it. I can't even begin to explain how much that meant to me. In fact, he didn't have much of a reaction at all."

A warm expression washed over Patricia's face as she asked, "So, there you were, completely vulnerable and exposed, and he seemed okay with you. What was that like?"

I hesitated momentarily, then replied, "It was like drinking the most refreshing lemonade but with a bit too much lemon."

Patricia furrowed her brow, seeking clarification. "What does that mean?" she inquired.

I attempted to explain, "I guess what I'm trying to say is that it was the best and worst moment of my life, simultaneously."

Patricia looked down, seemingly contemplating her next question. When she finally spoke, her voice filled with confusion and disbelief. "Did he truly accept your body, or was he just open-minded enough not to care?"

I shook my head, frustrated, while sadness filled my heart. "I don't know, I really don't," I said before adding, "All I know is that I will do whatever it takes to feel comfortable in my own skin."

Within the intimate embrace of our ongoing conversation, a delicate vulnerability unfolded.

Along this uncharted voyage toward embracing my physical congruity, the steadfast support of my dearest friend emerged as a radiant beacon of solace, a fragile glimmer of hope illuminating the tumultuous journey that lay before me.

CHAPTER
Twenty

ANATOMY OF SELF

Standing in front of the examination table, the distinct scent of antiseptic invaded my nostrils, triggering a sense of unease. Anxiety fluttered in my chest, intensifying as I grappled with the struggle to keep my gown securely fastened. The feeble string seemed to mock me, failing to maintain my modesty.

A sharp knock at the door interrupted my thoughts. "Come in," I called out, trying to steady my voice. Dr. Phil Mason entered, exuding calm confidence. With his smooth, youthful features reminiscent of actor Shemar Moore in his younger years, he carried a warm smile that was surprisingly disarming. For a fleeting moment, a spark of attraction flared within me, catching me off guard. I quickly pushed it aside, reminding myself to remain professional as his steady demeanor softened my tension.

"You'll be just fine," he said as he prepared for the examination. "You're in great hands."

I took a deep breath and settled onto the table, positioning my feet in the stirrups with a mix of apprehension and resolve. As the examination began, Dr. Mason's touch was clinical yet gentle, his steady presence grounding me. His tone remained professional, but I couldn't help searching his face for signs of judgment. Instead, I found only focus.

"You're doing great," he said softly, pausing to meet my gaze. His expression was calm and reassuring, a quiet confidence that settled some of my nerves. "We'll take this step by step."

I managed a small nod, my vulnerability laid bare. Moments later, he reached for the ultrasound equipment, explaining as he worked. "This will help us get a full understanding of your anatomy. The more precise the imaging, the better we can tailor a plan for you."

As he applied the cold gel to my skin, I tensed, bracing for the chill and the implications of what the ultrasound might reveal. Shades of gray formed shapes and outlines on the screen, a visual whisper of my internal self.

"Here's your uterus," he said, pointing to a small, shadowy structure. "It's smaller than average but intact. And this," he gestured to another area, "is your ovary."

He paused, glancing at the screen before continuing. "You also have a testicle here. It's the source of the elevated testosterone levels you've mentioned. Removing it would be part of the procedure we'll discuss."

As the screen shifted to reveal my miniature phallus, I winced, a wave of heat spreading up my neck and flooding my cheeks. My fingers gripped the table's edges as embarrassment collided with a lingering sense of shame. "I'm sorry," I whispered, my voice barely audible. "It's… been a source of pain my whole life—physically and emotionally. People see something like that and assume I'm… a boy. And the world doesn't understand."

I shifted on the table, my discomfort evident in my restless movements and the strain in my voice. "Too many people believe sex and gender are the same. They're not gender specialists, but they spread ignorance and prejudice, righteously citing third-grade, reductive biology."

Dr. Mason's expression turned thoughtful, his brow furrowing slightly as he met my gaze. His tone was calm yet resolute, cutting through years of internalized shame and societal ignorance. "Genitals are not the same as gender," he said. "Your body tells its own story, one that is unique and valid."

I swallowed hard, trying to process the magnitude of his statement. It felt like someone had finally said out loud what I'd been trying to articulate my entire life.

The rhythmic beep of the ultrasound machine filled the room as he continued to examine and explain, his voice a steady counterpoint to my racing thoughts. "It's important to understand that surgical interventions are highly personalized. Your anatomy, your identity—both deserve respect."

I nodded, unable to find words but grateful for his approach. His medical precision, paired with genuine empathy, created a space where I felt seen and not judged.

DR. MASON'S OFFICE WAS ENVELOPED IN A THOUGHTFUL QUIET as the conversation shifted. "This isn't a journey you'll take alone," he began. "Our collaboration with a gynecologist and urologist will ensure a comprehensive approach."

"Enhancing the vulva, realigning urological functions, and revising the clitoris—these aren't isolated changes but a unified vision," he continued, his tone steady.

The concept of such a comprehensive approach struck me deeply. I nodded, a shy smile tugging at my lips. "Yes, please. Let's go with your approach," I said firmly. It was a leap of faith, but one I felt ready for.

Dr. Mason's nod carried understanding. "What time range are we looking at for these procedures?"

"As soon as possible. Your next available surgical date works for me," I replied without hesitation.

His approving smile felt like validation. "Then let's get started."

A profound calm settled over me as I realized I was finally moving forward. The weight I'd carried felt lighter. The journey ahead was daunting, but I was ready to meet it head-on.

CHAPTER
Twenty-One

THE ROAD TO CLARITY

As the sun set on Sunday, I sought solace in a spontaneous drive, needing to clear my mind from the week's momentous events. The fading light and open road offered the comfort I craved.

The elegant strains of Adagio filled my sleek black Chrysler 300C as it glided across the Betsy Ross Bridge, leaving Philadelphia behind for the promise of New Jersey. The composition mirrored my emotions, its melancholic beauty tugging at my heartstrings as I contemplated my pending surgery—a decision I had delayed for years.

Adagio became a companion, providing solace on this soul-searching journey. My thoughts turned to my lover, Santé, and his silence after my revelation. Relief and concern mingled uneasily within me: Was his silence acceptance or suppressed outrage? It was an emotional minefield I navigated while driving south on Route 73.

Small towns like Pennsauken, Mount Laurel, and Voorhees passed by, their mini-malls and family restaurants dotting the highway. I envisioned a new life in this promising region, balancing proximity to Philadelphia with the comfort and safety I yearned for.

Dreams of reclaiming my production company floated to the surface, a vision for the years ahead after more time at Nybor Productions. The future loomed hazy but significant—a chance for wholeness and peace.

As twilight deepened, I spotted a gym and pulled into its lot.

A tear welled up as I confronted my long-standing fear of gym locker rooms, the politics, and the prejudice I had avoided for years—always at the expense of my own health.

I felt a kinship with trans individuals—that is, people with the medical condition formerly referred to as transsexuals, before the more inclusive, yet distorting, term transgender became popularized. I recognized our shared challenges on the continuum of sex and gender variations, so often demonized by society.

Leaving the gym parking lot, I wandered into a local Cherry Hill store, where the warmth of the people lifted my spirits. Returning to my car, I saw the outing as a preview of the life I aspired to—whole, authentic, and free.

Driving back to Philadelphia, the hauntingly prophetic song "It Can't Be the Same Anymore" by Barbra Streisand filled my car. The lyrics reflected my journey, a poignant soundtrack to my transformation. The combination of Adagio's strings and Streisand's powerful words etched an indelible mark on my heart.

As Philadelphia reemerged on the horizon, I parked my car and stepped onto its familiar streets with a renewed sense of purpose. The tears welling in my eyes were no longer tethered solely to past pain but glistened with hope, resolve, and the quiet strength of acceptance.

Streisand's words lingered in my heart, a testament to the beauty of change and the courage it demands. The road ahead would be as mysterious as it was promising, but I felt ready to face it—with pride, with grace, and with the undeniable certainty that life could never, would never, be the same again.

CHAPTER
Twenty-Two

UNWANTED PARTNERSHIP

I sat at my desk, the phone pressed to my ear, engrossed in a conversation with Roger Cartwright, the showrunner of one of our newer productions. We were tackling the challenge of reining in specific production costs related to a sitcom. The room was filled with the delightful aroma of cinnamon tea, its sweet and spicy fragrance swirling around me as I scrutinized the colorful budget spreadsheets displayed on my computer screen.

"Roger, we need to optimize the budget without compromising the quality of the show," I stated firmly but diplomatically. "I understand the creative vision, but we must be mindful of the financial constraints."

Roger's voice carried concern. "I hear you, Victoria. We'll look into areas for adjustments without sacrificing the essence of the story."

"Great," I replied, relieved he was receptive. "Let's find a solution that keeps the show's integrity intact while meeting our budgetary goals."

The intercom buzzed, momentarily breaking my focus. "Boss lady, Patricia is on the other line and wants to speak with you," Beth said, over the intercom. "

I asked Roger to wait a moment, pressed the hold button, putting Roger on pause, and responded to Beth, "Tell Patricia to hold on for a moment."

After wrapping up with Roger and assuring him we'd continue later, I switched lines. "Hey, what's up, girl?"

Patricia's voice carried excitement and a hint of mischief. "I was planning to go back to work today, but things have really heated up between me and Jagger."

Intrigued, I leaned closer to the phone, a playful smile on my lips. "Oh, I was due for a break…spill the tea. What happened?"

With a saucy tone, Patricia replied, "Let's just say it was gooood."

I giggled, feeling like two schoolgirls sharing secrets. "Girl you're such a tease! I need details," I said, my voice lilting with playful curiosity.

Patricia taunted jovially. "Wouldn't you like to know?"

"You bet I would," I retorted, curiosity bubbling. "Come on, spill the beans!"

Patricia chuckled before relenting. "Okay, fine. Let me tell you about Jagger's chest."

Before I realized it, I yelled, "Forget his damn chest. What's that dick do?"

Patricia laughed a little nervously. "Well, it does a lot and for a very long time. He started fucking me about five this morning, and what time is it now?"

I scrambled to find the clock on my desk. "Bitch, it's eleven-twenty, damn near noon."

"Precisely. I don't think I need to say more," Patricia replied.

"The hell you say? Think again," I yelled.

Patricia giggled. "I can't get into too much detail. He's in the bathroom, but the shower is on, so I'll give you this…"

My anticipation quickened as I tightened my grip on the phone. Patricia lowered her voice but spoke clearly.

"Jagger is a slow lover," she teased. "And his dick is larger than I'm used to but I'm a soldier, so I'm gonna keep taking all I can."

Pat's imagery sent my senses reeling as the cinnamon tea's sweetness mingled with the room's excitement. Patricia described Jagger's deliberate rhythm and his insistence on eye contact.

My temperature rose. Patricia's explanation of her sex life with Jagger left me wondering if I'd ever experience such joy and abandon. Her multiple climaxes, which left her light-headed, sent us both into joyful laughter.

Without notice, Beth knocked on my office door. Breaking protocol, she hadn't used the intercom. I placed my hand over the receiver and addressed Beth's head peeking through the door. "What is it? I'm on the phone."

Beth opened the door wider, revealing a piece of paper in her hand. "This was just delivered. I think you'll want to read it." I motioned for her to bring it over.

I removed my hand from the receiver and said in my most professional tone, "The event you described last evening sounded quite enjoyable."

Patricia immediately knew I wasn't alone. "Somebody came into your office?" she asked.

"That would be correct," I replied, scanning the letter Beth handed me. Its meaning hit like a punch.

> "Effective immediately, Ken Rutherford is hereby named Co-Vice President of Production. We anticipate great things coming from the teamwork between Vicky Robbins and Ken Rutherford, collectively the new Vice Presidents of Production."

Patricia was speaking, but I couldn't process her words. The following paragraphs blurred, though I caught the last one:

> "If there are any questions regarding this executive decision, I will be available upon my return from the Paris Film Festival next week. Thank you for your cooperation in implementing these changes in our corporate structure. A new Junior Vice President will be named within the coming weeks.
>
> Sincerely,
> Terrence Murray
> CEO of Nybor Productions Inc."

My hand shook audibly. Beth's concerned frown mirrored my internal turmoil. My heart pounded—not from excitement but rage. I'd been Vice President of Production for less than a month, and Ken was already encroaching on my space.

My mind whirled, trying to decipher Ken's behind-the-scenes maneuvering. I also weighed whether this change meant delaying my surgery plans or using the shared responsibilities to heal before returning to the fight.

Patricia's voice pierced my inner dialogue. "Victoria, are you still there?"

I replied hastily, "Yeah, girl. I gotta call you back."

Patricia asked, "Is everything okay?"

"No," I replied, hanging up. Turning to Beth, I said, "That bastard is moving faster than I expected. The question is, how do I stop him?"

Beth's puzzled face mirrored my inner conflict.

CHAPTER
Twenty-Three

A STEP TOWARD WHOLENESS

Monday, October 1, 2018, the big day had finally arrived, a moment that seemed to take a lifetime to reach. Patricia's unexpected question caught me off guard as I sat in the passenger side of her White Honda Accord, cruising down the early morning streets of Philly.

"Are you doing this for Santé?" Patricia asked. The world outside whizzed by, but I was stunned into silence, unable to find the right words to respond. After several seconds, I was able to gather my thoughts.

"No human being on earth could ever make me do what I'm about to do," I finally replied, my voice steady with determination. "And no human being on earth can stop me either."

Patricia looked over at me, a knowing smile on her face as if she understood the depth of my resolve. The rest of the car ride to the University of Pennsylvania hospital was spent in silence, each of us lost in our thoughts.

Upon arrival, the surgical suite waiting area greeted us with its sterile atmosphere. The faint scent of coffee lingered in the air. Only two other patients were waiting, their presence somehow adding to the anticipation in the room.

I felt uneasy about taking time away from work, even for such an important procedure—especially with Ken-Doll's behind-the-scenes antics. But then I reminded myself that this kind of misplaced prioritizing was exactly how I had gone decades without addressing my most agonizing physical challenge. I had become conditioned to put everything and everyone ahead of my own needs.

I rationalized that not having a personal life justified minimizing the importance of resolving my issue. It was as if I needed external reasons to care for myself. Santé's sudden return had provided that spark of timing. But as I had told Patricia, I was aligning my body and mind for myself first— even if I looked forward to the peripheral pleasures it might bring with Santé.

The time was now. If Ken was going to share the title and salary of Vice President of Production, he could damn well share the workload. This was the perfect time to force that balance, to hold him accountable while I worked from home during my recovery.

After I officially checked in, I joined Patricia on the long tan couch in the waiting area. Her warm hand reached across to rest on mine, a small gesture that brought immense comfort.

"You're so brave," she said gently.

"Don't make me cry," I replied with a faint smile, willing my emotions to stay in check.

I shared my estimate of the procedure's duration—seven long hours. Patricia nodded, her expression calm and resolute. "It doesn't matter," she said. "I'm not going anywhere. I'm here for as long as you need."

The sincerity in her words unlocked a flood of gratitude within me. "I've cherished our friendship over the years," I said, my voice trembling slightly. "And I want you to know how much it means to have you here, no matter the outcome."

Patricia's eyes glistened with emotion as she replied, "I love you, girl."

"I love you too," I said, as tears lightly streamed down my face. I made no effort to wipe them away immediately. Instead, we held hands, letting the moment stretch between us.

Five minutes later, a male nurse called my name, signaling it was time to head to the pre-surgical area. Patricia and I hugged tightly, her unwavering support filling my heart with gratitude.

I wiped my face, stood tall, and marched toward my destiny.

In the pre-surgical area, I met with Dr. Mason to review the procedure. He reiterated both the best and worst potential outcomes, his calm demeanor reinforcing my trust in his expertise.

Signing the consent form was a profound moment—a tangible acknowledgment of the gravity of my decision. I thanked him sincerely, knowing I was placing both my trust and my life in his hands.

The anesthesiologist followed, offering reassuring words as she explained her role in the surgery. Her calmness eased my nerves, leaving me with a fleeting sense of stability.

Left alone for a few moments, I sought solace and clarity. With my iPod in hand, I selected a song that resonated deeply: Barbra Streisand's *It Can't Be the Same Anymore*. The lyrics mirrored my emotions and reflected the essence of my journey.

As the haunting melody filled my ears, a sense of inner peace washed over me. I felt ready to face whatever lay ahead.

When the male nurse opened the door and announced, "It's showtime," I smiled faintly. I left my device and earplugs behind, their comforting notes still lingering in my heart.

As I was wheeled down the long, cold hallway toward the surgical suite, the song's melody continued to echo in my mind, its haunting beauty offering solace. I embraced the certainty that, in the most fundamental ways, my life wouldn't be the same anymore.

CHAPTER
Twenty-Four

LET THE MUSIC PLAY

In a post-surgical haze, I clawed my way out of unconsciousness, only to be greeted by an agonizing fire coursing through my legs. The pain was sharp and relentless, consuming me in a way that defied my expectations. I had braced myself for discomfort below, but instead, my legs screamed with a ferocity that left me breathless, as if molten lava were flowing just beneath my skin.

The faint ache from the surgical site barely registered, eclipsed entirely by the searing intensity in my legs. Confusion mingled with the pain, as I struggled to reconcile this unexpected agony with the overwhelming fatigue that swept over me like a tidal wave.

Moments later, a cacophony of voices reached my ears, their words initially mere garbled background noise. Slowly, like a puzzle falling into place, I deciphered my name amidst the chatter, compelling me to pry my heavy eyelids open.

The brightness of the room caused me to wince. I could sense I was being moved as my eyes adjusted to the surroundings. It became apparent that I was on a gurney in motion. Finally, the gurney halted, and I focused on Patricia's presence, holding her hand tightly. Her voice and the doctor's words were distant, echoing through the haze as if spoken through a tunnel.

"Thank you, I love you," I managed to whisper, my voice faint and strained.

"Victoria needs her rest. You can visit her in the morning," Dr. Mason informed Patricia.

The next thing I remember was Barry White's deep baritone voice singing, "Let the Music Play." The song played in my ears from my iPod and through my pink earbuds. I placed the tune on a repeated loop, which serenaded me in the solitude of the private hospital suite.

Staring out of the expansive window, I could see the city below, the view far grander than that from my condominium. It was Center City, Philadelphia, and from my elevated floor, the entire cityscape lay before me like a living, breathing canvas.

The clock on the wall indicated it was 2:30 in the morning when I first awoke. The pain in my legs had subsided, but the intense burning discomfort in my groin persisted like a smoldering ember. Despite the enduring ache, it was not as unbearable as I had anticipated, and unexpectedly, a powerful gratitude overwhelmed me.

For the next two hours, I found solace in the melancholic rhythm of Barry White's song, tears streaming down my cheeks. I felt an intense serenity. The tumultuous journey of my life had finally led me to a place of profound inner peace.

At six in the morning, a young Caucasian nurse appeared, checking my vital signs and informing me about the morphine dispenser next to my bed. A single push would grant relief, but I staunchly resisted the temptation. No narcotic like morphine was going to taint my system despite the pain.

Soon after, another nurse, a large and cheerful African-American woman, entered the room. Attempting small talk, she inadvertently veered into a sensitive topic. "Are you excited now that your sex change is complete?" she asked, her lack of understanding evident.

My annoyance flared, mingling with bafflement, and my inner dialogue yelled, This surgery is not a sex change. It's an intersex surgery, and even transsexual surgery is more of a gender confirmation than a sex change.

I considered whether to voice my thoughts, but I chose not to correct her misconceptions. Instead, I responded with a restrained tone, "No, I am not excited."

The nurse paused, her eyebrows lifting slightly as a flicker of surprise crossed her face before she quickly masked it with professional neutrality.

I calmly continued, "I'm at peace." The nurse turned the corners of her mouth downward and provided a light shrug.

In moments like that, the frustration of the world's lack of understanding about intersex and our transsexual compadres weighed heavily on me. This state of affairs was only complicated by the newer, popular umbrella term 'Transgender,' which had become more of a political statement than a medical diagnosis, adding to the overall ignorance around gender complexities. Putting all of that aside, and in my vulnerable state, I knew I needed to preserve my energy for healing.

Shifting on the specially designed inflatable mattress, my body sought comfort and repose. The nurse, perceptive to my silent request for solitude, backed away, leaving me to retreat into the depths of my mind, my eyes slowly closing as the soothing music played from my iPod. The world outside the window may have been bustling, but at that moment, I sought solace within the confines of my thoughts and emotions while Barry White crooned, "Let The Music Play."

CHAPTER
Twenty-Five

SLOW DOWN MY FRIEND

The evening's stillness was interrupted by Patricia's unexpected revelation. "Victoria, can you believe it? Jagger wants us to move in together," she blurted, her voice a mix of excitement and disbelief.

My heart skipped a beat, a surge of surprise and concern. "Move in together? Already?" I asked, my brows knitting. "Patricia, that's…huge."

She perched on the edge of my bed, absently smoothing the pink fur comforter. "I know, right? But first, I want you to know I unpacked the groceries and put them in your fridge."

"You're amazing, Pat. Having you here means everything right now," I said, my gratitude evident.

Patricia smiled faintly, her expression warm. "You don't have to thank me. We're sisters, not just friends. Helping you recover and running errands is nothing."

Her words were a balm to my restless thoughts. "I just feel so…stuck. But having you here makes it bearable," I admitted, letting my guard down.

Patricia leaned closer, her tone firm yet comforting. "You're not alone in this. We'll get through it together."

I tightened my grip on the comforter. "But how did this happen? It feels like such a big step."

She leaned back, her gaze distant, as if replaying the moment. "It was late at night in his car. Moonlight streamed through the windshield, casting this silver glow on Jagger's face."

Her voice grew wistful, drawing me into her memory. "He was so quiet, Victoria. It made my heart race. Finally, I asked if he was okay."

"And?" I prompted, leaning in.

"He turned to me with this intensity in his eyes. It sent a chill through me. He said he'd been thinking about something important."

I felt myself holding my breath. "What did he say?"

Patricia's voice grew quieter. "He said he wanted us to move in together. Can you believe it? A few weeks in, and he's already talking about it."

"What did you tell him?"

"I was stunned. But he was so sure, Victoria. He said he felt a connection with me like never before, that he wanted to wake up beside me every day."

"That's…intense," I said, my voice quieter now.

She nodded. "I told him it was a big step. But he reassured me, said he understood my hesitation but knew what he wanted. He didn't care whose apartment we lived in, as long as we were together."

Her recounting painted a picture of both determination and vulnerability. "But I love my apartment, and my lease isn't up until December," she added.

"And what did Jagger say to that?"

"He respected it. Said he wouldn't want me to give up something I love but also talked about creating a space together—somewhere uniquely ours."

I could almost see it unfold, the push and pull of emotions in that car. "He didn't want to pressure me but made it clear he wouldn't wait forever. He said he knows his worth and won't settle for less."

The room seemed charged with the weight of Patricia's story. "So what did you decide?"

"I told him I'd think about it," she said, her voice steady now.

"That's wise, Pat. Make sure it's a decision that fills you with peace, not fear of losing him," I said gently.

Patricia nodded, her gaze meeting mine. "He's sincere, and I love that he knows what he wants. But this decision has to feel right for both of us."

"Exactly. Take the time you need," I encouraged. "Whatever you choose, I'm here for you."

The conversation softened into a reflective silence. Patricia began tidying up, her earlier flurry of words giving way to quiet thought. The peach hues of the room wrapped around us like a cocoon, holding space for friendship and the weight of life-changing decisions.

Despite the warmth and camaraderie, a lingering worry tugged at me. Patricia stood on the cusp of a transformative choice. While her blossoming romance thrilled me, a protective part of me feared haste might lead her astray. Watching her move with quiet determination, I could only hope her journey into this new chapter would bring her joy, not regret.

CHAPTER
Twenty-Six

A BOLD RETURN

Three weeks of physical recovery, working from home, with Diana Ross playing throughout my condo had come and gone. At almost a month from my work office, I knew it was time to return. Ken Rutherford's recent power moves had unsettled me deeply. If he managed to become co-Vice President of Production while I was present at the Nybor Productions headquarters, who knows how much he could undermine me while I was working remotely?

As I got ready for work, I took delight in slipping into some newly purchased form-fitting clothes. Losing a few pounds before my surgery had given me a sense of happiness, but I couldn't help but imagine how much better I'd look with another fifteen pounds gone. Thoughts of the gym back in New Jersey resurfaced, and I made a mental note to join it later that week, eager to transform my body further.

My laptop held all the recent notes, budgets, and email communication I needed for the day ahead. As I walked toward my door, ready to venture out into the world, a familiar sound chimed from my phone: a text message notification.

Curious, I glanced at the message from an unknown number. It read:

I get off at 5 PM and I wanna get off at 5 PM LOL.

The playful words sparked intrigue, and I couldn't resist but ask, Who is this?

The sender replied with one word:

Santé.

My heart skipped a beat, and excitement rushed through me. We hadn't seen each other in weeks and the text messages, including a few rounds of sexting, had all been exchanged from a different number. I was missing Santé but felt grateful that our physical distance allowed me post-surgical healing. Even sexting was painful at times, but now I was feeling better. His timing was almost perfect.

Feeling a newfound confidence, I caught a glimpse of myself in the full-length mirror nearby, I was unashamed and nude. A smile of anticipation spread across my face. It was as if the woman staring back at me had grown and evolved.

As I stepped out of my condo, the world seemed to come alive with vivid intensity. Feeling more self-confidence and even daring, I replied to Santé's text:

I'll be there.

CHAPTER
Twenty-Seven

HIGH STAKES, HIGHER PRESSURE

My first day back in the office had been going remarkably well. From the early moments of the Monday morning, as I stepped into my office, it was like entering a sanctuary of sophistication, with the scent of fresh lavender from a flickering candle delicately filling the air.

Settling into my plush leather chair, I was happy to be back in my office, home away from home. I started reworking the latest budget for our popular sitcom. My fingers danced gracefully across the keyboard, and the rhythmic clickety-clack of the keys created a symphony of productivity. The gentle tune "Long As I Live" from Toni Braxton played from my desktop speakers which provided a delightful backdrop to my tasks.

I turned my attention to the pile of fresh scripts on my desk. I flipped through the pages, immersing myself in the captivating stories they held. The satisfaction of a job well done coursed through me, filling my heart with pride. Even the behind-the-scenes squabbles that once troubled our most popular production had diminished after I spoke with both the executive producer and the star of the show. By day's end, I received reports from the set. A new harmonious atmosphere was described as invigorating.

Just as I reveled in the harmony that had settled over the production, A soft knock on my office door interrupted my moment of peace. My curiosity piqued, I called out, "Come in."

The door swung open, and there stood Beth, her expression suggesting urgency. She hesitated for a moment before speaking as if debating how to break the news. Finally, she took a deep breath and said, "Victoria, there's an emergency board meeting. It's about the rumors of the corporate merger. They seem to be real."

My heart skipped a beat, and my senses sharpened as I absorbed her words. "A corporate merger?" I asked, trying to grasp the magnitude of the situation.

Beth nodded solemnly. "Yes, that's what the higher-ups are discussing. It seems like a television entertainment powerhouse based in New York City is acquiring Nybor Productions Inc."

My mind raced with questions. What would be our role in this new setup?

Before I could ask out loud, Beth said, "The plan is to turn us into an in-house unit for reality programming." Her voice was tinged with unease. "It means we would be producing reality shows for the parent company."

"Reality programming?" I asked. The words hung in the air like a heavy fog, suffocating any hope of continuity and stability in my career. I couldn't fathom being a part of such a venture, and the thought of abandoning the quality programming that had been our hallmark weighed heavily on my heart.

"But there's a small consolation," Beth continued, trying to offer a glimmer of hope amidst the grim news. "According to the rumors, Nybor Productions Inc. will still retain its name despite the change of mission."

"Oh great. What the hell difference does that make?" I said, my anger showing. I couldn't find comfort in that detail. My mind was consumed with the implications of the merger. The anxiousness it brought to my role in the company, the potential loss of creative control, and the fear of being involved in something I strongly opposed.

An hour was all I had to prepare for a most pivotal moment. How could I gather my thoughts and emotions before stepping into a room where my career's fate would be decided? I also had no assurance that my presence would be welcomed or make any difference.

Lastly, I couldn't go to the meeting if I wanted to. According to the clock on the wall, it was already 4:30. I had to leave. I was to meet Santé in just a half hour.

Beth must have noticed the turmoil on my face because she continued, "Is everything okay, Victoria? You look worried."

I tried to hide my internal struggle, but Beth's concern was genuine, and I knew I couldn't deceive her. With a deep sigh, I nodded reluctantly.

"Is there something wrong with your mother? Is she sick?" Beth asked, her voice gentle and caring.

Again, I nodded, feeling a pang of guilt for the lie, but I rationalized my mother was indeed sick. Allowing Beth to believe that leaving work without attempting to go to that most pivotal meeting was due to my mother, was the only way I could leave the office without arousing suspicion and unwelcomed scrutiny.

"I'm so sorry to hear that," Beth said empathetically. "Family comes first," she added.

I asked, "Please get the minutes from the meeting for me as soon as they're available."

"Of course, I'll do that right away," Beth assured me, her voice soft with compassion.

As I prepared to leave, Beth hesitated momentarily before speaking again. "Oh, by the way, I saw Ken heading toward Mr. Murray's office just before I knocked on your door. He might be joining the meeting."

A knot of anxiety formed in my stomach at the mention of Ken. "Thank you for letting me know," I replied, trying to hide my unease.

With a heavy heart and my mind burdened with the impending merger and Ken's possible involvement, I finally made my way to the elevators. I knew that whatever choice I made would have consequences, and the trouble that could emerge from the board meeting weighed heavily on my mind.

Technically, I wasn't a board member, and there was no guarantee that I would even be allowed to attend the meeting. For a few tense seconds, waiting on the elevator's arrival, I wondered if I should try to join the meeting or at least be in the loop by staying in the building.

Bing.

The elevator had arrived. I glanced at my watch. It was 4:35 PM. My decision had been made.

As the elevator doors closed, I whispered a silent prayer for strength and guidance, hoping that somehow, amidst the chaos and conflicting emotions, I would find the clarity I needed to navigate the challenges ahead. My mind raced with contradictions. The ride down felt both excruciatingly slow and alarmingly fast.

CHAPTER
Twenty-Eight

FAMILIAR YET DIFFERENT

My car's wheels stopped precisely at 5 PM, a moment that seemed like a pause in time. I glanced over at the imposing warehouse on Fairlane Road, the gates to its parking lot wide open. It was just a matter of moments before Santé, my dream lover, would make his appearance.

My heart raced with conflicting emotions as I stole a glimpse of myself in the rearview mirror. Presentable, but beneath the surface, I felt a maelstrom of emotions and conflicting feelings. Chief among the duality, I felt riddled with an inexplicable sense of being out of control. My loyalty and commitment to Santé burned fiercely within me. Still, I was also sure my commitment surpassed his affection toward me.

It was a bittersweet realization that left me with a choice to make. Should I indulge in the fantasy of finding a mythical, unconditional love from another more appropriate man who may not exist? Or embrace the complexities of my connection with Santé, a man already entrenched in my heart?

Sinking back into my driver's seat, my pulse quickened as I awaited Santé's arrival with bated breath. And there, like a mirage materializing, Santé's majestic tan Chevrolet Suburban emerged from the warehouse gates. Our eyes made a brief connection that ignited a spark of excitement within me. With a blink of his headlights, I understood his unspoken signal as a beckoning to follow him.

My Chrysler 300C purred to life as I gracefully executed a U-turn, positioning my car behind his. Santé's lustful intentions were clear, but the location and lurid details were still mysterious. Yet, I found myself embracing the thrill of the unknown.

I trailed him through the streets of Camden, New Jersey, my excitement intertwined with suspense. The city was largely unfamiliar to me, like a puzzle with missing pieces. The neighborhood unfolded before me, with the sun painting the sky in hues of amber and rose.

Finally, his Suburban came to a gentle stop at the edge of a tranquil park, an oasis amidst the urban blight. Earthy scents and a distant, faint, babbling brook enveloped me, accentuating the contradictions of the moment. A cool breeze danced against my skin, carrying an adventure on its wings.

Santé stuck his hand outside his truck's window, waving me to join him. A thrill ran through me as I stepped out of my car and ventured toward him. As I approached his parked truck from behind, every step closer to the man I loved caused my pussy to twitch.

I had barely climbed in the truck before Santé tugged at his sweatpants, "Sup?" he said.

I looked at his growing bulge and replied, "I think you are, Papi." I then provided a cheeky smile. The day was rapidly surrendering to twilight. I fixed my gaze on his face, trying to memorize his handsome features just in case I found myself lost in the darkness of the encroaching evening. Before long, his sweatshirt was behind his neck, and his sweatpants were down at his ankles.

Unprompted, I moved in position, hunched over, face in his balls, facing his steering wheel. I felt Santé's hand tug at my leggings. With a measured and graceful motion, I swept my hands behind me, guiding my leggings down in a ballet of subtle disrobing.

My smooth, sandalwood-complected ass cheeks were exposed for his delight. His hand made contact with my bottom. Pap. He struck my rear end as if he held a deed to my rosy ass cheeks in front of him. Lest there be no doubt, he asked, "Who's ass is this?"

I dutifully replied, "It's your ass, Papi."

His fleshy, peach-toned nightstick enlarged as it brushed against my cheek. His smooth and sticky dick head tapped upon my lips as if knocking for permission to enter. Before I realized it, I had engulfed him whole. Santé's flavor invigorated my mouth and penetrated my soul. The taste of Santé was like my favorite meal, and his moans were my favorite song.

What unfurled over the next few moments was a tingle so exquisite that it outshone any sensation I had ever felt.

I could feel Santé's hands rubbing my ass and groping between my legs. All was perfect, but a single regret tinged my heart. My positioning denied me a glimpse of his reaction.

In lieu of sight, I was gifted with the sensation of his tender touch, his fingertips soft, his hands firm. Santé's exploration of the contours of my pussy lips was both frantic and fumbling. He felt like a traveler in an alien land, bereft of guidance yet thirsting to uncover the secrets veiled by the foreign terrain. Finally, his fingers touched my clit, and his frantic finger movements slowed to a caress. His touch seemed to echo a silent recognition, a sense of comprehension amidst the symphony of the unknown.

Engulfed in the wildfire of passion, lust, and deep diving on Santé's huge dick, I willingly tossed aside all vestiges of caution. Despite the new and dangerous dance of dick-sucking in semi-public, the call of the moment was irresistible, drowning out the whispers of restraint.

The simultaneous sensations of Santé's dick sliding in and out of my mouth and his fingers rubbing my clit brought me to a climax. It was the first time I had experienced the sensation post-surgery. It was also the first time the rush came from someone else's touch. I know I wanted to experience more. But first, it was Santé's time to cum.

I put all my energy and focus on the dick games Santé loved to experience. Tongue lashing, mouth gyrations, ball-licking, and throat masturbation for over twenty minutes culminated in copious amounts of my forehead sweat and Santé's explosion of jizz in my mouth.

Paralyzed in the hush of the aftermath, both of us luxuriated in the lingering afterglow. I busied myself, replenishing my oxygen supply while Santé patiently weathered the storm of involuntary muscle quivers.

Santé shattered the hush that enveloped us, his words trailing into the void. "So, I guess you're happy now?" We both knew, without the need for explicit articulation, that his utterance reached far beyond our shared euphoria. It was a veiled reference, a nod of acknowledgment to the metamorphosis my body had undergone since our last time together, a transformation that his touch was able to discern.

As Santé cleaned himself with a towel, I kept my eyes on him. With daylight's glow all but spent, I was denied the mesmerizing spectacle of his amber eyes sparkling, yet I could still feel the power of his presence. Santé wasn't a talker. Silence was more his signature. It only intensified the tension, igniting a spark of courage inside me that I didn't know I possessed.

It built up from my chest, making its way up my tired throat, giving me the voice I needed at the moment. As Santé pulled up his sweatpants, I finally let it out, "I want to lose my virginity…and I want to lose it to you." My declaration cut through the silence, echoing in the stillness of Santé's steamy Chevrolet Suburban.

CHAPTER
Twenty-Nine

CONFESSIONS AND CONCERNS

I sat in my cozy bedroom on a rainy Wednesday evening, curled up in my makeshift window seat, gazing out at the rain-soaked streets of Philadelphia below. The view from my condominium gave me a sense of detachment. Still, my mind was preoccupied with the conversation with my bestie, Patricia.

While Patricia's voice filled the phone line, I pictured her lounging on her tan leather couch, rocking those red cotton pajamas she loved. In the background, I could hear a commercial previewing upcoming programming for the BET network. That gave rise to the image of her sixty-five-inch TV casting a soft glow around her.

Pat mentioned preparing pork chops for dinner and eagerly awaited Jagger's return. I could almost smell the tantalizing aroma of pork chops wafting through her apartment, and my mouth watered at the thought.

The phone in my hand felt heavy as I contemplated approaching the more sensitive portion of our conversation. "Girl, I gotta talk to you about Jagger moving in so fast. Are you sure this is a good idea? Y'all just started dating, like, a hot minute ago."

She scoffed playfully, "I'm telling you the same thing I told him. I thought about it, and I've decided to agree. I've got a good feeling about this one. Jagger's not like the other dudes I've been with."

I shook my head. "I get it, but you know I gotta keep it real. Moving in together is a big deal, and I don't want you regretting it later."

Pat said," I hear you, but we're good."

Our conversation naturally shifted, and I hesitated again before sharing my own decision. "Okay, speaking of relationships, I gotta spill some juicy deets too." I took a quick breath, then announced, "I've decided to give my virginity to Santé."

I could practically hear Patricia's jaw drop. Her voice intensified. "Are you serious, girl? I thought that feeling would pass. That dude is nothing but trouble, and you really wanna give this clown your cherry? Hell nah!"

I stood my ground. "I know he did me dirty in the past, but things feel different this time. I think he's trying to change."

Patricia wasn't having it. "Girl, you got a habit of falling hard for him, and he only wants you part-time. That works for him and only for him. You need someone who's gonna give you the whole damn package, all of the time, and not just when things get rocky in their real relationship."

Pat wasn't one to hold back, and I pictured her shaking her head in disbelief, trying her best to convince me to reconsider. But, I held firm in my decision, "I get it, but I'm gonna do what feels right for me. It's my choice, and I'm willing to take that risk."

Despite not being physically present with her, I felt a strong connection as we discussed our emotions and decisions. Patricia's passion and concern echoed through the phone, and it was as if she was right there in my room, comforting me.

After a brief moment of tense silence, we agreed to disagree, knowing our friendship was bigger than any disagreement. "Alright, let's just drop it," Pat said.

"We don't see eye to eye on the details of our relationships, but girl, I got your back no matter what," I reassured her.

Patricia's voice sounded hurried as she said, "Oh, girl, I better go. I hear Jagger's keys jingling at the door. He's on his way in. I'll talk to you later in the week."

I agreed and ended the call. I turned my attention back to my bedroom. The soft peach walls were adorned with photographs of me, and a few of Pat and I, a reminder of the precious moments we shared. A new pink throw rug lay beneath my bed, adding a touch of warmth and femininity to the space. The lemon-scented candle on my shelf cast a gentle glow, creating a soothing atmosphere. This room was my haven, a place where I could completely be myself and find solace amid life's challenges.

The rain outside continued to fall, tapping gently on my windowpane. It was as if the world was mirroring the angst I felt about the future. Patricia and I had made our decisions. She would move at hyper-speed with Jagger, and I believed I had a real chance at winning Santé's love.

As I climbed into my bed and snuggled under my new pale gray fur covers, I couldn't help but wonder what the future held for both of us. In the early evening hours, I slipped off to sleep with the lemon scent of the room caressing my nostrils and the soft rain as my soundtrack, tacitly accepting the reality: only the future would reveal the wisdom or folly of our decisions.

CHAPTER
Thirty

BETWEEN DESIRE AND DEMAND

Awakened by the chime of a text message, I stirred from my slumber, enveloped in darkness. Groping for the mirrored lamp on my end table, the cold touch of glass beneath my fingers grounded me back to reality. I retrieved my phone, disconnecting it from the charger with a gentle tug. The screen lit up, piercing the room's shadows, revealing a message from Santé:

Hey, you up?

It was not the first time Santé had texted early, but 4:00 AM was unusual even for him. I typed back, half in a daze:

I was asleep, but I'm up now. You okay?

His reply came swiftly, laced with an apology I wasn't expecting:

Sorry to interrupt your beauty sleep. I wanna talk about what you said you wanted me to do.

The words on the screen ignited a blend of curiosity and eagerness.

Nestled in the plush embrace of fur sheets, I sat up, the luxurious texture contrasting sharply with the sudden alertness that gripped me.

What? I typed back, fingertips hesitating over the keyboard as my pulse quickened.

Your virginity, came his reply, simple and direct.

Oh. That single word felt laden with more meaning than I could unpack at the moment.

A subtle warmth suffused my cheeks, and not just from the heat of the room. My fingers paused, hovering over the phone. A moment's hesitation as I considered my reply.

Do you want to talk about that now, at 4 AM?

I typed back, incredulity mixing with a hint of amusement.

Yeah. I'm in the bathroom getting ready for work. If you want, we can take care of that this morning.

Santé's reply was practical to the point of being jarring.

I couldn't help but marvel at how men could distill something as intimate as losing one's virginity into something so… transactional as if it were merely another item to be checked off a to-do list or a grocery list. But it only got worse from there. Before I could reply, he double-texted.

If you want I can open you up before I go to work.

The pain of his cold detachment was searing. It felt like an abrupt chill against the warmth of my naïve love, a jarring contrast that momentarily threatened to awaken me from the spell he had so carefully and consistently enraptured me with.

That instant of cold clarity was quickly enveloped by a wave of rationalization, smoothing over the edges of his all-too-practical words that might have served as a stark awakening. Rather than sinking back into the plush sanctuary of my fur sheets and returning to sleep, I summoned a trace of boldness, intending to subtly confront his misogynistic tone.

Me: *I'm not a garage, Papi. Could you phrase it differently? This is special to me.*

Santé: *Got you, Princess. But remember, I'm a thug, so I only get but so soft.*

Despite understanding that I was far too mature for a 'Thug Papi,' there was an embarrassing truth I couldn't ignore; my heart acted like an uncontrollable magnet, irresistibly drawn to the rough edges of Santé's personality.

What followed was another predictable two-step in our customary dance. Santé offered a minor concession, and I, in turn, assigned it far more significance than it deserved.

Is today gonna be our special day or not? Do I have to leave for work early or not? Santé roughly and impatiently pressed his message.

It would be nice to see you, but I'm still healing.

My reply, a delicate balance between the longing to be close to him and the need to protect my vulnerability.

You know you have more than one hole, he texted.

My eyes scanned the words, but my brain wrestled with the glaring lack of empathy they conveyed. It felt as though I stood at the edge of a brook, yearning for the safety of its banks yet drawn by the deceptively gentle pull toward the center, even as the movement hinted at a waterfall just ahead. The battle between the instinct for self-preservation, the allure of his lust, and my longing for his love left me teetering on the brink of decision and desire.

The other virginity is not the virginity I'm offering.

I teased with a hint of serious resistance.

I want both virginities.

He insisted, revealing an expectation.

Not today, Papi.

I replied, my response a firm yet gentle boundary set against his pressing desire.

Fine, At least suck Papi's Big Dick right quick, but I won't be able to stay long.

As I read his message, a cloud settled over me, the acknowledgment of a relationship pieced together from brief, fleeting encounters. It was as though each stolen moment, while cherished, echoed the hollowness of what might never fully be. A new message arrived:

I'll be there at 5:30. Be ready.

The prospect of seeing and being near him once more swept through me, overwhelming my reasoning. At that moment, all reservations dissolved. As I had done so many times during our situation-ship, I acquiesced.

I replied:

5:30 AM. I'll be ready.

CHAPTER
Thirty-One

RUSHED PASSION

It was 6:35 AM when Santé finally arrived. My first thought was, how much time will we have? Although we had different jobs, we were both supposed to report to work at 7:00 AM.

But both thoughts quickly disappeared when I realized he was not driving his suburban truck but had pulled into my parking lot driving the blue Toyota. I was momentarily dumbstruck. I thought, How? Did he really come to see me in Jackie's car? I couldn't decide whether I should be appreciative or annoyed. I settled on neutral gratitude for his presence, irrespective of how he arrived.

Clad in my blush-pink bra and matching panties, I opened the door, and there stood Santé, hyperventilating, his face etched with stress. "Sup. I know I'm running late. She was tripping. I don't have a lotta time," he explained, his voice ragged with haste. He didn't need to specify to whom he was referring. The unspoken presence of Jackie's name lingered between us, a familiar undercurrent in the background of our relationship.

Santé stepped briskly into my condo, making a beeline for my bedroom without hesitation. Only pausing momentarily to secure the door behind him, I followed. I entered my bedroom just in time to see him shimmy out of his pants, his torso already bare. While our trysts were typically fleeting, the urgency felt unprecedented, even for us.

What occurred next was a high-energy face fucking that left me dazed and exhausted. I could tell my body was healing because patting my pussy while having my mouth stuffed didn't cause pain, only pleasure.

Seeing Santé in a pleasure trance sent a flood of tingles down my spine. But my pleasure while pleasing Santé wasn't simply vicarious. When he placed my head against my bedroom wall, I opened wide to receive all eleven inches of his man-meat. An intense wave of euphoria engulfed me, washing away every ounce of stress and fatigue built up over the previous weeks.

After dutifully swallowing his joy juice, Santé looked down at me and said, "I'll text you later from work, probably on my break."

Exhausted, I replied, "I'd love that. We can discuss the other things we'd like to do."

As Santé dressed, he caught my gaze and asked, "So you're running as late as me?"

I managed a smile and replied, "Yeah, maybe even more after that action against the wall my throat is sore. I need to catch a twenty-minute nap."

Santé laughed, his amusement filling the room. "Papi's dick wore you out, huh?"

I blushed as I replied, "Yeah, Papi." Then added, "Could you please lock up behind you? I can't even make it to the door."

Santé chuckled, a hint of cocky bravado in his voice as he said, "I got you." That assurance, along with his ego-driven laughter, lingered in the air. Those were the last things I recalled from the early morning hours of Friday, November 9th, 2018.

JACKIE KNOWS

The harsh light of noon cut through my room like a surgical knife, pulling me from the gentle arms of sleep into a waking nightmare. Bleary-eyed, I glanced at the red, unforgiving numbers of my digital clock: 12:04 PM.

Panic bubbled up as I realized I was hours late for work. My body was filled with fatigue, but the fear of repercussions from my job urged me to reach for my phone. I needed to check and see if they had called or texted.

What I found was a message from Santé. The instant I made sense of the words, my world stopped:

Santé: *Jackie knows something's going on.*

My breath seized, and my fingers flew across the screen: *How? And how bad is it?*

Santé replied within seconds:

She knows I didn't go straight to work. Her car has a locator on it, and it can be turned on when it's parked.

As I exhaled, my body vibrated. A cold, electrifying sensation froze my heart. The room seemed to close in on me, and the taste of fear was sharp in my mouth.

So what do we do?

I managed to text, but every letter was a struggle.

I don't wanna lose my house and my kids.

Santé's response hit me with a powerful realization. Suddenly, it wasn't just about us. It was about his family, his home, his entire life. A torrent of empathy washed over me, a soul-deep understanding of his fear. My own loss, as profound as it was to me, seemed small in comparison.

With trembling hands, I offered a lifeline:

So does this mean we need to take a break?

An off-ramp. Not an end, but a delay. A chance for him, a chance for us.

A tense ninety seconds stretched into eternity before his reply came, a simple, devastating word:

Yes.

In the harsh light of noon, I fell back onto my bed, tears spilling down my cheeks. I grappled with the loss of what might have been, overshadowed by the unimaginable loss he could be facing. The scent of Santé lingered on my sheets—a bitter reminder of a phenomenal morning we shared but one which may have forever altered the course of our lives.

CHAPTER
Thirty-Three

REGRET AND CONSEQUENCES

The sharp sting of regret pressed on my heart, intensified by the memory of a weekend spent drowning in anguish over a love that was never really mine. Each thought a tantalizing "What if," a cruel reminder of my choices. Instead of being in the office on Friday, I surrendered to my grief, letting every tear and choked sob claim my weekend. The bitter scent of jealousy and loss still lingered in my nostrils.

Walking through the grand glass doors of Nybor Productions that Monday morning, I felt the world shift beneath me as if the ground had tilted ever so slightly. The gentle murmurs of the employees carried an undertone of gossip, and my shoes clicked a melancholic rhythm against the sleek marble floors.

I paused outside the imposing mahogany door that led to the office of the CEO, Mr. Murray. I took a moment to steady my breathing, drawing in the rich scent of polished wood mingled with the distant aroma of freshly brewed coffee. With a soft sigh, I pushed the door open.

The vastness of the room was overwhelming. The enormous floor-to-ceiling windows allowed the early morning sun to illuminate the room, making the luxurious red carpet glow. The walls, adorned with tastefully chosen art pieces, seemed to echo with whispers of power and influence.

Mr. Terrence Murray sat behind his grand desk, papers scattered all around, and behind him, the expansive view of the city stretched out like an artist's canvas, painted with skyscrapers and busy streets. I could almost hear the faint sounds of the city buzzing below, the distant hum of engines, and the occasional honk of a car.

Then there was Ken, lurking in a shadowy corner of the room, his face masked by a veil of inscrutability. I could taste the tension in the air, metallic and sharp, as I shot him an icy glare. Without knowing the details, I blamed him for me being called there.

"Demoted!" My voice pierced through the room's hushed atmosphere like a gunshot, echoing repeatedly in my ears. I felt the prickling heat of indignation rise in my cheeks.

As if reading from a script, Mr. Murray's voice carried an apathetic finality, "Victoria, given the circumstances of last week, we've made our decision."

The words felt like an anchor dragging me down. Yet, I had to know for sure. "Can you clarify that for me, Mr. Murray?" I asked, my voice tremulous but resolute.

Ken shifted uncomfortably, a barely audible sigh escaping his lips.

Mr. Murray's eyes met mine, attempting to emulate understanding, though they held a clinical detachment. His words fell on me with chilling precision. "Victoria, Friday's unexcused absence was just the latest event in a string of circumstances which necessitated the need for action. Your mother's condition, which has caused you to be away from the office so frequently, is understandable, but the combination of absences and tardiness has brought us to a crossroads."

I swallowed hard, feeling my throat constrict as he continued. "A group decision was made that, to be fair to your personal needs as well as the other team members who need more attentiveness, we must allow Ken Rutherford to act in the role of Vice President of Production solely. He has shouldered these responsibilities with a single-minded focus on many occasions."

I could feel Ken's smug satisfaction from across the room. My hands clenched into fists as Mr. Murray added, "Returning to your original position of Junior Vice President of Production will still allow you to contribute to the team without the same level of responsibility inherent in the job, which you clearly haven't had the time to dedicate exclusively."

My heart pounded in my ears. "Is this final?" I asked, my voice barely above a whisper. "Can there be further consideration?"

Mr. Murray leaned back in his chair, studying me for a moment before he replied, "I've made the decision, but I'm open to a review and the possibility of returning to a co-vice presidency in six to eight months."

His eyes drifted to the clock on the wall, and he stood, signaling the end of our conversation. "I have other meetings to prepare for. You both may leave."

I walked out of the office in a mental haze, my world collapsing around me. Losing the promotion and the love of my life in such a condensed timespan induced a bitterness I had never tasted before.

Ken's voice, dripping with insincere concern, interrupted my thoughts. "I'll be happy to instruct the staff to help you move back downstairs with the other junior vice presidents."

My anger flared. I held my hand out, stopping Ken in his tracks. "Ken. Not now, not now."

"Of course not. Not right now," Ken replied, his voice dripping with venom. "I wouldn't think of having all of your belongings tossed out of that wonderful corner office." Ken moved closer to me, his breath hot against my ear as he whispered, "You have a week to get your shit downstairs, or I will personally throw it in the hallway."

His smug smile was a knife to my gut. As he walked away, I stood motionless in disillusioned befuddlement, the day's losses squeezing my heart. I thought, *Today was indeed a bad day.*

CHAPTER
Thirty-Four

FRIENDLY DIFFERENCES

Tuesday evening at 7 PM found me seeking comfort in the company of my dear friend Patricia. The day had left me raw, my emotions frayed and tangled. My condominium's dimly lit living room became a sanctuary, with soft gray upholstery and a cream mohair carpet underfoot. We sank into plush cream lambskin leather reclining seats, the chairs hugging our forms in a gentle embrace.

A vase of white lilies glinted in the soft light, filling the space with their delicate fragrance. Nearby, two glasses of sparkling blush Belvoir Organic Elderflower and Rose Cordial water fizzed gently, a light counterpoint to the heady scent of truffle popcorn.

"I'm sorry I can't give you anything more than truffle popcorn," I apologized, embarrassed. "I haven't gone shopping recently, and I'm not in a mental state for cooking."

Patricia reached for a handful, her eyes filled with empathy. "Don't worry about it, Victoria. This is perfect." After a moment, she added, "But I'm going to be honest—I want to separate the loss of Santé, who, in my opinion, isn't a loss, from the loss of your promotion."

I sneered jokingly, trying to lighten the mood. "Shouldn't we be talking about Jagger, your roommate?"

She grinned, her eyes twinkling. "Yes, we will, in a little bit. And by the way, soon he may be more than a roommate."

I froze, my hand filled with popcorn. "You're not considering marriage, are you?"

Patricia blushed. "Neither one of us has talked about it, but for the first time, I'm open to the possibility."

I managed to smile, happy for her but secretly envious. We fell into silence before I finally said, "Well, there's no need to talk about Santé with you since you'll never understand my connection to him."

Patricia replied firmly, "I know exactly why you want him in your life. But what you don't understand is that you're free from your own restraints. There's a whole new world available to you if you just reach out for it."

I let the silence stretch, then finally admitted, "Perhaps, but I should focus on my career right now. Technically, he didn't say we were over forever, but who knows how long it'll be before I hear from him."

Patricia's hand found mine, her grip firm and reassuring. "I'll continue to support you, but my support for this Santé madness has its limits. You deserve better."

I forced a small smile. "I thought we weren't talking about Santé anymore."

"You're right." Patricia smiled, her eyes warm. "That was my last comment on him for today."

The truffle popcorn crunched as we shifted the conversation to lighter topics. "Let's watch the latest show from Nybor Productions," I suggested, eager to escape the intensity of our earlier discussion.

The sixty-five-inch screen illuminated, and we settled into comfortable silence. In the soft glow of the television and Patricia's steady friendship, I found a bright spot in an otherwise dark time.

CHAPTER
Thirty-Five

DOWNWARD DESCENT

T hursday afternoon found me sequestered within the sleek, impersonal confines of Nybor Productions's corporate headquarters, ensconced in the room where I'd once wielded power as Vice President of Production.

Bitterness gnawed at my very marrow as I surveyed my corner office, filled with its sterile gleam of glass and steel. A discordant hum from the city below laced the air with a constant reminder of the world moving on.

As I instructed Beth on logistics, my eyes caught the dim glow of the sun dancing across the glossy desk. It was laden with items that needed relegation to the downstairs office—a place for those beneath the senior executives.

"That painting," I said, my voice cold, pointing to a colorful canvas, its vibrancy now mocking me, "and my framed photographs should return to their original locations in my downstairs office."

Beth's face, usually pale, looked ghastly, like the life had been sucked out of her. She let out a soft groan, a sound of her own downfall. The realization hit me then, as acrid as burnt coffee lingering in the air—she, too, was facing a demotion.

Beth stood ready, her notepad in hand, her perfume—a sweet floral scent I'd grown accustomed to—now tainted with an undertone of despair. Then, my office phone rang like a shrill note from an unwelcome intruder.

"May I?" Beth asked, her voice quivering slightly, motioning to the phone.

I nodded, granting her permission. Her professional greeting resonated through the room, a veneer over her uncertainty. She looked at me, eyes wide and a frown pulling at her lips. The silence that followed seemed to thicken, heavy as a winter fog.

"It's the rehabilitation center for your mother," she whispered, her voice cracking like thin ice beneath our shared burdens.

I reached for the receiver, and my fingers trembled. The world seemed to close around me. This was my new existence, where power, luxury, and control had slipped through my fingers like sand.

My hand clenched the receiver, my breath trapped in a moment of foreboding as a soft voice from the other end of the line spoke.

"Miss Victoria? This is Susan from Moss Rehabilitation Center in Elkins Park, Pennsylvania. I'm calling about your mother's afternoon therapy sessions," she began, her voice carrying an undertone of hesitation. "We'd like you to attend if at all possible. Her rehabilitation goals have changed."

A cold shiver ran down my spine, and I tightened my grip on the phone. "Changed? What does that mean, exactly?" I inquired, my voice sharpening.

There was a pause filled with the disquieting hum of the line. Then Susan's voice returned, hesitant and soft. "Our staff is less certain we'll be able to achieve the original level of recovery we discussed at the beginning of your mother's rehabilitation plan. The clinicians would like to go through and modify the plan, along with expectations based on her physical capabilities and her demonstrated willingness to achieve the benchmarks."

Her words were a sucker punch, and I felt the room spin around me. Not again, I thought. I'll have to leave the office once more. Just when everything's falling apart here. But then I thought, maybe it's the best time to go. I've already been demoted, and my superiors have offered their token empathy regarding Mother's condition.

I tried to keep my voice steady as I responded, "I understand, Susan. What time do you need me there?"

"Three o'clock would be ideal, Miss Victoria."

"Very well," I said, ending the conversation with a curt goodbye.

I placed the receiver down with a click, feeling the news settle heavily upon me. Beth's eyes met mine, filled with concern.

"Beth," I began, my voice breaking, "The staff at the rehabilitation center isn't sure they can achieve the original recovery goals for my Mother. They want to modify her care plan. I need to be there this afternoon."

Beth's face paled even further, but she kept her composure. "I understand, boss," she said, her voice filled with restrained but sincere compassion. "I'll continue with the moving of the office items while you attend to your mother."

I grabbed my black leather Gucci purse, its luxurious texture lost on me in that moment. As I walked toward the elevators, a wave of annoyance and disheartenment washed over me. A tide of disappointments. Bitter, I said to myself: *And the hits just keep coming.*

The soft ding of the elevator was a stark reminder of reality, pulling me from my thoughts. I stepped inside. My reflection in the polished steel looked like a stranger's face, worn and defeated. The doors slid closed, and I was left alone with the silence and the overwhelming sense of everything I'd lost.

CHAPTER
Thirty-Six

FOLLOWING SECRETS

As "Long As I Live" by Toni Braxton played softly through the speakers as I drove in the far right lane, the song's haunting lyrics mirroring my sorrow. Santé had moved on, his life continuing without me, a thought that left my heart shattered once again. I liked the song, but the pain it conjured was too intense, so halfway through the song, I reluctantly turned off the radio silencing the melody and my heartache.

The only sounds remaining were my tires against the asphalt of Cottman Avenue, Route 73, heading westbound on the grim march toward the Moss Rehabilitation Center.

Although my eyes were on the road, my thoughts were with my mother. I imagined her lying patient and fragile as an old photograph.

Suddenly, a Tan Chevrolet Suburban, similar to Santé's, snapped me from my inner thoughts, it was just a few car lengths ahead.

Over the years, those trucks had become mere background noise, but that one had a presence that demanded attention.

My foot pressed down on the gas, eagerness guiding me closer. The license plate, once obscured, unveiled itself, there it was. The familiar sequence of numbers and letters, like a secret code only I could decipher. Adrenaline surged. It was Santé's license plate. It had to be him.

My vision narrowed, the world reducing to the road ahead and the Suburban just ahead of me.

I maneuvered closer, my car's engine roaring in harmony with the wild beat of my heart. Luck struck. A red light froze the truck.

But when I pulled alongside, expecting to find Santé's familiar face. It wasn't Santé's face behind the wheel at all. It was hers; It was...Jackie's.

Santé's girlfriend.

She was immediately recognizable. The realization struck with the force of a thunderclap and my world shook like a magnitude eight earthquake.

It was unsettling to have a familiarity with a stranger I'd never met. I had glimpsed Jackie in a single photograph over the internet, years before.

I debated if I should stare longer, I didn't want to draw attention to myself. So I looked away briefly. Then a thought—

The red light would be changing in mere moments. I needed to see more, I needed to see her.

My eyes slyly returned to Jackie. It struck me how ordinary and yet how extraordinary she looked simultaneously. Time seemed to slow as I drank in every detail of her. The way her eyes glanced nervously at the road, the curve of her lips, the graceful tilt of her head.

There, locked in a fragile connection, imperceptible to anyone other than me, I contemplated how we were interwoven by irony, lies, and secrets. Suddenly, it was too much, too real, I turned away.

Even that fleeting encounter with Jackie threatened to muddy the pure, albeit naïve love for Santé, to which I clung.

I could sense storm clouds of confusion and moral complexity gathering at the edge of my consciousness—unsettling the detached bliss I held when Jackie was nothing more than a distant concept.

I took what I'd hoped to be one last peek at her before retreating to my ranch of rationalizations. I knew she was Santé's live-in girlfriend; he had told me that a few years prior. Then I noticed the glinting ring on her finger, which told a darker truth. Oh Shit—Jackie was Santé's wife!

Green light!

AND JUST LIKE THAT—THE SLOW-SPEED CHASE WAS ON, DRIVEN by a curiosity that refused to abate.

With every block, the tension grew. The Suburban was almost pulling me along, just as it had the many times Santé would lead me through the streets of Camden, New Jersey.

This time was different however, I was no longer his imagined second girlfriend; It was official, I was his mistress.

Santé's Suburban, driven by his wife, signaled left, turning onto St. Vincent Street. I hesitated a few seconds before making the same turn, following her from a cautious distance.

My heart pounded with conflicting emotions battling for dominance as we drove down the unfamiliar road. My palms were clammy against the steering wheel. I swallowed hard, and with every block, the tension grew.

My internal ranting filled with second thoughts and moral niceties became an annoyance. I told myself, *Shut up bitch, you're in this now.*

I had no idea what I was doing or why, I just knew it was too late to turn back now. I did extract one self-promise—if I saw Santé I'd get the hell outta there—fast.

Finally, after several blocks, Jackie finally pulled over near the corner of Lawn Street, the truck settling into a space by the curb. My heart leaped into my throat as I drove past, pretending not to notice her, afraid that stopping might reveal I had been following.

A block later, I made a sharp U-turn, the tires protesting with a squeal. My chest felt tight, my breaths were shallow.

Parking half a block away, far enough to avoid suspicion but close enough to see. I saw him. Not Santé, but an unknown man emerging from the stone-faced house at the corner.

The stranger's stride was confident and purposeful. He reached the sidewalk just as Jackie stepped out of the truck.

Questions whirled: Why was Jackie driving Santé's truck? Why here, during work hours? Where were Santé's children?

My pulse roared in my ears as their hands brushed, their fingers entwined with an intimacy that sent chills down my spine. Each mysterious interaction between Jackie and the stranger drew me further into a dark space.

Then, as if to answer all my questions with a single, shocking gesture, the man leaned down and kissed Jackie on the lips. A visceral jolt—a realization coursed through me, a cold clarity cutting through the confusion.

Jackie wasn't just living the life I could only dream of, as Santé's wife; She was also living another life entirely—with another man.

I could taste the betrayal, bitter and lingering. The compassion I had been tempted to feel for Jackie and the traces of guilt trying to surface, because of my love for Santé, vanished.

It was replaced by a righteous anger that burned hot and fierce.

The green door closed behind them, leaving me alone with my frenzied feelings, and one undeniable truth: Jackie was cheating on our man!

CHAPTER
Thirty-Seven

THE OTHER MAN

Who was Jackie's lover, and what would I do about it? I sat on the edge of my bed, the soft pink satin sheets cool beneath me, my mind a battlefield of love, hatred, guilt, and judgment.

The rush of the forced heat pushing through my condominium's vents was a distant murmur. The dim glow of my bedside lamp cast a soft halo around the room. A faint scent of lavender from a nearby candle infused the air. My hands clenched and unclenched, the physical manifestation of my internal struggle.

The world around me had become distant and unimportant. The only reality was the searing knowledge that I was no longer alone in my participation in infidelity. My love for Santé remained unshaken but more complicated, the landscape of our relationship irrevocably altered by what I had witnessed.

I stood and began to pace, my bare feet on the shag carpet, the sensation both comforting and grounding as the questions circled in my mind. What now? Could I keep silent? Did I need more proof of Jackie's infidelity? Would I let Santé know?

My reflection in the mirror caught my pale green eyes, my expression a mix of determination and vulnerability. The decision pressed down on me heavily. My peach-colored walls seemed to close in as I grappled with what lay ahead.

Ten minutes later, I came to a halt, my soul resonating with clarity. The answer was there, solid and undeniable.

I would expose Jackie and her lover, but first, I needed proof.

I took a vow, a promise to myself that I would see this through, no matter where it led. The room was still, the world outside was irrelevant. Only the path ahead mattered now, and I was committed to walking it, whatever the cost.

CHAPTER
Thirty-Eight

SHADOW PLAY

The air was thick with the faint scent of polishing chemicals as I entered the towering Nybor Productions headquarters. It was 6AM on a Friday, and the lobby was nearly empty.

Sunlight bathed through the two-story-high floor-to-ceiling windows, casting a tranquil dance of light and shadow on the immaculate gray and white marble floors. The soft hum of electricity and the occasional shuffle of the early morning staff whispered in the air, creating an ambiance of serene solitude as if the world was gently waking up to the promise of a new day.

I spotted Chuck Daniels, the head of security, down the end of the hallway. The low murmur of his radio reached my ears, the lingering aroma of his coffee filled the air, and I could feel the hard, cool surface of the marble beneath my kitten heels.

"Chuck," I called, the click of my heels echoing through the space as I approached, "do you still do private investigative work?"

His eyes widened momentarily, and he looked at me, a bit flustered. "I haven't been into private investigating for two years, Victoria."

I moved closer, my voice lowering to a near whisper, tinged with challenge. "No longer have the skills to find out information on a person? Perhaps provide surveillance?"

Chuck looked around nervously and guided me further down the hallway to a dead end. He was frowning now, his face set in lines of determination and curiosity. "My skills are just fine," he said softly, "but my license has lapsed."

A small smile played at the corner of my lips. I posed a hypothetical, my voice teasing yet serious. "If no one would find out, would you be willing to make a quick couple thousand dollars?"

His eyes sparkled, intrigued. "What would be involved?"

I grinned, feeling the rush of excitement. The taste of victory was almost palpable. "Surveillance, photos, and positive identification of a man who lives on the corner of Lawn Street. I can get you the exact address along with a general description."

He rubbed his chin, his eyes narrowed. "So, based on the description, you want me to follow him?"

I nodded, feeling the impact of what I was asking. "I need you to trail him, but mainly, I need you to stake out the house and take pictures of any female guests that arrive—especially a Latina woman driving either a Chevy Suburban or blue Toyota."

Chuck took a deep breath. I could hear his apprehension. After a moment, he agreed, his voice firm. "And how do we work out payment?"

I detailed the plan, then said, "Once you deliver the pictures and the positive identification on the male, send an invoice directly to my secretary, Beth, in a sealed envelope. The description of services should read 'character development research cost for Red Desire Alley.' Beth will cut you a check within twenty-four hours."

Chuck's eyes narrowed, a spark of realization dawning. "So you're billing the company?"

I nodded, unable to suppress the triumphant smile that spread across my face. "Yes," I confirmed, the taste of victory almost sweet on my tongue. "It's all in the name of research, isn't it?"

We shook hands, the grip warm and firm, a pact sealed in confidence and trust. Chuck took my cell phone to add his number. A pause was filled with the sound of Chuck tapping on my phone, and then he handed it back.

"Text me the address and general description of the dude. If you have a general description of the woman, that will help too, but it's not necessary," Chuck said, his voice filled with professionalism.

I agreed, promising to send everything in about an hour, and we parted ways.

I headed toward the gold-toned mirrored elevators. Passing through the metal detectors, I scanned my ID, entered the elevator, and pressed the fifth-floor button.

The doors closed, and I was alone, my reflection staring back at me, my face filled with determination.

I held the handlebar behind me, feeling the cool metal under my fingers. Exposing Jackie became my new commitment, and I told myself I was dedicated to the truth.

In retrospect, the quivering in my stomach was likely a sign that things were more complicated—and that they were about to get much worse.

CHAPTER
Thirty-Nine

DANGEROUS JUSTIFICATIONS

The cold office phone pressed against my cheek while I was in a heated conversation with Patricia about Santé, Jackie, and the dangerous game I'd been playing.

I looked out the window as Patricia's voice, usually so soothing, carried a harsh edge. "I can't believe you, Victoria! Following Santé's wife through the dangerous streets of Philly like that? You could have been shot or, at a minimum, had your feelings hurt!" Her anger came through the line like hot poker in my ear.

"I know what I'm doing, Patricia," I tried to explain, my palms sweating, a tingle of anxiety rushing down my spine. "Jackie doesn't even know what I look like."

"You have no idea what that woman knows!" Patricia's words stung. "When Santé left you back in 2016, didn't you think Jackie pretended to be him, asking for a picture of you by email? You may have been heavier back then, but she may still have an image of you in her head."

I felt my face heat up at the memory, and my voice wavered as I tried to defend myself. "Girl, no matter how you look at this, I wasn't completely wrong."

Patricia's voice hardened, her words as cold as the November wind outside my fifth-floor window. "You were in a dangerous situation, Victoria, and you are contemplating making it much worse."

I was livid, my breath coming faster. "How could you say such a thing? You're supposed to be my friend! I knew and loved Santé first. This woman came along after. And speaking of 2016, when she found out about us, I did her a favor."

Patricia was puzzled. "A favor? What the hell are you talking about? A favor by having sex with her man?"

"Yes, a favor," I snapped, feeling the anger boil inside me like a kettle on the stove. I knew Santé first, loved him first. If not for me, he'd still be dangling her along. Jackie had been begging him for years, had his children, and yet he only married her to cover his tracks. Without me, he would've stayed unclaimed and free.

Patricia took a deep breath before speaking, her voice filled with concern. "Victoria, how do you know you were the only one he got caught with? You know what? I won't dispute what you've said, but what you're doing is rationalizing. None of it was right."

Patricia's voice quickened. "Maybe Jackie is getting paid back for manipulating Santé into marriage by him running the streets with you and probably others, but that doesn't take away from your wrong. And I'm telling you, if you go too far into this, I will not be there for you when this entire debacle threatens to destroy more than your career. It could destroy your entire life."

Her words hit me like a Mack truck. The room suddenly felt cold, and I could taste the bitter tang of fear.

I couldn't take it anymore. My voice was ice as I ended the conversation. "Look, Pat, I love you, but if that's how you feel, then perhaps we shouldn't talk about this. I have to go. I didn't get the support I expected, but that's okay. I have to return to work."

I didn't wait for a response. I slammed down the office phone, the sound echoing in the room like a gunshot.

CHAPTER
Forty

LINES DRAWN IN THE SAND

The crisp echo of my knife against the cutting board filled my condominium, a familiar crackle amid the Sunday evening's quiet. Under the glow of recessed lighting, my kitchen—its clean lines and subtle under-cabinet illumination—was a culinary jewel.

The sun's retreat had surrendered the stage to artificial light, dimming the once-sunlit warmth to a cooler ambiance. As I laid salmon pieces upon the baking tray, its rich pink breaking the monochrome spell of my marble countertop, I found myself lost in the rhythm of meal preparation.

My phone vibrated against the smooth surface, a sudden intrusion. Swiping the screen, I balanced the phone between my ear and shoulder, continuing my task. "Hey, Patricia," I said flatly.

"Vicky, we need to talk." Her voice carried a tension that made me pause, my salmon momentarily forgotten.

"What's going on?" I asked, trying to keep my tone light despite the heaviness creeping into my chest.

"It's about your plan…with Santé and Jackie," Patricia plunged in, no preambles. "I told Jagger."

"I know you're fucking lying?" The words came out sharper than I intended, my breath catching, my heart skipping a beat, as a cold shiver raced down my spine.

"I had to tell someone, Vicky. Jagger's my boyfriend now," she explained, her voice breaking slightly. I pictured her eyes darting around.

"And you chose to share my personal business, what the fuck?" I asked, my fingers tightening around the edge of the countertop, the smooth surface offering little comfort while the scent of basil from the jar on my counter offered a mere temporary distraction.

"Vicky, he thinks—he says you're getting too involved. He says that it could end badly for everyone." Patricia's voice wavered, the usual firmness replaced by a subtle tremor.

I picked up the bottle of avocado oil, pouring it over the salmon as I processed her words. "So, now Jagger's an expert on my life?" The oil shimmered, catching the overhead light, while the tightness in my stomach pushed me forward.

Patricia's voice rose in pitch. "He's been through something similar, Vicky. It's not about being an expert." As she continued, she lowered her volume, and her words flowed at a noticeably slower pace. "He's just worried, and honestly, so am I."

I grasped the smoked truffle sea salt in my hand. The dispenser felt heavier than usual as I seasoned the fish, "Worried enough to consider betraying a friend?" I asked, scattering the truffle sea salt, more out of habit than focus.

"It's not like that. I'm stuck between you and what I think is right." Patricia's voice sounded strained with intensity. "Vicky, I think meddling in Jackie's marriage could cause more harm than good. Can't you see that?" Patricia's pitch again rose and fell, as she achieved a tone of softness and sincerity that begged for understanding.

I slid the salmon into the oven, the heat a welcome contrast to the chill settling over me. "If their marriage is strong, it'll survive. I'm not the villain here for exposing the truth," I protested.

Patricia sighed, "But what if you're wrong? What if this destroys more than it reveals?"

I leaned against the counter, feeling the cool marble through my apron. "Then that's on them, not me. I'm just bringing the truth to light."

There was a heavy silence, filled only by the distant soothing sound of Janet Jackson crooning, "That's the way love goes," from the living room speakers.

Patricia's voice pierced the momentary peace, "Vicky, if you go through with this…I don't know if I can support it. It's one thing to think it, another to act on it."

I slammed my oven door. The sting in my chest exposed another fracture to my delicate heart, though I refused to admit that directly. Straining my voice, I yelled, "So, your morality is based on what you think is best for Jackie, a woman neither of us has ever met? And that's more precious than our friendship?"

"It's not about choosing, or what's precious, Vicky. It's about doing what's right." Patricia's voice was firm, a steel spine beneath the softness.

I closed my eyes briefly, the complexities of our situation pressing in. "I'm not asking you to choose, Patricia. But I thought you'd at least understand." The phone line was quiet for a moment, both of us lost in the gravity of what was unfolding.

I opened my watery eyes as Patricia said, "I understand more than you know, Vicky. But understanding doesn't mean agreeing. It also doesn't mean I have to stand by and watch you potentially ruin lives."

Before I could reply, Patricia heaved deeply. "Vicky. Jagger said something that stuck with me." Her voice deepened slightly, her words spoken with measured pauses.

I leaned against my center island, tapping my fingers to a nervous rhythm. "And what's that?" I asked, tilting my head to the side, the heat from the nearby oven barely penetrating the growing cold between us.

I placed the call on speakerphone just as Patricia told me, "Jagger said fucking with someone else's marriage and trying to manipulate the outcome never ends well. Not for anyone involved." Her words echoed in my kitchen, bouncing off the cheerful yellow cabinets and settling heavily in the air.

I scoffed, unable to help the bitter laugh that escaped. "Since when did Jagger become the moral compass we're all supposed to follow?"

"It's not about following anyone, Vicky. It's about seeing the damage your actions could cause," Patricia said. I had to admit to myself, her persistence was admirable, even if it grated on my nerves.

"That's when our conversation spiraled into a dance of conflicting ideals, fraying our friendship. "If their marriage is as fragile as you think, then maybe it's better the truth comes out now," I argued, the conviction of my voice clashing with the fluttering in my belly."

Patricia sighed, her exhale thick as maple syrup. "Vicky, I'm worried about you. This…obsession with exposing Jackie, it's consuming you. Can't you see that?"

I shivered at the accusation, my wounded pride throbbing. "It's not an obsession, Patricia. It's about justice, about refusing to let Jackie play Santé for a fool."

"But at what cost, Vicky? Your safety, becoming more entangled with Santé? Or at the cost of your peace? And what about the toll on our friendship?" Her voice held a raw honesty, a plea for me to see reason beyond what she considered my tunnel vision of retribution.

My spacious kitchen suddenly felt smaller, as we navigated the treacherous waters of our disagreement. "I thought you, of all people, would understand the need to stand up for what's right," I said, disappointment accenting my salty tears while defiance dripped from my tongue.

"Standing up for what's right doesn't mean tearing others down, Vicky. There's a difference between justice and vengeance," Patricia countered, her words a gentle but firm rebuke nevertheless.

Our conversation reached a precarious imbalance—our friendship teetering on the edge of a precipice, one I hadn't anticipated when I first considered my righteous cause. "Patricia, if I go through with this…where does that leave us?" I asked, silently praying that my vulnerability remained concealed, shielding me from being left raw and exposed.

Her response was slow and measured. "I'll always care about you, Vicky. But I can't support this path you're on. It's not just about choosing between right and wrong anymore. It's about choosing the kind of person I want to be, and the kind of people I want in my life."

The finality in her tone was a cold splash of reality, "So, this is it? You're saying if I do this, I'm doing it alone?"

"I'm saying that I can't follow you down this path, Vicky. Not with a clear conscience." Patricia's voice was soft, regretful, yet unwavering in her resolve.

The silence between us filled the room. As I stared at the oven, the salmon inside now an afterthought, I realized that the choices I made next would not only define my relationship with Santé and Jackie but also the very fabric of my friendship with Patricia.

I stammered, "Patricia, I…I hear you, but this is my life and my love. But I will think about this. About everything you've said," I muttered while lowering my eyes.

"Please do, Vicky. Really think about it," she urged, a note of hope threading through the caution in her tone.

As we ended the call, my kitchen felt emptier, the vibrant yellow cabinets less cheerful, their warmth unable to reach the chill that had settled in my heart. The path ahead was murky, fraught with potential loss and heartache. Nevertheless, I felt directed by a moral compass, though conflicted and imperfect, pulled at me like a gravitational force.

PROOF IN PICTURES

The tranquil embrace of a Sunday night found me in my master bathroom, my private modern escape space. I was poised gracefully within the sunken embrace of my bathtub. The majestic flush mount crystal chandelier above glittered like stars, casting a cool bluish-white cascade of light that danced across the polished gray glass wall tiles, and the tinted jalousie glass divider. The frosted glass window lightly filtered the cityscape that sprawled below.

The proceeds from my successful lawsuit against Fexor-Media were well-invested in my condominium. Only the center city luxury condominiums in Rittenhouse Square or Society Hill could compete with my showplace.

The depths of my freestanding tub felt like another world, immersed in the soft, soothing liquid relaxation. The water, a gentle cradle, caressed me with its warmth, carrying the delicate fragrance of "Library of Flowers," willow, and water bubble bath.

It was an alchemy that kissed my skin with elegance, its fragrance weaving a story that only the most discerning would know. It was a tale of flora and water, a respite from the city life from outside.

Phyllis Hyman's voice soared through the air, "Somewhere in My Lifetime" emanated from the new built-in speakers, filling the room with a bittersweet soulfulness that resonated deep within my bones. Her timbre reached its crescendo, and then—an abrupt "bing" cut through the air, like an intrusion into my sanctuary of stillness.

I reached for my cell phone; a message from Chuck appeared on the screen. My initial thought was that it was fast. My fingers, still dewy with the scented embrace of my bath water, fumbled to open his message:

Check your email. Let me know if that's enough. I'll prepare the invoice.

With a languid elegance, I rose, the bath water cascading from my body as if reluctant to release me from its luxurious hold. Bubbles, sparkling like tiny jewels in the chandelier's light, clung to my skin. Adorned in pink-chrome polish, my toes gleamed as my feet met the dove-gray marble floor, cool and solid beneath my steps.

The path to my bedroom beckoned, curiosity driving me toward my laptop computer. Whatever Chuck had prepared demanded the respect of a larger screen than my cell phone offered. I was ready to transition from the tranquility of my bath to the assertive glow of my laptop nestled in my bedroom.

The darkness of my bedroom was pierced by the glow of my laptop computer, a beacon in the shadows. As I settled onto the bed, my pink satin sheets clung to my moist body like a second skin, a sensual touch that contrasted the task at hand.

I found Chuck's email. My finger trembled as I hovered over my keyboard. One press and everything shifted. Like a magnifying lens bringing the hidden details of a delicate painting into focus, I suddenly had stunning clarity. The light-skinned, attractive man holding Jackie's hand and kissing her lips had a name.

His name was Antonio Navarro. He was a Dunkin' Donuts manager. He worked in northeast Philadelphia. Apparently, he and Jackie met a few years back when they both worked at the Dunkin' Donuts in the Kensington section of Philadelphia. Back then, she was the manager, and he was her prized employee.

Jackie Limon Sabatino, Santé's wife, was thirty-seven years old and mother to three children. Two by Santé: one boy, a junior, and one girl, named Jovie.

They were married in 2016. In March, just days after his birthday and just one month after we got caught.

Then I noticed an attachment labeled photos. I took a deep breath and opened the attachment. Ten photographs were watermarked with the date: Saturday, November 17, 2018, Yesterday.

I could almost feel the narrative unfurling. I imagined Santé working at the warehouse on Saturday morning, forced to use her car so she could track his every move. At the same time, she drove his truck with no modern tracking features.

Timestamp 9:00 AM. Jackie arrived at the house on Lawn Street. She parked the car in the same position on St. Vincent, parallel to the side of Antonio's house.

I saw a photo of Antonio coming out of the green door of the stone-faced enclosed porch, the large windows cloaked by white curtains.

The next still shot was of their embrace. Then, pictures of the two kissing at the green door.

The following three images were taken two hours later, marked 11:07 AM. Jackie was back in the doorway, appearing to adjust what looked like a nurse's aide uniform shirt. Antonio, wearing blue boxer briefs, had his arms draped around Jackie's shoulders, kissing her neck.

There were more images of Jackie walking down the small pathway before reaching the sidewalk as Antonio stood on the last brick step leading from the porch to the path, barefoot.

In the following image, Antonio appeared to be adjusting his dick, covered by his blue boxer briefs as Jackie approached Santé's truck, looking back at Antonio with a smile. Her arm was extended with a vehicle remote in her hand.

As I clicked through the remaining images, it showed Jackie entering the vehicle and pulling away. At the same time, Antonio watched with a satisfied, loverly smirk on his face and a sizeable dick bulge in what I identified as blue Calvin Klein boxer briefs.

My mind raced with a million thoughts and a storm of emotional realizations. But triumphant and resolute, only one word escaped my lips… "Jackpot!

CHAPTER
Forty-Two

THE BREAKING POINT

The underground parking lot of Nybor Productions Inc. was a scene of chaos, filled with the echoes of car engines, the tangy scent of gasoline, and the scuffle of determined feet. People brushed past me, their hurried conversations mingling with my own thoughts, which drifted to the gym in Mount Laurel, New Jersey.

My body sculpting project had finally reached a point where I could honor my promise. I had signed up, and now it was time to lose myself in the rhythm of the workout.

I envisioned a schedule, my mind painting the sensation of sweat, the aching muscles, and the satisfaction I would feel. I could almost taste the success. But fate, or Patricia more specifically, had other plans.

As I made my way to my Chrysler 300C, my cell phone shattered my peace with its insistent ringing. Patricia's name on the caller ID was a cold reality check. Annoyance from our last conversation slithered in my gut, and I cautiously answered, the metallic chill of the car door seeping into my fingers.

"What's up, Pat?" I said, my voice careful.

"Victoria, child," Patricia's voice tinged with arrogance, said, "I just called to see if you had come to your senses. You ain't really gonna mess with Santé and Jackie's marriage, are you?"

The inside of my car welcomed me with the fresh scent of lemon air freshener swinging from the rearview mirror. I sank into the leather seats and threw my purse aside. Biting my bottom lip, I retorted, "Patricia, this conversation didn't go well the first time we had it. What makes you think it's gonna go well now?"

She snapped back, "Because, honey, I want you to grasp the high stakes of what you're doin'."

I sat up, rigid, an adrenaline spike waking my senses. "I'm grown, Pat. I know there's a risk with telling the truth about Jackie, but that ain't my burden."

Patricia's voice was a slap. "It ain't about holding her secret, Vicky. It's about being a damn homewrecker, tearing apart a family. Your disability doesn't give you the right…"

I gripped the steering wheel, cutting her off mid-sentence. "Dammit, Patricia, when did you get so high and mighty? Is this 'cause of Jagger? Is the dick that damn good?"

Patricia replied, "This ain't about dick, at least not Jagger's, But now that you mention him, Yes Jagger's dick is good, and yes I did talk to him."

"You what?" I yelled, incensed. "Why are you still telling my business to some man you've known for a lil over a hot minute?"

Patricia didn't flinch. "I'm trying to build something with him, Vicky. Together, we ain't putting up with no home-wrecking energy."

I couldn't believe her audacity.

We argued for an additional six minutes, our voices crackling with years of friendship strained to a breaking point.

Then she finally said it. "Maybe it's time we go our separate ways."

The words hit me like a slap, tears already stinging my eyes. I couldn't hold back. "You're throwing away decades over Jackie, a *bitch* you don't even know, and Jagger, a *fucker* you *barely* know?" My voice cracked, each word cutting as it left my lips.

I sobbed openly. With bitterness coating my tongue, I snapped in a moment of fiery courage, "Know what? Fine. If you wanna go your own way, do it. But understand, while you criticize me for risking everything over Santé, you're doing the same damn thing over Jagger."

Patricia offered a weak defense. "It's different, Vicky. Jagger wants to be with me."

Her words rang a hollow sound in my ears. I yelled, "Then I guess I'll see you when hell freezes over."

I ended the call with the single push of a button, the silence heavy in my closed car, and tears rolled down my cheeks. My sobs reverberated off the windows, a lonely sound in a bustling world.

For ten minutes, I sat and cried, the taste of betrayal lingering, the ache of lost friendship raw, and the determination to move forward burning brighter than ever.

CHAPTER
Forty-Three

SEALED FATE

The elevator doors opened to the fifth floor, and I darted toward Beth's cubicle. The tangy scent of office cleaners mingled with the faint whir of computer fans as I spotted her heels clicking rhythmically on the marble floor. Luck was on my side—Beth hadn't gone for the day.

"Beth," I called, my voice filled with urgency. "Can you come back to the office? Quickly?"

Her brows lifted as she followed me to her desk. The eucalyptus scent of her hand cream floated faintly in the air. I lifted a fresh manila envelope from the side of her desk.

"Write this address," I said, placing the envelope before her. "32 Pond Drive, Turnersville, NJ 08012."

She paused, pen hovering over the envelope. "Whose address is that, Boss?" Her voice carried a curious lilt.

I hesitated, then decided to let her in. "It's my ex-boyfriend's address." Pensively, I added, "I'm hoping he'll become my boyfriend again."

Her face brightened, and she smiled knowingly as she wrote the address in her handwriting. Handing the addressed envelope back to me, she said, "Good luck, Boss. Let me know if there's anything else I can do."

"Thank you, Beth," I said warmly. "I will."

BACK IN MY OFFICE, THE CLACKING OF MY COMPUTER KEYS filled the air as I pulled up Chuck's email. I printed the incriminating documents about Jackie and Antonio. The laser printer whirred softly, releasing the crisp pages of high-quality photos. Carefully, I slid everything into the manila envelope and sealed it.

By the time I started the drive to the Turnersville post office, the leather seat of my car felt unusually stiff. The cool steering wheel was steady beneath my hands, but my thoughts were anything but.

The first truth I had to face was sharp: I was weaponizing infidelity. The same tool Jackie had wielded against me, I was now turning back on her. The bitterness of it formed on my tongue.

The second truth was even more damning. I wanted Santé—as a prize, I desperately wanted to win back. My emotions were a whirlwind, a mixture of passion and rationalization. I could hear Santé's laughter in my mind, his taste in my mouth, and our shared memories—sparse but poignant.

THE TURNERSVILLE, NEW JERSEY, POST OFFICE LOOMED AHEAD, overhead lights spilling across the parking lot as I pulled to a stop. The manila envelope felt heavier than it should, its rough texture scraping against my fingers.

The sound of the stamps tearing from the sheet as I overpaid the postage—couldn't risk non-delivery, especially with no return address.

In the open lobby, I approached the Dropbox hatch and hesitated, holding the package in my hand. The scent of old mail and metal filled the air, each breath laced with my swirling doubts. My mind was a whirlpool of emotion, thoughts of Santé, Jackie, and myself crashing like waves.

My hand hovered over the open hatch, fingers gripping the weapon. I hesitated, a pang of guilt twisting in my chest. I pondered if even the smallest spark could ignite a firestorm. Though I had never known Santé to be violent, the thought of a shouting match in front of his kids haunted me. What if my actions caused pain I hadn't anticipated?

I didn't know whether it was from the tension in my hand or a subconscious desire, but the package slipped from my fingers, gliding into the chute with a soft thud.

The sound resonated in the quiet lobby like a gavel striking its final blow. My breath hitched. I felt like I had been gut-punched with a fist covered in a velvet glove.

Back in my car, the rich smell of leather did little to soothe my racing mind. The deed was done. The envelope was federal property now, untouchable even by my second thoughts.

All that remained was the waiting. The fallout could be a dud, a delayed explosion, or nuclear Armageddon. Whatever came next, I had crossed the point of no return.

CHAPTER
Forty-Four

SILENT ENDING

I had just closed the door to my condominium when the piercing ring of the telephone jarred my senses. "Hello," I said.

"She's had another stroke. Your mother, she's no longer at the rehab. She's been transferred to Einstein Hospital."

I recognized the voice right away. It was Katrina, one of my mother's nurses. "Thank you, Katrina. I'm on my way."

My heart drummed in my ears, and my mental and physical exhaustion seemed to solidify within me, but I couldn't resist my call to action. Ignoring the weariness, I headed back to my car for the emergency room, drawn by an invisible, emotional thread.

The glaring lights of Einstein Hospital's emergency room met me with clinical indifference as I passed through the hurdles of security and the registration desk.

Once in the emergency room, the strong aroma of iodine stung my nostrils—a pungent reminder of despair creeping into my heart. I felt my life unraveling, my hope slipping away—for my mother, for myself.

"Why have I been cursed from birth?" I wondered, my eyes stinging with self-pity. Unaware of my own gifts and uniqueness, I found myself trapped in a cycle of longing for what I lacked, entangled in a net of jealousy and betrayal. Patricia had found love with Jagger, while I planned to send secret packages to a married lover, desperate for his love and affection. The risk, the shame—it all tasted bitter on my tongue.

The bleak reality of my mother's situation hit me with a cold gust of sorrow when I reached Triage Area 22. A tangle of wires, machines beeping their heartless song, and there she lay, pale and lifeless.

I couldn't go another round with the woman who hadn't done right by her daughter; a pang of guilt felt like a sharp knife in my chest.

But a more profound sadness soon washed over me as the doctor, his eyes shadowed with suspense, explained that she wasn't conscious.

"Will that change?" I asked, my voice breaking.

"We don't know," he replied, his voice a somber melody.

Not now. Not my mother, not this week. The loss was too much—a void that threatened to swallow me whole. Patricia was gone, my promotion, Santé—now my mother too?

I stayed by her side, feeling the hours stretch and warp from Wednesday into Thursday morning. I watched her fragile chest rise and fall, listened to the clinical beeping of the monitors, and tasted the stale hospital air. The goal was to monitor her vitals and hope for consciousness while the medical staff measured the impairment from the stroke. A CAT scan was scheduled, but more suspense lingered, heavy and cold.

Driving to work later, I could feel the cracks in my psyche widening, the fragility of my heart and soul threatening to shatter. I knew I needed to slow down, but the fear of asking for time off gripped me. The relentless march of life didn't stop for grief or exhaustion. All I knew was that I had to keep moving, even when every fiber of my being screamed for rest—for a pause in this relentless, crushing tide of loss and longing.

CHAPTER
Forty-Five

LOUD CONSEQUENCES

Beth had just handed me notes from my recent focus group. They had watched the pilot episode of our most recent drama show. The air smelled of a hint of Beth's citrusy perfume. It was 1PM, and my stomach ached with hunger.

I hadn't eaten lunch. I had missed so much work over the last few weeks and was desperately trying to catch up. Though I never spoke of it, my taste buds longed for a meal.

I turned to Beth, my eyes narrowed with concern. "So, these are the most recent survey questions and interviews?" I asked, my voice conveying my urgency.

Beth hesitated, her blue eyes clouded with confusion . "I think so. There was only one focus group for that show."

Her answer should've been obvious, but it was another sign of how distracted I had become. My senses were dulled, my mind elsewhere, so caught in the week's losses and my mother's illness that I was slipping at work. Before I could regroup, the shrill ring of my cell phone sliced through my thoughts. It was the hospital.

"Hello?" I answered, my voice crisp.

The voice on the other line was controlled yet somehow empathetic. "Mrs. Robbins?"

I corrected him, "This is Miss Robbins." I paused, then questioned, my voice faltering, "Is this about my mother?"

The voice on the other end introduced himself, "Hello, Miss Robbins, I'm Dr. Stevens."

I repeated his name, clinging to formality, "Dr. Stevens, how's my mother?"

The doctor's voice remained steady but softened slightly, "I received the images back from her CAT scan, and the news is not good. She has not regained consciousness, and based on the magnitude of the damage in her brain seen on the CAT scan, it's very unlikely that your mother will do so."

My heart sank. The words rang in my ears. Just as I was about to ask what all of that meant, the doctor summarized succinctly, "Miss Robbins, your mother is in a coma, and you may want to consider hospice or end-of-life considerations."

I thought my heart would explode in my chest. My world swayed, and I fell back in my seat, the leather cool against my heated skin.

Full of worry, Beth's voice reached my ears, "Boss, are you okay?"

I replied with vacant eyes, my voice barely above a whisper, the taste of despair in my mouth, "I have nothing left."

The doctor's voice broke through, "Are you speaking to me?"

"I was not," I told him mechanically. "Thank you for your call. I'll come to the hospital soon to discuss options for end-of-life protocol for my mother."

I ended the call, the finality of the end call beep bouncing in my ears. I looked at Beth. My voice was hollow as I said, "I didn't know my life would turn out like this."

Beth's eyes dropped to the floor. She responded, with a blend of sympathy and shared grief in her eyes, "I don't know exactly what you're going through, but I can still relate to your pain. Two weeks ago, my mother was officially diagnosed with dementia, and she's already in the mid-stages."

I looked at Beth with fresh eyes. She was no longer the young Caucasian girl who brought my tea and helped me organize my workload. She was a real person, a sweet young girl with a decent-paying job but no promise of upward mobility, a young mother caring for her mother officially diagnosed with dementia.

"Beth," I asked, my voice choked, "would you like to take off early today?"

She looked confused, her eyes wide, and replied, "I would, but only if it won't put your workload further behind."

I reassured her, "There's no way I can work today. I didn't even know that this focus group was a one-sample-sized endeavor. I'm going to take the rest of the day off."

Beth's eyes softened, her voice filled with gratitude. "Thank you, boss."

I lightly corrected her, extending her license, "Call me Victoria."

Beth's face seemed to glow from the inside, and her eyes became visibly moist as she softly said, "I'll leave when you leave—Victoria.."

I nodded, touched by her loyalty, and continued, "I'll ask for some bereavement time in the coming days."

Beth's head shook. "I understand," she said, her voice full of compassion. Then she turned to leave me in peace. When she reached the door, she turned back and said, "Oh, by the way, I meant to tell you, Ken told me that all invoices have to be copied to him as well as accounting from here on."

Goose pimples formed up my arm. "When was this new rule announced?"

Beth replied, "It was shortly after Chuck presented me with an invoice for some work you had given him on one of the productions."

"What?" I exclaimed.

Beth clarified, "Yes, I was standing talking to Ken about something when Chuck dropped off the invoice. Ken questioned me, and I told him it was just a basic invoice and tried to finish the conversation so I could get back to work. That's when Ken told me that he wanted to see all invoices from the junior vice presidents and that I should send him copies of everything."

My voice quivered as I asked if she complied with his request.

She said, "Yes, I sent him everything this morning, so he should not be on our backs about anything. Her last words before leaving were, "I'll let you know if there's any additional hoops he wants us to jump through. In the meantime, go and take care of your mother. Everything here at the office is just fine."

Beth exited, and I stared straight ahead, practically catatonic. I lowered myself back into my executive chair, knowing everything was not just fine, just the opposite. Despite Beth's sweet words of reassurance, I knew another fire was about to ignite.

CHAPTER
Forty-Six

THE LAST GOODBYE

"**M**iss Robbins," the doctor began with gentle compassion, "I'm afraid your mother's condition has worsened."

I stood by my mother's bedside, the steady beeps of the machines surrounding her sounding like a chorus of mechanical crickets.

The doctor continued somberly, "We've done everything we can, but at this point, I recommend considering hospice care."

Despite the brief mention of the possibility over the phone earlier, the words still stung like an icy slap, leaving me momentarily speechless.

He reached out and placed a reassuring hand on my shoulder. "I'm truly sorry. She'll have palliative care."

The doctor left, his footsteps echoing down the hallway, and I was alone with my unconscious mother. Her skin was luminous even under the cold fluorescent lights. I reached out to touch her hand, feeling the fragility of her thin, dry skin.

I wanted to thank her for my life, to make peace, or at least make what could be her life's end about her. But all my adult intellectual understanding of how I should behave in this moment yielded to the raging child within. I struggled to maintain my composure.

"Mom," I whispered, tears threatening to spill over, "why did you do this to me? Why did you raise me like a boy when I told you I was a girl? The taunts, the names, the isolation… why? You could've helped me, Mom!" My voice cracked, anger and grief welling up. "If you had medically treated my intersex condition, you could've saved me from a childhood of ridicule and rejection. All those years growing up, feeling like an outsider, like a freak—I needed you. I needed you to understand, to help me, to guide me. But you weren't there."

I looked at her, the stillness of her form a stark reminder of the distance that had always existed between us.

"I never had dates, Mom. Never had boyfriends or Valentines. While other girls were experiencing love and romance, I was left alone, rejected and misunderstood."

The memories came flooding back, and I could almost taste the bitterness of those lonely years.

"Do you know what it's like to watch others fall in love, to see them celebrate anniversaries and special moments, while you're left alone, always on the outside looking in?"

I choked back more sobs, my voice brimming with emotion.

"I would watch the other girls at school, see them giggling and blushing, holding hands with boys, receiving flowers and chocolates. And all the while, I was left alone, never understanding why I was different, why I couldn't be like them."

I wiped my tears, the cool touch of my hand a small comfort against the raging storm within me.

"I wanted to be loved, Mom. I wanted to feel the thrill of a first date, the joy of a first kiss, the warmth of a loving embrace. But all I ever got was cold rejection and bigoted taunts." My voice was a mere whimper as I said, "You put me out—onto the mean streets of Philly because you couldn't handle the gossip and rumors.

I was eighteen before one boy overlooked me being a freak. But of course, because we lived in Philly, he got killed. So, I was back to being misunderstood, unaccepted, and alone.

My body involuntarily shook as I continued to tell my truth. "By the time you came back into my life, you didn't know any of what I had gone through. The first puberty was more male than female, and the second puberty, which never corrected the first, just made me more androgynous—a stage I got stuck in until I finally made enough money to begin medical treatment.

"You know what it's like to finally find someone who sees you, Mom? I found Santé. He was youthful, kind, sweet, and didn't pressure me. He was my first real lover, my first real connection. Now, he's all I have, and I have to hold on to him. If I can, maybe someone in this life will actually love me. By the way, you were right. Turns out I am a homewrecker—Santé is married. I know you think that means I should say goodbye to him. But I can't, Mom. I can't."

"It's time to say goodbye, Mom. But I'm not strong enough to say goodbye to both you and Santé," I said, choking on the words. "So, I'll say goodbye to the one who left me first."

I bent over and kissed her cheek, feeling the soft warmth of her skin, my tears leaving wet trails on her face.

"When you see God, ask him to give me the happiness that your choices denied me," I whispered. "You owe me that. Do that for me, and you have my forgiveness."

I left the hospital, the taste of loss bitter in my mouth and the chill of the night air enveloping me as I made my way home. My heart was heavy, and the world seemed to move in slow motion.

Ten minutes after I arrived home, the phone rang. After a brief greeting, the voice on the other end was sympathetic but impersonal.

"Miss Robbins, a few minutes after you left this evening, your mother died. I'm so sorry."

I stood frozen, my living room spinning around me, and the emptiness in my heart a gaping wound that nothing could heal. All that was left were memories, pain, and the haunting echo of a life that could have been.

CHAPTER
Forty-Seven

THE ENVELOPE THAT CHANGED EVERYTHING

My one day off, in fact, my first Friday off in six months, and this bitch wants me to work in the garage. Typical. If it was me stayin' home all fucking day, I'd be there to get the Amazon and UPS shit. But I guess that's just too much to ask. 'Cause Jackie's got so much to do while I'm breakin' my back payin' the bills. She wants me to install some fancy garage opener. Supposedly, the delivery guys gotta have access to my garage. As if I ain't got better things to do.

Just when I was tryin' to figure out this damn contraption, Jackie busted in. Her voice was like nails on a chalkboard. "Babe, Jovie wants you to walk her to the park." I looked up, face twisted in shock.

"What? You see I'm busy. Why can't you do it?" I snapped, the raw edge of irritation in my voice.

"She wants her dad," she whined. God, that voice, just like Jovie's. My daughter had to inherit something from her mom, and she got that whining voice. It could cut through steel.

I was desperate for some rest, or at least a good dick suck, but here I was, stuck with this. "Jac, either you walk her to the park or get Mark to do it. I'm busy."

"Babe, you know Mark is still on punishment for smoking weed. He can't go out, remember? You said no exceptions." She threw my words back at me...damn.

"Fine, let me finish the garage opener, then I'll take her," I snapped, wantin' to end the conversation.

Her smile made me grit my teeth cause she only smiled recently when she got her way. She said, "Thanks, babe. So the keypad outside, do we pick the code that opens the garage door?"

"Yeah, we can program four codes, but all the delivery guys gotta have one code."

"Sounds good. Thanks for doing this. I know we live in a good neighborhood now, but there are videos all over the internet showin' people stealing packages. I don't want that happening to us."

I took a deep breath, tryin' to keep my cool. "I know, Jac. Just gimmie a minute."

"I'm going to the supermarket," she said.

"Fine," I spat.

I assumed she'd take the kids, but I could hear Jovie and Junior arguing in the house. Their bickering hit me like a punch to the gut. I was stuck with 'em again.

Just off the ladder, a voice rang out, "Mr. Sabatino?" I spun around, instincts from my boxing days kicked in, fists up and ready to fight, but it was just my mailman, Gary.

He handed over the mail. I took it, grunting my thanks.

The garage closed, and I eyed the manila envelope. The rest was just bills. Nothin' new there.

Just as I was about to rip into the manila envelope, Jackie popped her fat ass into the garage again, like she was allergic to lettin' me have any peace. "Babe, while you're at it, can you get rid of that big dog cage? We don't have the pits anymore, and it's just taking up way too much space."

That damn cage was mine. Bought it years ago when we first got Bruno and Sasha, our two pit bulls. That cage was a fortress, built to last, bigger and badder than any dog pen in the neighborhood. But Jackie always griped about it.

Jackie's complaining kept going, "Seriously, it's too damn big. It was too much even for the pit bulls, and now it's hogging up half the damn garage. We need that space." Her voice was grindin' on me like sandpaper.

I took a slow breath, trying my best to muzzle the growl that wanted to come out. "Fine, I'll take care of it," I said, even though I had no intentions of parting with that cage.

"Thanks, babe. I'll be off to run some errands. Remember, the kids are in the house. I need you to watch 'em till I get back."

"Yeah, yeah," I muttered as she turned to leave. After she exited, I walked back into the house just to make sure Jovie and Junior weren't setting the place on fire or some shit– all clear.

Returning to the garage, I shook my head at her nerve. Jackie thought she could just decide what goes and what stays in my fucking house.

I walked over to a shelf on the garage wall and grabbed the two padlocks. Stridin' over to the cage, I locked the empty cage door first, then locked the cage to the wall as an anchor. Let her try and get rid of it now. My cage, my damn rules.

Back in the house, I crashed in the living room on my black leather throne, the seventy-five-inch screen playin' basketball in front of me.

I finally turned my attention back to the strange manila envelope. My fingers hesitated just a moment before opening it. Something was off about the manila envelope with no return address, but I ripped it open anyway. In an instant, that one piece of mail changed my life and the lives of everyone that mattered to me.

CHAPTER
Forty-Eight

RETURN TO HOSTILITY

Monday morning and my first day back after two weeks of bereavement leave was an assault on my senses. I was in a small conference room on the sixth floor of Nybor Productions, bracing myself for what lay ahead.

Ken Rutherford was due to arrive any moment. The very walls seemed to exhale anticipation, doused in the scent of stale cigarettes and old papers. The others waiting with me were, Grace who appeared edgy, her assistant Carol with suspiciously bright eyes, Andy, whose cologne wafted a fragrant trail, and Blake, the ever-nervous assistant to Ken, who eyed me with a peculiar intensity.

The tick of the clock against the room's silence was painfully audible. The atmosphere was filled with an uncomfortable silence, punctuated only by Carol's soft scribbling on her notepad and Blake's feverish tapping on his tablet. Andy's heavy musk cologne began filling the small space, inducing an artificial claustrophobia.

Finally, Ken Rutherford made his grand entrance directly from a gym workout. Wearing a black tank top and loose-fitting blue basketball shorts, he emanated a strong arrogance that matched his armpit odor and the distinct, heavy musk that could have only come from his sweaty balls. The aromas clashed immediately with Andy's cologne, reminiscent of Jovan Musk for Men. A tangible tension filled the small conference room.

"Shitty ratings!" Ken began, his voice laced with contempt. "The studio's itching to fire Howard Jensen. They think it might boost the numbers."

"That's a dreadful idea," I protested, my voice edged with disbelief.

Grace's first sentence was low, but then she forced her voice louder, "It's concerning, yes. But if the studio wants it, we must comply. We can make it work."

Andy, unfazed by the pungent clash of odors, added, "Focus groups, perhaps? Could help us understand the impact."

Ken's response was immediate and brutal, his scent intensifying as he leaned in. "Enough of this. Howard's done. I'll handle legal."

The ensuing discussion was a whirlwind, Grace's timid voice growing in strange bursts of forced confidence, while the room remained filled with the battling scents of Ken's body odor and Andy's cologne musk.

Amid the intense discussions, Andy began dissecting the latest episodes of "University Peers." I felt a pang of responsibility to realign the team. "Let's not forget the essence of 'University Peers.' It's not just about youthful college antics. It's a deep dive into young adults, navigating the turbulence of newfound independence, grappling with budding relationships and academic pressures, and making those big life decisions away from the safety net of home."

Andy said, "I agree. We should have a meeting with the head writer, but I'd also like to address the fact that the editing team is lagging behind. We need a faster turnaround." A fresh wave of his musk wafted in my direction.

Grace piped up, her voice quivering yet earnest, "Script revisions have been nonstop. We're making sure the storylines align with what the network expects."

Carol nodded vigorously, scribbling down notes, while Blake captured data points on his tablet, his fingers darting across the screen.

Seizing a brief lull in the conversation, I ventured, "What if we explored a subplot where Jenna's character faces a moral dilemma? It might resonate with our viewers, adding depth to her arc."

Andy, usually hesitant to embrace sudden shifts, surprisingly nodded. "That could work. It's a fresh angle."

Grace, forever in the throes of her timidity, wrung her hands. "Um, I... I'm not sure. It could be... a risk?" Her voice, although hesitant, carried genuine concern.

Ken's eyes, however, flashed with irritation. "Vicky, we're not here to reinvent the wheel," he said dismissively, his tone dripping with condescension. "We have a tried and true formula. Stick to it."

His words pressed down on the room, emphasizing the decision-making hierarchy and where my ideas stood in that pecking order.

Ken leaned forward, interlocking his fingers. "Let's remember," he started, his voice authoritative, "we're here to ensure quality while maximizing productivity. Andy, get your team in line. Grace, keep those scripts coming, but faster." He paused, surveying us all with a piercing gaze, clearly relishing the new power he held. "We're shaping stories, yes. But never at the expense of timelines or budgets."

After a few more minutes of rapid-fire discussions, Ken, with an air of finality, declared, "Alright, that's it for now. Meeting adjourned." He stood up, signaling the end of the discussion.

After dismissing the others, Ken turned to me, his eyes cold. The door clicked shut, leaving us alone in the small conference room, a blend of tension and lingering smells.

"I'd like to give you my condolences on your mother, Victoria," he said, his voice dripping with insincerity.

I shook my head, surprised by the sentiment, and began to thank him. But he cut me off, smirking, "I said I'd like to, but I don't give a damn."

I felt a surge of anger but managed to reply calmly, "I don't have time for your abuse, Ken. If there's something work-related, please tell me. If not, I'd like to go back to my office."

He sat down, his eyes gleaming with malice. "Actually, there is something. I've been looking into the accounting for some of your production invoices. There's something shady going on."

I fought to keep my face impassive, my heart pounding in my ears. "I don't understand what you're talking about."

"Oh, you will," he purred. "Accounting and legal are investigating. If there's even the slightest hint of financial impropriety, your ass will be fired. And if it's big enough, I'll see if we can press criminal charges."

The threat was a physical blow, his words lingering along with his unpleasant armpit odor.

"Is there anything else?" I managed, my voice a controlled tremor. He dismissed me with a wave, his arrogance following me out the door.

The elevator ride down to the fifth floor was a blur of emotions—a storm of grief and tension. My leg trembled involuntarily as the doors slid open, revealing my destination. My unraveling had become physical—a visceral response to a world twisted by loss, treachery, competition, raw ambition, and fear.

CHAPTER
Forty-Nine

BETWEEN LOVE, LUST AND LOSS

The past two weeks seemed like it sped by in a frenzied haze. Ken, always full of bravado, had assured everyone he'd take care of the "University Peer's" leading talent, yet I was the one thrust into those high-pressure conversations.

Navigating talks with the show-runner felt like tightrope walking, both of us aiming for the same goal: to resolve things without the looming specter of negative press that could jeopardize our show and one of the financial pillars of our production company.

At the same time, my personal life was reeling from its own blows. My mother, Sarah, had passed away, and making the heart-wrenching decision to cremate her remains was like navigating through a fog of grief. It was also a sharp reminder of the fragility of life.

But the universe wasn't done testing me. Patricia, my childhood friend, confidante and I had not spoken since our catastrophic falling out. Our once unbreakable bond was now marred with hurt and misunderstandings. The silence between us was deafening, amplifying the isolation I felt.

In this landscape of emotional upheaval, there was a faint glimmer of warmth. Beth, whom I mainly knew through professional circles, began edging into the role of a friend. We found solace in each other's company one afternoon, sharing stories over bowls of fresh salads at Salad Hut. It was a far cry from the elegance of Lorenzo's, but in that moment, it was exactly what I needed.

Yet, the nights remained challenging. Alone in the soft light of my bedroom, tears would find their way onto my satin sheets. The looming precariousness about me using company funds for the Jackie investigation was an ever-present dark cloud. And with Ken in the picture, I knew he wasn't just after rectifying a monetary issue with a quick reimbursement. He'd seize any chance to put me in a tight spot.

Adding to my stress, Santé's unsettling silence was like a stone in my shoe, a constant nagging presence. The unanswered questions around Jackie's betrayal and what she might have done or said to wriggle out of the situation clouded my thoughts. Trying to disentangle myself from the hope of hearing from him only deepened the chasm of loneliness.

Each morning felt like a challenge. Often, I'd find myself yearning for a sign, a hint that things would get better. On Monday, December 17, 2018, the universe seemed to send a response. Rushing due to oversleeping, I made a hasty exit from my condo at 6:45 AM.

Time was ticking, and in my rush, I tossed my purse onto the passenger seat of my sleek black pearl 300C. But just as I was set to drive off, a note tucked under my windshield wiper caught my eye. When I exited the car and looked at the folded note, it had one word on the front, one word which made my heart race— Santé.

Instantly alert, I scanned the parking lot, not quite sure what I was looking for. Taking a deep breath, I settled back into the car, my hands trembling slightly as I unfolded the note.

Meet me outside my job tomorrow at 5 PM. I want you to come get this BIG DICK!.

A rush of emotions flooded me. Though unsure of the details, one conviction stood strong: tomorrow, come what may, I'd be there, waiting for Santé.

CHAPTER
Fifty

CROSSROADS IN DECEMBER

At 4 PM, the waning sunlight painted my office with amber hues, casting a warm, soft glow on my documents. The scent of cinnamon tea lingered, soothing but unable to calm the restless energy within me. I stood and made my way toward Beth's cubicle.

The whirling of computer fans and the low murmur of office conversations provided a steady backdrop as I leaned in. "Beth, I have something to do. Cover for me?"

She arched an eyebrow, the hint of a knowing smile playing at her lips. "Something to *do*?" she asked, her tone playful as she stretched the word do.

I rolled my eyes, feigning annoyance but secretly amused. "Fine. I'm meeting an ex. But this is strictly between us," I confided.

Her eyebrows shot up, and her voice lowered, a smirk tugging at her lips. "The ex? Juicy. Don't worry, boss—I got you," she said with a wink. "Nobody will even notice you're gone."

I smiled, her reassurance settling the jitters in my chest. "Thanks, Beth. I owe you one."

She leaned back, giving a mock-contemplative look. "Don't worry, I'll open a tab to keep count," she added, winking once more.

I laughed lightly at her playful tone, shook my head, and gave her a warm smile. With a final glance, I walked away, heels clicking against the polished marble floor. As I neared the elevators, each step felt heavy with anticipation.

DECEMBER'S CHILL NIPPED AT MY SKIN AS I ENTERED THE PARKing garage. My fingers hovered over the keys, sparking the car to life, and warmth slowly crept through the interior.

Philadelphia's sounds enveloped me—honking horns, scattered voices, and the faint sizzle of street vendors. The aroma of roasted chestnuts lingered as I crossed the Benjamin Franklin Bridge, where golden city lights shimmered on the Delaware River below.

Traffic slowed to a crawl, engines grumbling in protest. Each pause stretched time, quickening my pulse as my thoughts churned: the package I'd sent to Santé, its contents, and the unease twisting in my gut.

His blue Toyota came into view outside the warehouse. When our eyes briefly met, a silent understanding passed between us—a familiar but unpredictable dance.

The drive unfolded like a mystery, each turn deliberate, until we reached the Audubon shopping center. Holiday shoppers and the jingle of a charity Santa's bell filled the air, jarring me from my expectations.

This wasn't the secluded space I'd anticipated. The public setting felt exposing and audacious. As doubt crept in, Santé beckoned from his car window, dissolving my hesitation.

Drawn by his presence, I parked two spaces away, my heart racing. Whatever came next, I was ready. I was all in.

CHAPTER
Fifty-One

VICTORIA'S TURNING POINT UNFOLDS

The ice-tinged air and the ringing of the distant hand-held bell provided a backdrop of holiday serenity, while Santé's penis, nestled in my throat, made it difficult for me to breathe.

My heart may have been full of hope, but my mouth was full of dick. Fortunately, I had years of experience attempting to swallow Santé Sabatino's eleven-inch Puerto Rican Pinga. By contrast, I had only recently dared hope to win his love.

Who would have imagined me, Victoria Robbins, ass-up, hunched over the gear shift of a Toyota Camry? Christmas shoppers traversed the parking area of the popular retailer while, just feet away, my tongue traced the head of Santé's dick for the tenth time. I sincerely hoped the customers and store employees of the Audubon, New Jersey, Bigstore would remain oblivious to the unassuming, blue Toyota at rest in the desolate rear parking lot, steeped in the emerging evening darkness.

My spirit gushed with pure joy as I witnessed the scant, warm light of dusk reflected in Santé's amber eyes. The illuminated yellow overtones, coupled with his green undertones and red hue near the center, provided a hypnotic visual. His eyelids slowly lowered, half-masked from the succulent delight I offered. Unadulterated validation rushed through my heart as I heard him utter a deep, gratified moan, sounding like a cat's purr.

Santé's head was cradled by the beige leather headrest. My green eyes surveilled his every facial motion. Though he had become skillful at masking his more demonstrative signs of pleasure, his involuntary facial tics and muscle contractions unintentionally disclosed his euphoric bliss.

The natural flavor of Santé's dick was reminiscent of butterscotch and a hint of caramel. Despite the stiffness of his shaft, his flesh was tender as a fine delicacy. I was fully intoxicated. Pumping my mouth with increasing fervency, I was barely aware that my dominating Papi had destroyed one of my last personal boundaries, public shame.

All of my conscious energy focused on satisfying his manhood. I slurped and sucked on the dick I had studied for a decade. I was a woman of better-than-average intellect. Nevertheless, I was only tacitly aware of how far I had fallen. As he partially watched for strangers, I fully increased my suction, and I rotated my lips in circles around his dick, just as Papi preferred.

"Yeah, like dat. Suck that dick bitch." His light Spanish accent softened his language's coarseness, but not too much. I was with a bad boy, and I knew it. Temporarily, at least, I also knew that he had chosen me. My pleasure sensors were on overdrive, matching or exceeding his, despite the fact he was the only one receiving oral service.

Sucking dick in a random parking lot wasn't much gratification for most girls and woefully less for most women. However, for me, giving Santé Sabatino pleasure and having him with me, even for a fleeting moment of lust, meant everything to me.

Bobbing my head up and down on Santé's dick repeatedly, my neck muscles contracted and released with a rhythm reminiscent of a musician meticulously playing an instrument. Around the twenty-minute mark of stretching my mouth wide enough to accommodate Santé's thick dick caused my jaw to sting, a reminder of the effort I was putting in. Every drop of sweat, every muscle twinge, or leg cramp paled in comparison to the profound contentment I felt being wedged between his thighs.

Shortly after, Santé's entire body convulsed as his cum leaped from his dick like prisoners executing a jailbreak. The moment Santé's cum touched my tongue, the world around me seemed to blur into insignificance. The thick texture melted in the warmth of my mouth, swathing every crevice and corner with a symphony of sensations. The initial sweetness of his ball juice cascaded like a gentle waterfall, serene and soothing. It played on my tongue. The faint, bitter undertones unveiled themselves, dancing forth like shadows at dusk.

The bite of his cum's bitterness was not overwhelming but a surprising partner to the sweetness, challenging and enticing in equal measure. Santé's blend of texture and flavors stirred something deep within me, causing my very soul to pulse with vigor. I felt more alive, drawn into an exquisite dance of flavors that left me yearning for more.

But it was over, and despite my reluctance to admit it, I knew the moment of forbidden pleasure had ended. Santé's hand touched my hair. I nestled my face against his bare thigh. The warmth of his skin radiated against mine, smooth with the faintest traces of soft hair that tickled my cheek. It was like pressing my face against the surface of a sun-warmed stone but with the intimate pulse of life coursing beneath. The aroma wafting to my nostrils was uniquely him: a blend of his testosterone-filled sweat, the remnants of his shower gel, and the indescribable scent of just…him.

Every part of the experience fed my soul, so I sought to embed every nuance of the moment deep within my memory. With every breath I took, I could feel our connection, the unspoken words, and the gentle cadence of his heartbeat that seemed to synchronize with mine. I had braced for him to distance himself and sever the moment's closeness. Yet, he remained still, tethering us even more.

The initial thirty seconds felt like a delicate dance of hopes and fears, each tick echoing our shared vulnerability. As the minute hand journeyed onward, the profound depth of our connection became palpable. The touch, though just a melding of skin, felt more profound, if only amidst the shared embrace.

Santé's fingers meandered through the maze of my curls. His touch was surprisingly gentle. The rhythmic motion was almost hypnotic, lulling me into a sense of calm.

Then, breaking the enchanting silence, he spoke. "I have to tell you something."

Santé's voice instantly brought me back to reality. It was like a cold gust of wind had blown through our shared space. I lifted my head, the comforting touch of his skin leaving me as I shifted to an upright position. My heart began to race, a proclamation of my anticipation. Every ounce of my being was on edge, preparing for what would come.

I said, "Yes, Papi," full of anticipation.

Santé pushed his lips together before saying, "I was thinking we could spend some time together, but I don't know."

I was at a loss for words. I stammered, "What, why? What do you mean?"

Santé replied, "Well, I was considering spending the night with you." He reached for a towel on his backseat next to his basketball.

I was instantaneously exuberant, "Yes, you can spend as much time with me as you want." I reluctantly added, "Well, as much as you can, considering your marriage to Jackie."

Santé stopped wiping his dick with the blue hand towel. "How did you know—" he stopped mid sentence.

His beautiful eyes held a storm of emotions: pain, disbelief, anger. "Jackie and I are a wrap," he confessed, his voice breaking very slightly. He took a moment, shaking his head as though he were attempting to clear away the remnants of his shattered past. It was clear the ending of his marriage was still settling upon him.

For a moment, I was transported. Santé's revelation had given me hope but also a poignant reminder of the twisted path that led us here. I had to suppress the rising tide of elation, pushing it back down into the depths of my heart. "Because of us?" I probed gently.

His chuckle was bitter, edged with irony. "Nah, that's the crazy shit. This ain't even about us," he revealed. "I found out that bitch was cheating on me. Tonight, I'm making it official. My marriage is over."

A multitude of feelings cascaded within me. Guilt for my secret role in his revelation, relief that he was attributing no blame to me, and the ever-present ember of hope that we could finally be together without any shadows lurking in the background. The intensity of the moment was almost over-whelming.

Santé suddenly balled his fist and struck the palm of his hand. The atmosphere inside the Toyota felt even more charged. The sound seemed amplified as it bounced off the steamed windows. His actions served as a punctuation mark to his raw, emotional confession.

Santé continued, "Jackie's punk ass side dude sent me some shit in the mail," his voice tinged with both disbelief and anger.

I tried to keep my face neutral, but my heart raced. I hoped Santé wouldn't detect my nervousness and with it my secret. The potential fallout from my covert actions had loomed over me for so long, and the fear of being discovered was never far from my mind.

Yet, just as I was sinking into a quagmire of guilt and anxiety, Santé's words offered a lifeline. "Do you think I could spend the night with you tonight?"

Pure, unadulterated joy swelled within me, erasing every trace of doubt, fear, or guilt. This was the moment I had dreamed of and hoped for, and it was finally here. With a smile that stretched from ear to ear, I responded with a fervor that could not be contained. "Yes. Absolutely. I'd love for you to spend the night, Papi. You can spend several nights with me, if you want."

Santé fastened the last button of his pants. As he did so, he looked across at me, and for a fleeting moment, our gazes locked. Though the cabin of the Toyota was now dark, I could still catch a glimmer of his distinctive and hypnotic eyes. At times, those eyes told stories, lied, and held secrets, but in that moment, they held promise.

Santé's fleeting smirk was almost lost on me, but as it grew, transforming into his signature grin, I felt the tug of its charm. "Good." His voice was deep and confident, his single word echoing in my ears. He added with intention, "I'll be coming by around eight o'clock."

As he spoke, those amber eyes twinkled with a blend of mischief and earnestness, setting the tone for the promise of the evening that lay ahead.

CHAPTER
Fifty-Two

INTO THE HEART & HOME

The ambiance of my condominium whispered of sophistication, but on that evening, it was a canvas of organized chaos. With only thirty minutes left until Santé's arrival, a surge of adrenaline raced through me. The soft gray upholstered walls beckoned for attention. I quickly ran my hand over them, ensuring they were free of any marks or dust. I felt a new appreciation for how the upholstery of the walls contributed to the room's tranquil yet sophisticated atmosphere.

Beneath my hurried steps, the soft gray fluffy rug felt like a comforting embrace. Still, I didn't have the luxury of savoring its plushness now. I zipped around, adjusting the plush, tufted sofas and armchairs to their prime angles. I ensured they offered a perfect view of the framed poster-sized photos and the black-and-white photographs of iconic architecture on my walls. Each frame held a moment of captured allure, and they had to shine just right for Santé.

The glass table drew my attention next. Beside the vase, now sparkling with its yellow crystal core and crowned with sweet-scented lilies, an assortment of crystal decanters and small sculptures were meticulously arranged, each reflecting the soft glow of the overhead chandelier. I swiftly wiped the table clean, the fragrance of the flowers filling the air and momentarily calming my frantic heart. The grand chandelier above, a stunning cascade of crystal and chrome, dimmed slightly to cast a warm, inviting light throughout the room, accentuating the muted grays and lavenders of my carefully chosen color scheme.

The kitchen was up next. Time seemed to speed up here, with each clock tick echoing off the light wood floors. Those vibrant yellow cabinets always caught my eye—they really brought the energy. I quickly swiped the induction top, admiring how the ceiling lights bounced off the counters and made everything glow. The place was designed with a sleek, handle-free look that somehow made scrambling to get dinner ready feel a bit more chic.

I popped open the fridge to rearrange—strawberries, Perrier, and a few Puligny Montrachet bottles. Everything had to be just so. As the aroma of seasoned rice and beans started to fill the room, I glanced over at the island. There was my little green oasis—a potted plant next to the olive oil and a clear bottle, all set on a wooden board, ready for action. It's funny how a few simple things can make a kitchen feel like the heart of the home. I hurried to plate the chicken, arranging the veggies with a chef's eye. Every moment counted.

With everything in its place, a fleeting glance at the clock told me I had mere moments to spare. I took a deep, steadying breath, the scent of white lilies and a hint of lavender from the sofas grounding me. Santé would be here any minute, and everything was perfect. The anticipation was almost too much to bear.

With not a moment to spare, my doorbell rang.

I SWUNG OPEN THE FRONT DOOR AT 7:50 PM. THERE HE WAS, Santé, standing before me with his jet-black duffel bag, a vibrant lime green shirt that practically radiated energy, perfectly fitted jeans that seemed sculpted to his form, and a smile that could light up the night.

"Hey," he greeted, his voice a warm melody that greeted my ears like a familiar tune.

I welcomed him into my condominium. The anticipation of his presence had been simmering since our semi-public tryst a few hours earlier, and now he was here. A buzz of excitement coursed through me. He made himself at home on the couch, his presence effortlessly commanding attention.

"Something's smelling good. You order out?" he asked.

I said, "No, Papi, I cooked for you."

Santé lowered himself onto my couch, his arms opening wide as he leaned back.

"Thanks, Boo. I like that," he complimented with a smile.

"My pleasure, Papi. I'll be right back." My giddy laughter punctuated the end of my sentence.

As I exited to put the finishing touches on dinner in the kitchen, I could barely contain my joy.

Aromas wafted through the air, the sizzling of chicken breast and the earthy notes of seasoned rice and beans intertwining with the faint scent of sweet lilies that adorned the living room.

I plated Santé's food, then sauntered into the living room. My attention was drawn to Santé's fingers dancing across his phone's screen as he finished a text message. I watched as his gaze wandered to the poster-sized photographs of me that adorned the walls. He lingered on those images. I gently placed the plates on the glass coffee table.

"Why didn't you ever consider stepping in front of the camera?" Santé asked, his voice a mix of curiosity and intrigue. Then, as if adding an afterthought, he continued, "You've got the looks and the talent."

The magic of his amber eyes shone sincerely as they met mine. My heart skipped a beat at his compliment. The years of friendship and collaboration, the unspoken stories that lingered between us, gave his words an extra layer of meaning.

I chuckled softly, flattered. "I've always been more focused on helping models shine," I added. "Besides, I never felt pretty enough to be a real model." My eyes lowered momentarily.

Santé tilted his head before saying, "Hey, you're beautiful."

Just like that, years of pain and insecurities seemed to melt away. My breath slowed, and I felt at home in my skin. Santé was a man of few words, so for him to offer me a compliment so directly was as welcomed as it was rare.

Involuntarily I blushed, admitting, "Being behind the camera shooting models like you was where I felt most at home."

Santé grinned, that captivating smile I could never resist, and mused about the path he'd chosen instead of modeling, "You know," he continued, his gaze returning to the photographs, "I miss those early days sometimes. I probably should've stuck with modeling instead of diving into this whole welding shit."

Sympathy welled up within me as I looked at him. "But you've become quite successful along your chosen path," I countered, adding, "And I have to say, you've always had a certain charisma that translates well into whatever you do."

Santé grinned, a playful light dancing in his smile. "You always had a way with words, Victoria."

The fondness between us was unmistakable, the unspoken memories of our shared history coloring the air with camaraderie. Santé looked at the photographs again, lingering on them for a moment longer before returning to meet my eyes.

"It's never too late, you know," I said softly, the words slipping out before I could stop them. "Even though I'm no longer actively involved with a modeling company, I'm still connected to the industry as a photographer. If you ever wanted to explore modeling again, I'd be more than happy to help."

Santé's eyebrows lifted slightly, surprise and contemplation all over his face. Pulling himself to the couch's edge, he looked at me as if reassessing his possibilities, "You think I could still pull it off?" he asked, a note of skepticism in his voice.

"Absolutely," I affirmed with conviction. "You're gorgeous," I blurted. Feeling the heat rise to my cheeks, I quickly corrected myself, "I mean, you're very handsome."

We both shared a playful smile, my embarrassment receding.

I continued, determined to steer the conversation in a more focused direction, "Your eyes alone have a uniqueness that's hard to ignore. Besides, age is just a number, and your confidence would be your best asset."

Once more Santé leaned back on the sofa, a thoughtful expression settling over his features. "I'll admit, with my marriage ending and everything changing, I've been thinking about what's next. Maybe it's time for a fresh start."

I offered a reassuring smile. "Fresh starts can lead to amazing opportunities. Just remember, you've got potential beyond what you might imagine."

Santé eyed me up and down slowly. He sniffled and with a serious undertone, he said, "Thanks for always believing in me."

Once again my eyes dipped demurely, and I softly replied, "You're welcome, Papi."

Our conversation became the bridge between the past and the nebulous future, held up by shared memories and newfound possibilities.

After a few minutes, Santé took a bite of the delectable dinner I'd prepared. The sounds of his fork against the plate and the cadence of our dialogue became the backdrop for more moments of rare connection and my much-desired quality time.

Santé looked at my plate, then back at me, a playful glint in his eyes. "Are you planning to eat?"

With a mischievous smile, I replied, "I thought you'd never ask." I slid underneath the glass table which held his plate and ornaments above. Moving on my hands and knees, I reached Santé's lap and slowly unzipped his jeans. I looked up at him, his face revealing a sly grin. He lifted his body at just the right moment to allow me to remove his jeans and underwear.

Santé's dick popped out of his underwear; he was already semi-hard. I kissed his balls gently, and I said, "Thank you for the appetizers Papi. They are absolutely delightful."

Santé laid back on the sofa, "Oh yeah, that's it bitch."

Santé took a fork full of my grilled chicken breast, and I devoured his dick under the table. I teased and tantalized his meat with my tongue. Then I deep-throated him, moaning deeply so he would feel the vibration through his shaft down to his balls. It was Santé's first night in my home, and I wanted to treat him like the King he was, in my heart.

He finished his entire meal, as did I. He served me the dessert of his man cream. I later served him ice cream. We were both thoroughly satisfied.

JUST BEFORE SANTÉ'S ARRIVAL, I HAD SWAPPED MY PINK SATIN bedding for a black jersey cotton set, as soft and comfortable as a favorite T-shirt. When Santé entered my slumber chamber, he threw himself onto the bed, his playful demeanor evident. "So, where are *you* sleeping?"

I was almost sure he was joking, but I took a moment of silent consideration anyway. My mind stuttered as I tried to find the right words, but Santé gave me a reprieve. "I was just joking. You better not think you're going anywhere." Santé said before undressing and sliding under the sheets, a contented smile on his lips.

The sight of Santé naked and in my bed there brought a surge of joy that was unmatched. The room seemed to shimmer with a newfound intimacy, that only intensified the connection between us.

Because Santé had to get up at four in the morning, I didn't expect any more sex. Instead, I joined him in bed hoping for a few shared words before sleep.

Impetuously, Santé said, "Wait a minute, there's something I want you to hear." He rolled to the edge of the bed and grabbed his cell phone from his pants strewn across the floor. "You gonna love this," he added, his voice uncharacteristically gleeful.

Curiosity sparked within me, but I didn't have to wait long. From the tiny speaker came the first few chords of a tune I couldn't forget.

Recognizing it immediately, I smiled as the familiar vocalizing emerged: *"Ooh na-na... ooh na-na-nev'r let go."*

My facial recognition was likely obvious, but Santé asked anyway, "You remember this?"

"Oh my God, I didn't think you'd remember." I said with surprise, my eyes tingling with emotion.

"Me forget this? Nev'a", he replied, a playful grin spreading across his face. Santé conjured our past. "We'd been kickin' it for about a year, and I decided to turn things up a bit."

I placed a hand over my mouth, the memory no longer painful but wistful. Lowering my hand, I said, "Yeah, you put this song on and did a little striptease."

"That's right, boo." He chuckled. "But you thought I was gonna stop at the Tommy Hilfigers."

I laughed. "You showed me—and I mean, you really showed me."

He grinned. "I knew you always loved looking at my dick." After a beat, he added. "In fact, I could tell you loved me."

His words caught me off guard. It was the first time Santé had ever acknowledged knowing that I loved him. I sat silently on my side of the bed as the tune played, the moment settling over me like a soft blanket.

After a few beats, his gaze shifted to the sound system in the corner of my room. "You got Wi-Fi on that thing?" he asked.

"Yes," I replied, already anticipating where this was headed, I got up from the bed. Reaching my touchpad, I located his cell phone within the syncing options. After a few permissions, the song Never Let You Go poured from the speakers, filling the room with its rich, nostalgic melody.

I stood there, caught in a dream-like trance. Was this moment real, or was I dreaming?

As if answering my unspoken question, Santé patted the bed beside him. I sat down, and as the song approached the refrain— "You're the one I return to, again and again..."— he said, "That summer afternoon turned into one of the best afternoons of my life. That was before Jackie, the kids, or any other complication in my life."

Bashfully, I dipped my head as the song ended. Santé reached out, using his index finger to lift my chin. His eyes met mine as he said, "I didn't want that day to end, but I knew it didn't matter if I left that night or however many times I left. I'd always come back. Because I'd always be your Papi, and you'd always be my baby."

I smiled, my voice soft as I affirmed, "You'll always be my Papi."

"And?" he prompted.

"I'll always be your baby," I replied.

We didn't technically cuddle that night, yet the warmth of our bodies close to one another radiated a comforting energy. I felt Santé's presence in a way I hadn't before, and for the first time in a long time, I found myself at peace.

The devastation of so much loss, and the weight of everything that had gone wrong, seemed to lift as I lay there with the man I loved.

For the first time in years, I slept through the entire night, wrapped in the quiet grace of Santé's presence. My last thoughts before drifting to sleep were ones of gratitude for the connection we shared. The simple moment I had longed for was suddenly real.

For a fleeting instant, I felt hopeful. *Despite all the pain and loss, could things finally be changing? Could my life, at last, be turning toward the dreams I had only recently dared to imagine?*

CHAPTER
Fifty-Three

TONIGHT'S THE NIGHT

I walked through my Wednesday in a gentle haze, only half present in my meetings and phone calls. I knew I was on a Santé high when even the dirty looks from Ken-Doll didn't phase me as we stood in the elevators earlier in the day.

The entire day was a countdown to five o'clock. I wanted to get back home to my man…Santé. At 4:30 PM, that desire took on a new hue after receiving a text message.

Santé:

Leaving at 5. Text you when I'm coming across the bridge.

BTW, Your virginity is mine. Tonight's the night.

I immediately felt flush. Excitement and nervousness tangled together in a ball of energy, filling me with a new sense of certainty as I quickly sat down. I was just a few hours away from my first sexual experience and it was going to be with the man I loved, and in my own home.

MY FINGER FRANTICALLY FUMBLED ON THE DOWN BUTTON AS I waited for the elevator. "Goodnight, boss," Beth's voice called out from behind me.

Just as I turned to reply, the doors to one of the elevators opened. I waved at Beth hurriedly. "Night, Beth, gotta go."

My clacking kitten heels sounded like applause as I rushed through the interior parking garage toward my car. As I touched my car handle, the automatic locks unlocked the 300C, and I caught my breath. Slowing down for a moment, I took in the world around me, savoring the last few moments before the night's events unfolded.

Tonight's the night, I thought again, taking a deep breath as I eased into the car seat. After many years of wondering and dreaming, it was finally happening. The nervousness was there, but it didn't change how much I wanted this. Santé was my man, and this was our moment.

I WAS JUST FIVE MINUTES FROM MY CONDOMINIUM. TECHNICAL-ly, I still had a few more weeks of recommended healing time before sex was advised, but I felt ready—nervous, yes, but ready. My heart raced, my sweaty finger leaving moisture on the touchscreen as I navigated to the next song.

As if reading my mind, Janet Jackson's soft voice flowed from the speakers, crooning "Tonight's the Night." My tires hugged the last city block before stopping in the parking lot of my condo. I kept my hands on the wheel, letting the song's last note linger.

Just then, a new message appeared.

Santé:

Coming across the bridge.

My legs shook slightly, and I let out a long breath.

It was almost showtime.

CHAPTER
Fifty-Four

THE FIRST TIME

I opened the door, and there stood Santé, hyperventilating, his face etched with stress. "Sup. I know I'm late; been a long day. Plus, she called my phone, tripping. I told her the shit was a wrap, stop calling me."

Clad in my blush-pink bra and matching panties, I simply nodded. He didn't need to specify to whom he was referring. The unspoken presence of Jackie's name lingered between us. Santé stepped briskly into my condo, making a beeline for my bedroom without hesitation. Pausing momentarily to secure the door behind him, I followed. I entered my bedroom just in time to see him shimmy out of his pants, his torso already bare.

Seconds later, he lay fully naked on my bed. The sight was a feast for my eyes. Things began routinely, the kisses to his balls, working my tongue up the shaft of his growing dick. The joy of taking him into my mouth, the delight of his flavor, feeling his body relax then periodically convulse.

The change came quickly. Santé made eye contact with me, then told me, "Turn around and lay face down, ass up." I followed his instructions without commentary. I knew the moment had come.

During one of our previous sexting sessions, we had agreed on how my first sexual experience would play out. The understanding was he would give me that big beautiful dick in at least two positions: doggy-style first, Santé's request, then missionary, my preference. Spontaneity would guide us from there.

As I positioned myself doggy-style, I moved to the far right edge of the bed. I had placed a standing mirror in that area to see us in action, specifically Santé, behind me. I wanted to see his face as he entered me.

When Santé rubbed the head of his dick up and down across my inner and outer pussy lips collectively, it felt like a smooth, electrified touch that danced across my skin. He activated nerves deep within my dermis, which sent pleasure impulses all over my body and collected in my brain.

His dickhead put pressure on my entry, causing a bit of pain, blunted by pleasure. The remaining discomfort quickly subsided at the sight of him in my mirror. My pussy slowly stretched to accommodate him but reached its limit quickly.

I took a minute to fully comprehend what I was feeling. Santé was inside me for the first time, a foreign and inexplicable pallet of sensations followed. I felt swollen from the inside, bloated, and intoxicated. I thought he had filled me completely, but I also knew I had only taken a small fraction of his dick. Embarrassment and frustration loomed.

Just as I was about to say something, I felt an internal pop accompanied by a sharp, swift pain. In that instant, Santé was able to gain further entry into my love tunnel. It was so sudden he briefly lost his balance and had to grab my hips for stability.

Naïve and in shock, I quickly abandoned the images in the mirror, opting to see his face directly. I turned and looked over my shoulder, asking, "What was that?" foolishly assuming that he could feel what I felt because we were taking this journey together. Naïvely unaware that he had his own sensations, which were very different from mine.

"I just got the head in," he said with a grin.

"What? All of that was just the head?"

Santé chuckled before telling me to turn around. He added, "I got you."

I placed my hands under my chin and prepared to receive the rest of him. I was moist but not super wet by any means. In preparation, I had placed a bottle of lube on the nightstand. Santé grabbed the bottle and added more moisture.

He pulled his dick all the way out and then put himself back inside of me. I jumped, and he remarked, "Damn, you're tight."

I reminded him, "You're my first, Papi."

When he pushed his dick back inside of me, I was a bit more elastic.

Over time, I focused less on how much of his dick I could fit inside of me, instead centering myself around the experience and the sensations accompanying him filling my vacancy. Slippery tickles, swollen eroticism, and the pleasure-pain paradox of my internal stretching provided a one-of-a-kind experience.

I could feel his dick pulsating inside me, and I was exhilarated. I had expected us to change to the missionary position at any moment. Instead, Santé grabbed me by my waist and fucked me harder. What initially felt like a deep sea internal probe slowly stretching me quickly resembled an internal boxing match in which Santé's massive, heavy, weight dick delivered several uppercuts to my lower stomach, reverberating deep in my pussy in my lower gut.

I stole a glance into the mirror, and the reflection told a tale of two contrasting experiences. On Santé's face, pleasure was etched in every line, his eyes shining with heightened focus, lost in the throes of the moment.

My image painted a different story. The tussle between pain and pleasure was evident, and it seemed the pain was gaining the upper hand. My eyes, wide and filled with tension, and the tightness around my mouth bore testament to my experience. The mirror candidly showcased the dichotomy of our moments, his deep immersion in pleasure, and my struggle with discomfort.

Just as I was about to ask Santé to change positions, he said, "This pussy is tight as fuck. You gonna make me cum."

I thought that couldn't be. We hadn't been screwing for long, about six or seven minutes in total. It was feeling good at times, pain in the moment, but I didn't want the whole experience to stop. Besides, I hadn't received the missionary position I wanted.

The missionary position was where I had imagined I could look at him directly. I felt instinctively that element would intensify the enjoyment of the sexual experience for me. Nevertheless, when Santé increased the speed of his thrust, I knew he was working toward his finale.

The tingling sensation in my pussy increased and seemed to envelop my whole lower region. After about thirty seconds, I felt warm beads of sweat forming on my forehead. A different type of tingle was developing—from a deeper source. A realization washed over me: I might be ready to climax. Before that could happen, Santé pulled his dick out of me and told me to turn over. I did as I was instructed.

Laying on my back, I watched as Santé stood on the bed straddling me from above. He looked down at me as he jerked his dick, a tantalizing and slightly intimidating sight. A few seconds later, his knees buckled somewhat. Reflexively, I extended my arms just in case I needed to catch him if he fell.

Instead, Santé let out a groan, then heaps of cum leaped from his dick and fell down upon me like warm rain. His head reared back for a moment. Heated heavy drops splatted upon my face, breast, and my stomach. His load was much more voluminous than usual. A realization I mentally noted and to which he commented when he looked back down at me fully painted in his ball juice and said, "Wow, turns out I'm a shooter, huh?"

I smiled up at him and replied, "I guess so, Papi." I was pleased yet slightly disappointed that it would be too late to try to discover one of the sensations I felt emerging, my climax. *One step at a time,* I thought. *I had my first sexual experience. Maybe next time will be my first climax during sex.*

But for that moment, at least, our experience was done. I braced myself for Santé's usual hurried exit, but then I remembered he was living with me, at least temporarily. I was in an uncharted territory.

He lowered himself next to me on the bed. I saw a glimmer of satisfaction in his eyes, a contentment that mirrored my own, and that, in turn, filled me with a quiet joy.

I looked at him, a lingering tentativeness in my eyes, and asked, "Did I do everything I was supposed to?"

He smiled warmly. "It was good. You were good," he assured me. Then, his amber eyes sparkling with curiosity, he asked, "Did you enjoy yourself?"

I couldn't help but grin, a playful energy bubbling up from within me. "I did," I confessed, and then, with a triumphant flourish, I announced, "I'm not a virgin anymore."

A grand, satisfied smile spread across Santé's face, filling the room with a shared joy. "No, you're not," he agreed, his voice rich with pride and a modicum of affection. "Not anymore Bae," he added.

I told him that I wanted to learn more about sex and how to please him. He smacked my ass and said, "We'll get to that. But what I really want is that ass." Fear struck my soul. I realized he was talking about having anal sex with me.

In a panic, I said, "Papi, I could barely fit you in my pussy. Actually, you never even got the whole thing in my pussy. How would you get all of that dick in my ass?"

Santé snickered lightly, though it seemed he was holding back a more boisterous laughter. "I'll make it fit, don't worry," he said, a teasing glint in his eyes.

The look of terror in my eyes must have been apparent, for his expression quickly softened. He reached out, gently touching my arm, a soothing balm.

"Don't worry about that right now. Just enjoy the moment," Santé reassured me, his voice calm and comforting, his smile genuine and warm.

And with those simple words, my fear dissipated, replaced by the trust and connection that had drawn us together. At that moment, in Santé's eyes, I found the strength to let go, be present, and savor the intimacy we had discovered in each other.

Santé bent down, bringing his face level to mine. Reflexively, I puckered my lips. Santé snuffed my hopes for a lip-locking kiss with a disapproving shake of his head and a hushed injunction. Santé delivered his audaciously arrogant words so cavalierly I didn't feel the punch to my ego. "If I have to wait to fuck your ass, you'll have to wait to taste these lips."

The bruise left by his words caused my heart to wince. Numbed by the afterglow of the loss of my virginity and Santé's magnetic presence, I froze, unknowing how to respond.

"Can you still feel me inside you?" he asked, his voice a soft murmur, his eyes locked on mine.

"Yes, Papi, I can still feel you," I replied, my voice seasoned with a deep warmth.

"Good," he replied, his eyes twinkling with satisfaction.

The object of my desire, joy, and pain offered a consolation prize. He tapped his index and middle fingers to his cheek. Santé's instructions was clear. I understood the gesture to mean he wanted a kiss, but not on his lips.

It was unusual that after sharing such an intimate moment, he would want a kiss on the cheek rather than the lips. But I didn't question it or complain. Instead, I pressed my lips to his soft cheek, feeling the subtle scratch of his sparse stubble against my skin.

Surprisingly, I felt contented. There was something tender and genuine in that simple kiss, it was unique, memorable, and deeply personal.

That cheek kiss, so unconventional yet so fitting, seemed to capture the essence of us, an asymmetrical love yet an affection we had built together, held together by mutual trust.

"I had a good time, but I'ma go shower. Mind if I watch TV in your living room after?" Santé asked.

I held my breath briefly, then replied, "I don't mind. There's towels in the bathroom and ice cream in the fridge."

"Cool," said Santé, gathering his clothes from the floor. He strolled to my bedroom door and looked back at me, his gaze lingering, his eyes soft. He seemed to be drinking in the sight of me, committing the moment to memory.

"Get some rest, watch TV, either way, think of me," he said, his voice gentle, almost wistful.

I blushed, my smile innocent yet knowing, and replied, "I will, Papi."

Then, encouraged by the intimacy of the moment, I took the risk of saying, "I love you."

He tilted his head slightly to the left, and a sliver of light illuminated his eye. I could see the specks of green amongst the yellow amber.

His voice warm and accepting, Santé simply said, "I believe you."

Santé turned and walked away; the soft click of my bedroom door followed, leaving me in the peaceful silence of the early evening.

CHAPTER
Fifty-Five

FROM SUGAR TO SHIT

The motherfucker fired me, and I was trying to find one good reason why I shouldn't burn that entire office building down to the goddamned ground. My freedom, that's it. I don't want to go to jail. I had never been to prison and reminded myself that was the last place I wanted to go.ike a swarm of anxious bees.

At my office door, I found it locked, my keypad code useless. A glaring yellow Post-it directed me to 605, a small meeting room on the sixth floor.

Inside, Ken, Beth, and Chuck waited. The room felt airless, the buzz of fluorescent lights and Chuck's walkie-talkie creating a low, oppressive hum. Beth's tear-streaked face hit me harder than I expected.

Ken's smile was sharp, his voice cutting. "Victoria, don't sit down. You won't be here long."

I froze, my sense of stability hanging by a thread.

"Affirmative action ends today," Ken announced coldly. "The investigation is done. You charged personal investigative services to the company. Now, I get to say what I've wanted since your second day here: Victoria Robbins, you're fired! Return your credentials. All of your shit will meet you at the curb.""

The words hit like a sledgehammer. Chuck avoided my gaze, and Beth broke into sobs.

Leaving the building, daylight mocked me. My belongings were strewn on the curb, my past uprooted and discarded. Each item I loaded into my car felt heavier than the last, my heart breaking a little more.

Back at my condo, I collapsed onto my bed, tears soaking the pillow. A half-empty glass of water sat on the nightstand, its stillness unnerving. It mirrored my unraveling.

The hours dragged as I absorbed the weight of my losses: my mother, friendships, now my career. Each had carved its own devastation into my life.

And then there was Santé—the only thing I had left. But how could I tell him I was fired for charging investigative services to expose his wife's affair? That I'd known and said nothing? The enormity of my deceit threatened to destroy us.

The thought of confessing filled me with dread. Hiding it felt equally impossible. The absurdity of needing him while concealing the truth sent a fleeting, bitter smile across my face.

Time marched on, the confrontation looming. As I clung to the hope of Santé's return, a question lingered: Could I hold on to him when the truth could tear us apart?

CHAPTER
Fifty-Six

BETWEEN GUILT AND GRATITUDE

Lies are downright ugly, but lies of omission were only unattractive. That rationale guided my tongue as I withheld from Santé the entirety of my termination narrative. I trained my focus on the undeniable direct truth: Ken Rutherford, an unabashed racist, orchestrated my ousting from Nybor Productions Inc. Any pretext would have caused my dismissal, so I didn't provide a specific reason. Instead, I generalized.

Santé came breezing into my condominium with a question dripping with raunchy humor, "Victoria, why weren't you on your knees to meet me at the door?" His tone bore humor, yet that was a mirage. The tears perched on the edge of my bottom eyelid prompted his inquiry.

"What's wrong? That was just a lil joke." Santé lied and we both knew it. His seriousness was a cunning chameleon.

I unfolded the account of my unemployment, weaving it with the recent mourning of my mother and the estrangement from a once cherished friend and confidant.

He gestured toward my couch, urging me to sit. The setting sun's last gasp bathed Santé's face in a warm, tangerine glow. A single ray of that warm light danced within his eyes. I discerned the rich palette of gold hues reminiscent of a sun-kissed landscape with streaks of lime green woven into the horizon.

Santé's voice, uncharacteristically tender, said, "Right now, we gotta back each other in these hard-ass times. We're both takin' big hits. You lost your mom, your gig, your home-girl, and me? My whole damn family's fucked up."

Guilt, like an immovable boulder, settled in my gut. Yet I chose silence, allowing his monologue to unfold without interruption.

Santé's support continued, "It's probably a shit move to go solo right now. If you're down, you can crash at my place starting next week."

In that fleeting moment, the world whirled, tipping in my favor. Victory was so close. Was this the culmination of my story, a triumphant climax? My hands quivered, and my answer slipped out as an unsteady murmur, "Absolutely, Papi," I added, "I'm on board with your plan. But, could it be dangerous for me to stay at her place?"

Santé's anger flared up like a blazing fire. "Fuck you mean her place? I pay the bills at my house."

I rushed to apologize, but as swiftly as his anger ignited, it ebbed away.

More composed, he said, "All I'm sayin' is the house is mine. Cause she messed up, I might dodge the alimony bullet, but child support? That's a whole other story. I already got a lawyer on it, so for now my wallet's staying sealed."

My voice soft and my tone meek, I said, "I'm sorry, Papi. I didn't mean to add to your stress. I'm always here to add to your peace, not your pain."

Santé reached for my hand. "You're really special… you know that?"

I blushed. "You inspire me, Papi."

I offered, "I have rice and beans ready, but I could easily prepare some salmon if you preferred something more substantial."

Santé rubbed his small belly. "Rice and beans would hit the spot." I smiled just before he pulled me into an embrace that calmed my spirit.

Santé headed to the kitchen, and I informed him that I would join him in the dining room. I added, "You can enjoy your meal at the dining room table, and I can greet you appropriately, as you wanted when you first arrived…on my knees."

Santé's smirk emerged as if he were claiming victory in a sports game. He said, "Like I said, we gotta live together, pronto." The last twinges of guilt ebbed away. Santé's words permitted me to revel in the victory that was finally tasting incredibly sweet.

CHAPTER
Fifty-Seven

A CHRISTMAS OF TRANSITION

On Christmas Day of 2018, I meticulously packed several suitcases, my hands moving over the smooth surfaces of clothing and possessions, each piece carefully chosen and placed. The air in my condominium was infused with the scent of lilies, cardboard, and anticipation—a mixture of old memories and new beginnings. Every item I touched seemed to emit the energy of change, the faint echoes of a future about to unfold.

As I moved through each room, nostalgia unfurled with every touch, bittersweet and vivid memory. My hands brushed against surfaces, caressing them with a sense of farewell. Not merely a condominium, these walls held echoes of laughter, whispered secrets, and a myriad of emotions.

The gentle sound of forced heat pushing through my vents and "Ave Maria" performed by Hauser pouring from my speakers serenaded my senses, underscoring the gravity of the changes ahead.

Tomorrow marked the day when I would cross the threshold of Santé's house for a week or perhaps a lifetime, intertwining our lives in ways beyond mere shared spaces. The thought of his impending divorce sent ripples of concern through my thoughts, like the faint rustling of leaves in a gentle breeze. My heart wrestled with empathy for his children, wondering how they would navigate the waves of change. Yet, even amidst these currents of worry, a quiet happiness took root within me.

My mind wandered into the realm of whimsy, conjuring vivid scenarios where Santé shed his aloof veneer. In my dreamscape, he transformed from a figure of calculated detachment into a paragon of romantic devotion. I could almost taste the flavors of meals I would craft with care, their fragrant aromas enticing his senses. Cooking his favorite meals would become an art, a labor of love transforming ingredients into something truly special.

I saw myself folding his laundry with the precision of a caretaker, each garment a testament to my dedication. And his desires, those secret wishes he might never voice, would become my compass, guiding me with unwavering purpose.

My gaze drifted to the window, and my thoughts momentarily strayed from the sentimentality of my interior. Beyond the glass, the world was a muted living portrait of winter magic. Crystal snowflakes descended from the heavens, dancing gracefully to the ground below. Each flake was a delicate, unique, fleeting masterpiece, much like the moments with Santé.

As I watched the snow's silent descent, the question lingered: should I hold onto this sanctuary, this haven that had been my retreat for so long? Was the victory of love I had won with Santé long-lasting enough to rent or sell this symbol of comfort and familiarity? My condo, once just a place of solitude, now held the echoes of a thousand dreams that had led me to my crossroads.

CHAPTER
Fifty-Eight

LOVE & DUTY

It was Friday, December 28, 2018, at 3 AM, and my eyes were blinking open, still adjusting to the early hour. The darkness in the room was tempered only by the soft glow of the digital clock on the nightstand and the moonlight that filtered through the cracks in the curtains.

Santé was still asleep beside me, his face a portrait of tranquility I had adored. I eased out of bed as quietly as possible, throwing on my robe before tiptoeing to the bathroom. Years of artistry had taught me how to apply makeup with the precision of a surgeon, but doing it so early in the morning felt like a sacred ritual. It was my private endeavor, almost as if I were painting a new day, not just my face.

After that, I moved to the kitchen, every step a careful choreography to avoid any sound that could betray my efforts at silence. I started to prepare his lunch—grilled chicken salad and chicken tacos with mild taco sauce on the side. I felt my new life wrapping around me like a cocoon.

It was a series of small but significant adjustments, like learning the rhythms of Santé's house and the texture of the life I hoped we were building. I was getting used to it, like a favorite song you hum without realizing, like a subtle perfume you identify as your own scent. And though it was painstaking, waking up at that ungodly hour just to put on a façade before he woke up, it was a labor born out of something quietly profound.

Each lettuce leaf I washed, and every piece of chicken I grilled was like stitching another thread into the fabric of this burgeoning love story. And so, as the sun prepared to rise, I felt my own dawn breaking too, still fragile but full of light.

With the kitchen enveloped in the comforting aroma of grilled chicken and spices, I quietly made my way upstairs to the master bathroom. The marble tiles were cold beneath my feet; in stark contradiction to the warm anticipation bubbling inside me.

I lined up Santé's bath gel, shaving cream, and a neatly folded bath towel beside the sink, placing the washcloth last with reverence. Everything had its place, each item a small but essential part of his morning ritual. I filled a cup with water, placed it next to his toothbrush, and took a moment to appreciate the symmetry of it all, this carefully orchestrated prelude to his waking moments.

Slipping back into the bedroom, I eased into bed beside him as gently as possible so as not to disturb his slumber. My eyes flicked to the alarm clock: 3:57 AM. The anticipation settled over me like a fine mist. His day would soon begin, inaugurated by the alarm's chime. The digital numbers seemed to crawl forward in slow motion, each second stretching out as if equally reluctant for the spell of the night to be broken.

But I waited, feeling the warmth from his body beside me, hearing the soft cadence of his breath, and enjoying every second. Finally, at 4AM, the alarm rang. Another day, another dance in the delicate ballet of our newly shared life. And as he stirred awake, I felt a sense of fulfillment, a silent joy in the rituals we were weaving together, one early morning at a time.

STEAM DRIFTED FROM THE MASTER BATHROOM AS SANTÉ emerged, his skin glistening from the shower. Over the short time I had lived in his house, I had grown accustomed to this sacred ritual.

The alluring scent of his Versace Eros Invigorating Shower Gel always lingered, intoxicating the space between us. Notes of green apple and zesty lemon mingled with the soothing undertones of mint and the warm trace of geranium, creating a fragrance that seemed to define him.

He lay down on the bed, his muscles warm and relaxed from the hot water, surrendering to the moment. I would straddle him gently, my senses alive and my pulse quickening. Everything about Santé had a way of igniting a flame within me.

On this particular morning, my hands found their way to his arms first. Their strength always astonished me, and as I began kneading his muscles with firm, rhythmic strokes, I felt the tension ease beneath my touch. Each press of my fingers deepened the imprint of his rich aroma, etching it into the air and my memory.

Moving to his shoulders, I let my thumbs draw slow circles, coaxing away the working man's stress he carried so quietly. Each muscle I touched seemed to surrender fully, evidence of the trust we were still building—fragile, yet profoundly felt.

I turned around, facing the back of his legs, my pulsating wet pussy on his back, surveying the landscape of his calves and thighs. His muscle tissue yielded under the pressure of my warm hands, and I could hear the soft exhale of his breath, signaling his approval.

My hands worked their way up and down his lower body, shifting my focus to his calf muscles, feeling them loosen under the pressure of my fingers. After several minutes, I watched as he rolled over to glance at the clock. Santé's dick was rock hard. The time was 4:25 AM.

With only five minutes before he was supposed to leave for work, I wondered if he wanted the morning blowjob I had been providing as my loving duty.

I didn't have to wait long for my answer. Santé sat up, pulled me close, and then pushed my head to the center of his body. I knew my duty. I was officially Papi's bitch, which meant I had the honor and responsibility to suck his dick on demand. So I opened wide ushering in a new day of love and duty.

CHAPTER
Fifty-Nine

VICTORY IN CHAINS

As I moved through Santé's house, every detail whispered of quiet elegance. The scent of his lemon-infused living room mixed well with the underlying masculinity of his basketball lying nearby.

His kitchen, steeped in hues of sophisticated gray and accented by the dove gray, white, and silver glass tile back-splashes, wasn't just a room. It was an intimate gallery of the man I was falling so deeply for—Santé.

Buffing the stainless-steel appliances had an oddly therapeutic effect. As I wiped them down, their sheen seemed to wink at me like old friends sharing a secret.

Opening the refrigerator to clean it, my heart sank. What I found was an emptiness that transcended physical space: a few bottles of water, a loaf of bread, butter, and beer. My fingers gently touched the barren shelves, and a heavy realization flooded me. This was a visceral, aching display of what Santé's divorce cost him. He was sacrificing, and this stark reality, the absence of food, the bare minimum, was its symbol.

I glanced at the clock; Noon. A fragment of my current reality nibbled at the edges of my adoration-soaked chores. I needed a job. I had yet to replace the one I had lost. I reached for Santé's tablet, lying on the kitchen counter. Its surface was slightly colder than expected but warmed under my fingers as I navigated through job listings.

Unintentionally, I looked at the list of Santé's favorite websites in his browser. Most were adult sites and a few were sites to rent female escorts. I was certainly not a prude, so I wasn't bothered by his general interest in adult entertainment.

The escorts and the specific selection of videos on his tablet desktop were more concerning. Women bound while intimate was the pattern. There was also a disproportionate emphasis on an alternative type of sex. I shuddered to think these were his secret fantasies, and fear struck my heart at the possibility he secretly expected me to fulfill any of these unorthodox needs. I stopped watching and tucked my concerns away within the safe fortress of denial.

From the upstairs loft area, I looked down on the living room. The high ceilings amplified the room's airiness and echoed a sense of endless possibility. There, I could explore my business ambitions and job searches in an office-like setting. While below, Santé's furniture looked minuscule, like pieces on a chessboard waiting for the next move. The only exception was my lover's seventy-five-inch television.

"Santé will be home soon," I whispered to the emptiness as though the house could hear and share my anticipation. The walls, imbued with fresh coats of muted gray, seemed to murmur back in assent.

This was just the prelude, I realized, And as I stood there in the home that was just Santé's and not ours, but soon might be, I realized I had never felt more ready for the next chapter to begin.

IT WAS ALMOST THREE IN THE AFTERNOON THAT FRIDAY, December 28, 2018, before my efforts at job hunting showed promise. Because I had no agent, I personally made nearly fifty calls, and placed over forty online applications, before my phone rang.

The name Tamala Mochasford flashed on my cell phone screen. An old colleague, now a television executive, was calling. She saw my name in a list of applicants. She wanted to contact me personally, a departure from her standard protocol.

Tamala presented me with a job offer that seemed too good to refuse. Except it came with hooks. First, I would have to move to the Los Angeles area within the next two weeks and commit to doing it within the next twenty-four hours. The second hook only reinforced the first. This job of President of the television production for her new joint venture with Paramount Television Group would offer no remote work opportunities. Ending the call, my chest tightened with conflict as I paced the loft before sinking into a welcoming chair nearby.

The panoramic view of the two-story living room below me painted a vision of domestic bliss that we could share. I could almost hear Santé's laughter and practically feel his body's heat next to mine on the plush couch below. Was I ready to trade this unborn promise for the glaring lights of a distant city?

Suddenly, my thoughts were shattered. The immediacy of preparing dinner became my anchor. With car keys in hand, I drove to the ShopRite on Route 42, and every item I placed in my cart felt like a manifesto: a commitment to this life, to this man, to us. Paying with my savings debit card felt like a sacrament, as if I was already contributing to our shared future.

The act of cooking turned into a spiritual ritual. Basil, garlic, and ground beef combined in a sizzling pan, their aromas climbing higher like prayers. By 5:30 PM, the pasta pomodoro was ready, its scent mingling with the ambient fragrance of the home we were building. Just then, the rumble of the garage door pierced the atmosphere, causing my heart to accelerate like a drumroll.

Drawn as if by a magnetic force, I moved toward the door that led to the garage. Anticipation of Santé's appearance was palpable. After a few moments, he opened the door to find me on my knees. A smirk appeared on his face. "I see you've learned how to greet Papi when he comes home." His seriousness was wrapped in a gentle veneer of irreverent humor.

I said, "Yes. Welcome home, Papi. Your meal is ready, and I'm ready for mine." The sound of Santé's zipper opening echoed around the lower level of the home.

I NEVER EXPECTED TO BE HANDCUFFED, ESPECIALLY WHILE GETTING fucked. Santé had barely finished his heaping helping of Pasta Pomodoro when he said, "Hey Sexy, I wanna fuck you." While it wasn't the most romantic of gestures, laying in his bed with just my fuchsia bra and panties and looking at him stark naked, his crude remark was elevated to a poetic overture.

"I'd love to Papi," I said, relishing the chance for greater intimacy.

Just before Santé approached me, I noticed him reaching under the mattress on his side of the bed. He pulled a pair of handcuffs. "Hold out your hands," he instructed.

I hesitated, reluctant and fearful.

His words brimming with confidence, Santé said "Come on, you're gonna like it. I already know you will" he smiled. "Okay, Papi, I trust you.," I said, but was still reluctant to bring my hands forward; I waited for Santé to take the lead. I did not have to wait long.

Within seconds, he took one of my wrists, locked the handcuff around it, placed me on my knees, my face forward, and locked the other cuff onto the bed. He then stretched my arch. He repeated the process, attaching the other end of the handcuff to the brass frame of the bed.

As my panic sored, I watched Santé reach into the table and retrieve a second pair of handcuffs. With those, he locked my other hand and connected it to the brass frame just as he'd done with the first pair.

My nervous laughter was meant to camouflage my enormous fear and anxiety. I felt Santé sliding my panties off. The cocktail of lust and fear was intoxicating. I felt the man I love mount me from behind. Although I knew I could not move, I tried, just to feel the restraints of the handcuffs.

Santé's sticky dickhead rubbed against my pussy lips, sending thrills up and down my spine. The feeling was exhilarating and new. As he slid himself inside me, I felt myself stretching, the warm skin-on-skin action enveloping my senses. I gasped for air, took a deep breath, and exhaled, releasing stress, tension, and my small amount of control.

Suddenly, I was an extension of his body, a canvas on which he could express his sexual desire. My pleasure tunnel, warm and wet, behaved like Santé's personal dick mold, created just for his desire, rhythm, and intensity.

With my face down and ass up, Santé picked up the speed of his stroke. My body practically convulsed. I was cumming already, but how could that be?

Santé slapped my ass and rode me like a thoroughbred horse. I thought I felt him in my gut. My legs shook involuntarily. I think he suspected I was about to lose my balance and fall onto the bed. He said, "Don't you move that pussy an inch." He added, "You came two times. The next one is mine."

For the next ten minutes, Santé pounded my pussy like he was trying to turn it into jelly. He worked his hips like a gyroscope, tapping every centimeter of my internal walls. My tunnel was sensitive and on sensory overload.

My legs trembled again, this time much harder. Within a few seconds, I realized another orgasm was emerging, This time deeper and more robust than the previous two. No longer holding my balance, I screamed into the pillow as I fell onto the bed.

Santé was livid. He followed me and fell on me as I flattened onto the bed, pulling my hair, he said. "I told you not to move that pussy." He jackhammered me, and I felt increased lubrication.

At first, I thought he had come, but then a heat wave flushed my body, and perspiration popped from every pore. It was apparent to me that the climax I almost had during my first sexual experience, I was actually having at that moment.

The warmth intensified and suddenly, I was levitating just a few inches above the bed. It was only my fear that I might be dying and leaving that connected me back to my body with shock.

Seconds later, Santé demanded, "Turn over." Instinctively, I tried to follow his directions, but I was still handcuffed. Only my neck could turn to face him. Santé removed himself from me, moved up on the bed, and jerked his dick so close, his arrow tip almost touched my nose. Without warning, heaps of cum leaped from his dick onto my face. One wallop hit me in my eye. Momentarily, I was blinded, unable to wipe my eye, I shook my head. I said, "Papi, my eye is burning."

Although it appeared to be a mistake, something about the way he angled himself suggested a different explanation. An internal whisper told me it was punishment for falling and not maintaining my position, as he had demanded. Too difficult to accept such a petty motive during such a passionate moment, I ignored my inner whisper.

The next thing I remember, Santé was removing the handcuffs. There was tissue paper on the bed, though I don't recollect seeing him retrieving the tissue. I had experienced pleasure tinged with discomfort, and it was a potent elixir. Little did I know that the contradictions I felt that evening would only intensify.

CHAPTER *Sixty*

FATED FORSAKEN

Santé's arms felt warm around me, a cloak of false security that had lured me in time and time again. His words hung in the air, a toxic perfume, as he nestled his face in the curve of my neck.

"Vick, you get me, you know? You understand me in ways no one else ever has." His voice was low, a rumble I felt more than heard.

The words should've been comforting. In some twisted way, they were. But they were also the nails in the coffin for what I'd hoped we could be. Bursting my bubble of false dreams, he said, "Jackie never got it. I was never built to be a one-woman man. You get that, right?"

His words were like ice water, shocking me from the warm haze. I had long suspected that infidelity was endemic to the culture of an alpha male like Santé. I had seen it manifest in various ways. But hearing him say it so unapologetically unraveled the threads of my fantasies.

I clasped for an answer I could accept. "Does that mean you'll never settle down with anyone?" My voice quivered as I posed the question, dreading the honesty he was capable of.

"I don't think so," he said, his words a soft punch to my gut. "After what Jackie pulled, I'll never marry again, trust me."

Santé shifted his weight, rolled on me, and kissed me gently. "Thank you for being the only woman to love me for who I really am. No matter what happens between us, it's never goodbye. At worst, it's see you later."

As he spoke, a single tear slipped from the corner of my eye, a quiet recognition, an emblem of shattered dreams, wilting fantasies, unmet expectations, and a future that now seemed definitively unattainable.

Yet, I clung to the vestiges of my delusions like a life raft in a stormy sea. Santé, for his part, seemed to think we were having a bonding moment. His affection, as flawed and limited as it was, appeared sincere. But it wasn't the kind of sincerity that builds futures. It was the kind that prolongs moments, stretching them until they snap, leaving one to pick up the pieces of what could have been.

So there I was, held close physically but feeling far away, touched but not moved, accepted but not chosen. As Santé's breath deepened into sleep, my heart fought a quiet battle between the agony of reality and the fleeting comfort of my faded delusion.

CHAPTER
Sixty-One

FRAGILE TRIUMPH

I had settled into my morning routine of preparing Santé's bath, providing early morning pleasure and breakfasts. I had his work clothes freshly prepared and his packed lunch ready. But on Saturday morning, after Santé went to work for a half day, my unemployment felt like a scar that wouldn't heal.

The phone buzzed on the kitchen counter, its vibrations pulling me from the mental maze I was navigating. I saw Beth's name flash on the screen and hesitated before answering.

Should I pick up? What more bad news could she possibly bring? No, don't think like that. Beth's a friend.

"Hello?" I said carefully.

Beth's tone was soft, "Victoria, hey. How are you?"

I thought, *I could lie and say I'm fine, but what's the point? No, it's better to keep it positive but vague.*

"I'm managing," I said, choosing to airbrush reality a bit. "You know, I've got the love and support of my boyfriend, so that's something."

"That's good, Victoria. You're incredibly talented, you know? You'll bounce back," said Beth.

Really? Will I? Maybe Beth's right. There may be hope for me yet.

"Thanks, Beth," I said, touched by her words. "How's everything at the office?"

"If I can be frank, it's a mess." Beth's voice was thick with frustration. "Ken's morphed into a full-blown asshole. I've been demoted to his secretary's assistant. We don't have days off anymore, and the atmosphere is just toxic. I'm not sure how much more of this I can take."

So Ken's still ruining lives. I'd escaped his orbit, but poor Beth was still caught in his shadow.

"I'm so sorry to hear that, Beth. You're wonderful at your job, and I wish I could offer you another opportunity so you could leave that place."

"That means a lot, Victoria," Beth said, her voice softening. "There are rumors about more corporate shake-ups, so who knows?"

Sounds like a sinking ship, I thought.

"Speaking of which," Beth continued, "the chairwoman of the board somehow got wind of your departure. She's asked that a letter and a box be forwarded to you. I have both with me."

A letter and a box? From the chairwoman? Should I be flattered or worried? No way am I setting foot in that building again, not if I can help it. I felt a mix of curiosity and apprehension.

"Thanks, Beth. How about we meet up for lunch or an early dinner in a couple of weeks? We can catch up, and I can get the stuff from Robyn then."

"That sounds wonderful. I miss you, Victoria," she said, and I could hear the emotion in her voice.

"I miss you too, Beth," I managed to reply, my voice only cracking at the end.

We hung up, and I sat there holding my phone against my chest. It felt good to reconnect, even if the conversation was a stark reminder of how much had changed. Thoughts of Patricia, my friend since my teenage years, filled my mind. We hadn't spoken, and I missed her; she was another casualty of my new life.

I wondered if the sacrifices I was making, including distancing myself from long-standing friendships, were truly worth it. Was my life with Santé enough to offset the isolation I was feeling? The voice in my head spoke with haunting emotion. *I am winning, aren't I? So why does Victory feel so different than I had imagined?*

CHAPTER
Sixty-Two

THE COST OF NON-COMPLIANCE

It was Sunday, Santé's day off, so I thought I'd have an opportunity to rest, too. But after four hours of frantic fucking all over his house, I was more exhausted than ever. My pussy throbbed like a toothache. Santé fucked me in all five bedrooms of the house, which was particularly creepy because that list included his children's rooms. Sex in the kid's room was a complete turn-off.

The entire bizarre room-to-room sexual escapade made me profoundly disturbed by how my moral center had been lost for quite some time. It was as if I'd been reprogrammed to suppress my own sense of right and wrong. Santé's needs preceded things like good or bad or even my previous morals and boundaries.

Although I loved having sex with Santé, it was difficult to feel only like a sex toy. Blowjobs and banging were the principal activities of our time together. On rare occasions, we had sprinkles of casual conversations, but only a handful of times had we shared moments that could be considered intimate conversations.

Santé was still naked when he swaggered into the kitchen like he owned the place. Well, actually—he did own the place. But his words caught me off-guard as they cut through the warm aroma of lemon tea lingering in the air. "I've been thinking, you need to get rid of that condo of yours."

I felt a knot in my stomach. "What? Why? Where would I live?"

"Here, with me, silly." His grin was playful, but his eyes held a seriousness that made me pause.

I was happy to live with him full time, but not elated. My condo was more than just a property. It was a piece of my past, a sanctuary that had seen me through heartbreaks and triumphs. "Oh, okay. But do you think I should sell it? It has sentimental value."

"Yeah, but it also has financial value, and that's what we need right now."

I opened my mouth to say something, but Santé was already rolling along like a freight train loaded with conviction.

"Look, I don't mind supporting us because I am the man, but I also have a family to support and maybe even an ex-wife soon. If we're in this together, we need to be in this together. I know you're attached and all, but right now, we don't have time for sentimental value. We need cash."

"Can I think about it?"

"What is there to think about? I told you what I needed, and you're living in my house."

His words, cold and calculated, stung more than I cared to admit. "I understand, and I will give you my answer soon. It's just…"

Santé puffed air through his lips, his frustration materializing in a single audible sigh. "When you're ready to have this conversation, I already have a realtor. That's all. I don't really have anything else to say."

"At all?" I asked.

"You heard me." He said.

And with that, Santé left the kitchen.

I was alone, leaning against the sink, trapped between the walls of our home and the boundaries of our relationship. The faucet seemed to mock me, dripping in rhythm with my inner turmoil.

The prospect of his looming silent treatment hung in the air, heavier than any words he could've said. As I traced the condensation on my lemon tea cup, I wondered how we had gotten here. How did love and cohabitation become so… transactional?

I walked into the living room, balancing a plate of six tacos in my hands, my feet cautiously navigating the short distance from the kitchen. Santé's eyes were glued to the football game blaring from the massive television screen. "Here you are, babe," I said, trying to inject warmth into my voice. "Where would you like me to place these?"

Santé's eyes remained locked on the screen. He pointed a dismissive finger at the coffee table in front of him as though words were suddenly too precious to waste.

My heart stung, a mixture of hurt and confusion knotting itself around my ribcage. I quietly placed the plate on the table and took a deep breath, attempting to ward off the rising emotion. "Would you like something to drink with that?" I asked, forcing a smile onto my lips.

Santé glared at me, his gaze lingering on my face for what felt like an eternity before he stood up. Without a word, Santé walked past me into the kitchen. I heard the fridge open and close, and he returned holding a beer. Settling back into his leather throne, he cracked open the can and took a swig, his eyes returning to the television as though I were nothing but a temporary, insignificant interruption.

I stared at him momentarily, my gaze shifting to the television and then back to him. My initial hurt morphed into something more complex—a blend of disbelief and astonishment. I had never recognized this side of Santé before, the petulant child hiding within the frame of a man. His actions showed a kind of sinister immaturity, an intentional withholding of words and feelings simply because things weren't going his way.

A new clarity washed over me. It wasn't just a football game he was watching on that screen. It was the playing field of our relationship, where he had just shown me how little he was willing to engage when I dared to displease him even in the slightest way. Despite his silence, his petty actions spoke volumes.

CHAPTER
Sixty-Three

MEET SANTÉ'S ASS

The night of Sunday, December 30, 2018, changed the contours of my inner world. A sudden click cut through the room's tranquil ambiance—the bedside lamp on Santé's side sprang to life. The LED bulb flushed his face in a cool, daylight hue, transforming his features into a surreal portrait of contrasts.

His words crashed into the atmosphere like jagged ice. "So, are you gonna sell the damn condo or not?"

My senses were a tangled web caught between the sterile LED light and the sharper, more abrasive tension that now saturated the room. "You know what, Papi, I don't think it's the best financial decision for me in the long run, but I understand your point of view. So if you want me to sell it, I will."

I waited for a nod, a smile, some fleeting acknowledgment that my concession mattered. Instead, his voice sliced through the air, colder than I'd ever heard him before. "Then why the hell did you ruin my entire Sunday? My one day off, we spent not talking because you had to play power games with your real estate."

His words left me disoriented. Confusion brewed within me, its taste a bitter cocktail of self-doubt and bewilderment. "I'm sorry, Papi," I found myself saying, even as I grappled with the realization that I didn't entirely believe I was wrong. Yet his conviction, acrid and palpable, had a way of over-shadowing my own perceptions.

"Prove it," he said, his voice an iceberg that seemed to absorb all the warmth around it.

Without another word, Santé kicked off his bed sheets to reveal his naked body. I suspected I knew what he wanted, another bedtime blowjob. But to my surprise, Santé threw his legs into the air. He moved into a yoga position often referred to as a happy baby pose, laying on his back and holding his feet in the air.

Santé then said, "Come over here and lick my ass."

I was frozen in disbelief. Although not entirely innocent, I was also far from sexually advanced. And if I heard him cor-rectly, what he asked me to do was the least sexually appeal-ing thing I had ever imagined. Placing my face in the crack of a man's ass, or any ass for that matter, was a non-starter.

The already frayed threads of my emotional fabric ripped even further apart. While every instinct screamed against complying with Santé's demand, I knew all too well that my compliance had been the longstanding currency of our relationship, the most glaring justification for my presence in Santé's bed.

I felt diminished, reduced to a begging shadow of my former self. "Do I have to, Papi?" I asked sheepishly.

Santé's face transformed into a scowl. His voice was devoid of the slightest hint of empathy. "I thought you wanted me, but if you don't, you don't have to do shit for me." Santé pulled the cover over himself, and I was left shattered.

For the second time, within mere minutes, I felt compelled to apologize for behavior that I didn't believe to be wrong. But this time, the words that escaped my lips were steeped in a painful brew of duty and internal conflict.

"I'm sorry, Papi. I'll do what you want."

It would take considerable time for me to grasp the profound implications of what he said next. "Good bitch. If you'd had that energy earlier today, you might not have to do this now," he declared, his tone dripping with self-satisfaction.

Before I could even begin to unpack the layers concealed within his choice of words, he gestured for me to come over, giving me no space to absorb the depths of dysfunction and disrespect his sentiments had just revealed.

The texture and taste was reminiscent of the underside of a mushroom head. Relief and gratitude surged through my mind when the only scent I could detect was traces of his body gel. Nevertheless, I knew where I was, and so did he. I couldn't tell if the pleasurable, relaxed look on his face came from the sensory reaction to my tongue on his butthole or the subjugation of my position.

Typically, sex with Santé placed me in a meditative state, present, focused, and centered. This experience, however, invited detachment. I found myself embarrassed not just at the moment, but I imagined the irresistible temptation for Santé to tell his guy friends, "Dude, she actually ate my ass."

It took ten minutes before he placed his legs down. Instinctively I moved upward toward his dick.

"No! Just kiss the balls," he ordered.

I lightly placed butterfly kisses on each ball. Santé dismissively said, "Thanks for the goodnight kisses... all of them." He rolled onto his stomach, adjusted his pillow, and groped for his bedsheets.

As I moved to my side of the bed, I felt like I was in a trance. The waves of disorientation, pain, and a new sense of humiliation crashed over me, different from all the instances before. I recalled the parking lot, the park, and those early morning rendezvous' at my condo. What I once deemed romantic now seemed tainted. While those moments felt unique and dear, a dawning realization emerged. Their significance was largely one-sided, cherished by me but not by Santé.

I had willingly, albeit unknowingly, entered into a covenant—a silent agreement that dictated even the slightest displeasure or dissent I caused Santé would subject me to degradation and dehumanization.

How had it all gone so wrong? How had I failed? I had achieved the goal, of winning Santé, hadn't I?

The urge to cry was overwhelming, yet fear and shame held my tears at bay. Instead, I choked back my emotions and rested my head on the pillow in a bed I had strived so fervently to occupy. And as I closed my eyes, I couldn't help but wonder how my victory had become much less victorious.

CHAPTER

Sixty-Four

KEYS TO THE PAST

It was the last day of 2018. I stood by the door that Monday evening, watching the clock tick closer to 5:30 PM. I was a bundle of nerves. My stomach churned with anticipation, regret, and something close to relief. When I saw Santé's truck pull into the driveway, I took a deep breath, steadying myself.

"Hey, babe," Santé greeted, his face lighting up as he stepped through the door. "Ready to go?

"Ready as I'll ever be," I said, managing a smile.

We drove to the realtor's office in relative silence, the implications of what we were about to do settling between us like an unspoken secret. I kept staring out the window, trying not to let my apprehension show.

Once we arrived, a man in a crisp suit greeted us warmly. "Hi, I'm Peter, your realtor. You must be Santé and Victoria?"

"That's us," Santé replied, shaking his hand.

"Victoria, Santé told me that you want to sell your condominium as soon as possible. He mentioned you're trying for a ten-day closing. Is that accurate?" Peter asked, glancing between us.

I felt a jolt of surprise but masked it quickly. *Ten-day closing? When did we decide that?* My inner thoughts raged. I looked at Santé, who was nodding encouragingly.

"Um, yes, that's correct," I said hesitantly, folding my hands to stop them from shaking.

"Any particular reason for the rush?" Peter queried, tilting his head.

Before I could speak, Santé jumped in. "No, she just wants out of the property. We now live together, and she wants to get rid of old memories. The sooner, the better."

I glanced at Santé, feeling a slight sting at his words. I mimicked his confident posture, forcing a smile on my face and nodding in agreement. I pretended I was also eager to erase a part of my past.

"Alright then," Peter nodded and said, "I specialize in quick closings, but I must admit, ten days is quite a challenge. Do you have any objections to posting pictures of the property online?"

"No problem," Santé answered, even before I could open my mouth.

"And how soon can we get the keys for photos and viewings?"

Santé looked at me this time, signaling me to give up the keys. I reached into my bag, felt the cold metal of the keys against my palm for one last time, and then handed them to Peter.

The rest of the afternoon was a blur. Discussions about property value, open houses, and buyer interests filled the room, but it all seemed distant and unreal. Before I knew it, papers were being thrust in front of me, and I signed where I was told to sign.

Santé was buoyant as we left the office, his eyes sparkling with a happiness I hadn't seen in a while. "Let's go celebrate. Dinner's on me."

The following two hours were unexpectedly pleasant. We dined at Texas Roadhouse. Santé animatedly talked about his day, complimented my appearance, and told me about his plans to bring the New Year in with his work buddies later in the evening. But, despite the joyous atmosphere, the sale of my condominium hung over me like a dark cloud.

When the cheesecake arrived at our table, I took a bite and looked up to meet Santé's happy amber eyes. The cheesecake's sweetness felt at odds with the bitter aftertaste of surrender, a flavor I was growing accustomed to. At that moment, I consciously decided to latch onto his joy, to let myself live in the present experience and treasure it. Tomorrow would bring what tomorrow would bring. And I would face that too, just as I had faced everything else in my life, with or without the keys to my past.

CHAPTER
Sixty-Five

STRENGTH AT MIDNIGHT

I sat alone in Santé's high-end kitchen, surrounded by what should have been the trappings of a perfect New Year's Eve celebration: shrimp neatly arranged on a platter, cocktail sauce at the ready, and a bottle of Dom Pérignon chilling in an ice bucket. The vibrant glow from Santé's seventy-five-inch TV illuminated the adjacent living room, where the New Year's Rockin' Eve show was in full swing.

Just hours after signing the papers to list my condo for sale, I regretted the decision but knew it made Santé happy. However, I soon had to face that despite my huge sacrifice, Santé was not celebrating with me. Just hours before the new year and after I signed the papers to list my condo, he announced, "I'll be back shortly after New Year's," breaking

317

the news that he'd be spending the evening with co-workers instead of with me. Those words played in my head repeatedly, each repetition sharpening my sense of isolation.

I checked the time. 11:30 PM. A heaviness settled in, pulling me deep into my thoughts. Only last year, on the brink of 2018, I was in my own condominium, full of ambition and daydreams about a future with Santé. I had a fulfilling career and my friendships were genuine—the kind where I didn't have to give up pieces of myself to keep them going. Even my troubled relationship with my mother held a glimmer of hope for reconciliation.

But now, sitting in Santé's kitchen, it felt like I'd strayed far from the path I'd imagined for myself. My job at Nybor was over, and my future was uncertain. I had likely lost the chance to restart my career in Los Angeles. I had turned down the one chance to start fresh, in a new city because leaving Santé behind was outside of my consideration. I had always thought of my loyalty as a virtue. I was left contemplating whether it may also be a vice.

The man I'd thought Santé was seemed to be dissolving before my eyes. Parts of him were as I'd fantasized, but there were moments when he felt like a stranger. This duality left me in a cloud of confusion, unsure about what 2019 would bring.

Shaking myself back to the present, I saw it was 11:58 PM. Time had slipped away unnoticed. I grabbed the Dom Pérignon and my bowl of shrimp, uncorking the bottle with a satisfying pop. Champagne fizzed into my glass as the countdown on the TV began.

"Thirty, twenty-nine, twenty-eight…" The numbers counted down, each taking a sliver of the past year.

"Three, two, one…" Fireworks burst onto the screen, and couples on TV shared their New Year's kisses. I was in Santé's home, celebrating a milestone, but he was nowhere to be found.

Raising my glass high, I shouted, "Victory!" as the clock struck midnight. The word was a cocktail of irony and hope. I downed my champagne, feeling the bubbles tickle my throat on the way down.

2019 lay ahead, an unwritten story.

Whatever the year would bring, I knew it would be pivotal, setting the course for the rest of my life. I set down the empty glass and, at that moment, understood that—for better or worse—there was no turning back.

THE TENSION IN THE AIR WAS PALPABLE AS SANTÉ STUMBLED into the house at seven a.m. The champagne bottle of Dom Pérignon lay empty on the kitchen counter, evidence of the hours I'd spent waiting for him. My head buzzed from the alcohol, but the fog couldn't mask my mounting irritation.

"Is this the way it's going to be?" I asked, unable to keep the edge out of my voice.

"Happy New Year, Victoria," he slurred, avoiding my gaze.

"It won't be a happy new year for either of us, Santé, if you intend to treat me like this."

Annoyed, he snapped, "Treat you like what? Like you've always wanted to be treated? You're now officially my bitch. You live in my house, and I fuck you every night. You suck this big dick three or four times a fuckin day. Isn't that everything you've always wanted?"

"I think you're missing a few things," I shot back.

"Like what?"

"Like respect. Like some appreciation and affection," I articulated, each word tinged with a simmering anger.

He lumbered into the living room and plopped onto the couch. "Don't worry about those things, Victoria. Trust me, they're overrated."

At that moment, I heard my late mother's sarcasm echoing through Santé's words. I knew I had to take a stand.

I followed him into the living room, daringly raising my voice. "I'm serious, Santé. You mean everything to me, but I've sacrificed a lot for us."

He barked, "I never asked you to sacrifice anything for me."

"Yes, but you know I have, and you never deterred me," I countered, struggling to control my emotions.

"Is that a fancy way of saying I owe you? 'Cause I don't owe you shit."

"Are you trying not to understand me?" I asked incredulously.

"No, I'm trying to relax after a New Year's celebration. Are you trying to fuck up my new year on the very first day?" he retorted.

Gathering my courage, I said, "No, Santé, I'm trying to set the tone for the new year. Before I go to settlement and sell my home, I need to know that I have a home here. One where I'll be respected, if not loved."

"So what are you saying? You don't want to sell your condo anymore? I got a text from Pete. He may already have us a damn buyer. That man is working his ass off, and this is the shit you pull?"

"I'll repeat what I said before. I never wanted to sell my home, but I'm doing so to live here with you. I just want some respect while I love and honor you. If that's not possible, then I won't go to settlement. I'll just go home."

A single tear rolled down my face. I leaned against the wall, bracing myself for Santé's inevitable verbal onslaught. To my surprise, he hesitated and looked down as if in deep thought or contemplation. After a tense twenty seconds, he stood up, walked over to me, and kissed me softly on the lips. "I'm sorry," he said, his voice a quiet revelation.

Reflexively, I replied, "I accept your apology, Papi."

"Good. Now let's go to bed," Santé said. Then he took my hand, and we climbed the stairs to his master bedroom. A new year and perhaps a new beginning for the first few hours of 2019.

CHAPTER
Sixty-Six

A FUTURE SIGNED AWAY

The settlement office had that stale smell of photocopied paper and ink. One wall was painted in a bright, off-putting yellow that clashed with the room's overall drabness. Santé and I sat across from Linda, our closing agent. Piles of documents were strewn across her cluttered desk like fallen leaves in autumn.

Santé's leg bounced up and down, brimming with anticipation. I could see it in his eyes—he was excited for our future while I was awash in a melancholy I couldn't shake.

"Alright, Victoria." Linda adjusted her reading glasses and flipped through the stack of papers. "Just a few more signatures and initials here, and you'll be all set."

Bart, the buyer, smiled silently as he had already signed his paperwork.

"Of course," I said, picking up the pen. My hand hovered over the paper. This was my condo—my independence, my solitude—drifting away from me forever.

Each signature felt like a chisel, carving away pieces of the life and self I had carefully constructed, leaving me raw and increasingly bound to my lover. But then, I glanced over at Santé. He was grinning from ear to ear, his eyes gleaming with plans and dreams.

"You're doing great, babe," he said, squeezing my hand. "This is the start of something wonderful for us."

I smiled back, though my heart felt heavy. With a final flourish, I signed the last document. Linda put the papers in a folder and handed me a settlement, certified check for $206,000.

"Congratulations, you two." She beamed. "Best of luck in your new chapter."

THE RIDE BACK WAS A STRANGE MIX OF EUPHORIA AND REGRET. As Santé drove my car, he couldn't contain his excitement as he spoke about future projects and possibilities.

"We should go to the bank," he said, turning into the parking lot of a TD Bank. "Why don't we open a joint account? A fresh start for the new year and all."

I looked at him, surprised. "A joint account?"

"Yeah." He grinned, parking the car. "Think about it. We're merging our lives together, so why not our finances? I'm planning on starting my own welding company by the end of the year. Having our funds together would really help speed things up. What do you think?"

He was all smiles and dreams, his words woven with a charm that was hard to resist. I felt cornered, though. It was a huge step I hadn't anticipated taking so soon. But looking at his hopeful face, I found myself nodding.

"Okay," I whispered. "Let's do it."

We walked into the bank, hand in hand. Within an hour, we had a joint account. Santé transferred $2,000 from his $2,210 savings while I deposited my $206,000 settlement check, bringing the total to $208,000. As the teller handed us our new savings book statement, Santé's eyes lit up like I had never seen before.

He held my hand, intertwining his fingers with mine. "Thank you, Victoria. This means the world to me."

I SETTLED INTO THE PASSENGER SEAT OF MY CAR AND MY LIFE, numb as I watched Santé gleefully take the wheel of both. After ensuring I was comfortable, he closed the door and returned to the driver's side. The car roared to life, and we headed back to his house.

As we drove on, each mile widened and closed the gap between us. My heart was a complex mix of emotions, like a painting splattered with contrasting hues, beautiful yet indecipherable. As I stared out the window, pondering the beautiful yet complex mix of joy and sorrow that had become my life, I realized I had everything I had ever wanted, but it was nothing like I had envisioned. I'd reached the life I'd always longed for, but now achieved, it lay before me twisted and unrecognizable.

CHAPTER
Sixty-Seven

BETRAYED BY DESIGN

I stepped out of the factory in Camden, New Jersey, worn out from a long day of welding. Fuck, man, that job never gets any easier. I wiped the sweat from my brow and climbed into my Suburban. The engine roared to life, and just as I was about to pull out, I noticed this dude outside the gate. Fucker was acting weird, waving his arms around, like he was tryin' to flag me down or some shit.

"Who's this motherfucka?" I muttered. Never seen him around here before. He didn't work at the job, that was for sure. My gut told me to keep drivin', but then again, my gut also told me to eat that old burrito the other night, and that didn't work out too good.

So, I drove up to him, cautious but curious. I lowered my tinted window just halfway—enough to look him in the eye but not enough to put me in danger. My eyes met his. I wanted to know what kind of game this dude was playing.

"You Santé?" he finally blurted.

"Who wants to know?" I asked, my voice sharp with suspicion.

"I have some information about Victoria that you should know," he said.

I figured Vicky might have a hater, and I wasn't about to let him tell me something I already knew—something Vicky and I had already dealt with between us.

"I'm cool," I said, dismissing him out of the gate. I was about to roll up my window and jet, but then he dropped the bomb.

"I just thought you should know the truth about your divorce."

My hand froze on the window switch. "Da fuck'd you just say?" I lowered the window all the way this time, fully revealing myself.

"Man to man, I have some information you need to know," he continued. "Meet me at the McDonald's parking lot, and I'll give you all the dirty details."

I don't know what it was about dude, but something about him seemed like he could be the real thing. I would at least hear him out. I nodded and pulled over to the curb while he got into his car.

I chilled for a moment before tailing him. He turned the ignition, and I saw him check his side mirror to see if I was behind him, I was. We drove down Fairlane Road, past some apartments, and finally pulled into a McDonald's parking lot.

His blue Charger barely had time to come to a stop in the parking spot when I pulled up beside him. I got out of my car. I adjusted the strap in my waistband, the handle near my tailbone.

Even before his window was fully down, I was already asking, "So who the fuck's you supposed to be? And what do you know about me and Victoria?"

Dude stayed in his car and didn't make any sudden moves. I narrowed my eyes, tryin' to figure him out.

He said, "I'm the dude sent here by his girl to play the reuniting-best-friend type shit. But bro code told me it was more important to tell you why your marriage really ended—and how Victoria set the whole shit up."

Homeboy had earned his right to be heard. I said, "Okay, bro, you got the floor. Say your peace."

The dude stepped out of his car and introduced himself as Jagger. We walked to the front of his Charger. As Jagger spilled the details, my blood heated to a boil. This Jagger dude, that I had never met before was giving me the trifling dirt on Victoria, my ride-or-die.

Turns out that bitch was scheming behind my back. Hiring someone to follow my damn wife? Snapping pictures of her with another nicca!

But the real kicker was how she mailed those damn pictures to me anonymously, hopin' to drive me and my wife apart. She wanted to end my marriage, slide into my life, and take my wife's place.

As wild as Jagger's story sounded. I knew deep down it was true.

I had a brief flashback to Audubon—in the car. Victoria had just finished sucking the fuck outta my dick, it was one of her best performances, and that's saying something—because she was always the best. I had secretly decided to break things off with Jackie and figured I needed a place to stay, somewhere to let things cool down after the explosion I knew would follow calling it quits on my marriage. Hanging with Victoria made the most sense, so I asked her if I could spend time with her.

I remember she said, "Yes, you can spend as much time with me as you want." She was practically giggling with joy. But then she added something strange: "Well, as much as you can, considering your marriage to Jackie."

I remember I froze mid-motion, the blue hand towel still clutched around my spit-sloppy dick. I was fucked up for a second. I had never told Victoria about my marriage. Not once. I even started to question her: "How did you know—" But I stopped mid-sentence, unwilling to draw more attention to the fact that she knew something she shouldn't have.

I tried to convince myself I had heard her wrong. Or maybe she was guessing, grasping at straws. But she wasn't guessing. She knew. Victoria knew I was married because she had already put her plan in motion to destroy it—And damn it, it worked.

My fists clenched, knuckles white, "Victoria masterminded this whole damn scheme?" I blurted, trying to wrap my head around the bullshit.

"Exactly." Jagger nodded. "It was her game from the get-go. She wanted your wife out of the picture, and she made that shit happen."

My hands clenched into fists, my knuckles turning white. I felt betrayed, not just by my ex, but now by the bitch livin' under my roof, sharin' my life. The tremor in my leg raged like a volcano about to erupt, but I forced myself to keep it together.

"Man, this is some next-level fuckery," I finally muttered, my voice filled with a bitterness I couldn't hide.

"For sure bro," Jagger agreed, lookin' genuinely sorry for bein' the messenger of the bad news.

My emotions were everywhere: rage, betrayal, and a weird sense of relief. At least I finally knew the truth. And knowin' the truth, as ugly as it was, gave me a new sense of power.

When he was done spilling everything, we shook hands. Any tension between us was broken. Jagger had given me the key to my past, a way to make sense of all the madness. And while my head was still spinning from betrayal and fury, at least now I could start puttin' the pieces of my life back together.

Jagger was alright. In a world full of snakes, meeting someone who worked for pest control was good.

As our vehicles went separate ways one thought pounded in my head. *I have to figure out how to snatch my life back from that bitch, and get my swerve back on track.*

Victoria was about to learn exactly what happens when you piss off the wrong motherfucker. Teaching her that lesson would be downright delicious. Because the one you never, ever fuck over is—Santé Sabatino.

CHAPTER
Sixty-Eight

RAGE AND RETRIBUTION

I heard Santé's car pulling into the driveway. An inexplicable and unsettling feeling came over me like a dark omen. Santé's temperament was delicate as a butterfly's wing and unpredictable as the wind. One moment, he could be captivating and inviting. In the next, he was as volatile as a sudden lightning strike.

The door to his master bedroom swung open violently, and there he was, clearly enraged. Santé's presence was imposing, electrifying, and deeply unnerving. His eyes met mine, and I saw none of the affection or lust that once dwelled there. The eyes that looked back at me were a vast, empty yellow-green tundra.

"Victoria," he began, uttering my name like an accusation, "is there something you wanna tell me?"

A shiver slithered down my spine. "I don't know what you mean."

Santé balled his fist, "Don't play me for a fucking fool!" His voice was a whip, slashing through the fragile silence, a sound reverberating off the walls long after his mouth closed.

Terror gripped me like a hand clenched around my throat. I felt crushed, as if the walls were closing in on me. Was this how it would end?

"I thought you were different, Victoria," he hissed, his words loaded with an icy disdain that frosted the room. "I thought you were my rock through this hellish phase in my life. But you…" His voice broke, but not with sadness. It broke with a raging fire of anger, of betrayal. "You bitch! You were plotting, scheming behind my back!"

My senses were in overdrive. His voice was not just a sound but a physical entity, each word a slap against my face. I could smell the bitterness in the air, pungent and acidic, as if the room itself was souring.

"What are you talking about?" The words tumbled out of my mouth, struggling to catch up with my racing thoughts.

He slammed his hand against the dresser. The whole structure quivered, and a crystal trinket given to him by his daughter, Jovie, which read "World's Greatest Dad," fell, shattering into a million pieces. "You hired someone to follow Jackie, didn't you? Took pictures of her with her side dude, didn't you? My God, the damn nerve of you!"

My mouth went dry. The taste of impending doom was coppery, like blood. The room tilted at a sickening angle. "Santé…"

He silenced me with a roar. "You mailed those damn photos! You evil bitch! And you sent them to me anonymously, as if they were a Goddamned gift."

Standing frozen, my leg lightly touching the sheets, I nervously watched Santé pace at the foot of the bed, where he yelled, "Were you trying to claim some moral high ground? You wanted to destroy my family? Take Jackie's place like some vulture circling overhead?"

The accusation was sharp and cruel, a sword piercing through any defense I might have had.

But I had to try. I felt my knees buckle, as the room spun I exclaimed, "I saw her by accident and I didn't know what to do."

Santé was thoroughly unmoved, "You should've told me the moment you saw her," he spat, pacing back and forth, his footsteps rhythmic drumming. Maybe then I might've believed it was an accident, but not now. Not after you've put this entire scheme together, and for what? To play the innocent?"

His words carried an unbearable heat, a scorching judgment that no tears could quench. The air grew thick with unspoken recriminations, a smothering fog that made breathing hard.

"I don't know how to defend myself. I didn't want to see what I saw," I said. Santé waved dismissively. "I can't believe a damn thing you say."

Then, Santé delivered the ultimate insult, the knockout blow. "You're just as bad as Jackie, maybe worse." At that point. I just wanted it to end and I wanted directions toward our exit.

"So, what's next?" My voice was barely a murmur, buckling under the strain. "Are you kicking me out?"

He looked at me, his eyes no longer aflame but cold as the most unforgiving winter. "No," he said, shaking his head with a twisted smirk. "That would be too easy. You'll stay, but not here, not in this room. You'll be staying in the basement like my dogs used to. That's where bitches stay."

My heart ached, and I cried out, "The basement? Santé, please."

With maximal disdain in his voice, he said, "The basement is where you'll be stored until I figure out exactly how to deal with you."

His verdict was final, each word hammering down like a nail sealing my coffin. I was to exist but not live, to breathe but not feel, sequestered away until he deemed me worthy of his judgment.

As he walked out, leaving me alone in the room that used to be 'ours,' each step sounded like a clock ticking, marking time, distance, and the end of something irreplaceable.

And I stood there amidst the shards of a shattered relationship, my skin tingling with the raw, unsettling realization that our love, even in our most twisted form, had come undone. And the wreckage was beyond comprehension, beyond repair, a devastating portrait of just how far we'd fallen, how far I'd fallen, from the edge of something that once felt like destiny, now only doom.

CHAPTER
Sixty-Nine

CASTÍGALA... PUNISH HER

"Castígala!" Santé's words sliced through the silence and the darkness of santés basement.

Had I understood Spanish better I might have been prepared for what was to follow but I didn't so I was completely unprepared when the basement door's lock yielded with a loud clunk, its opening accompanied by a flood of blinding light.

Wordlessly, as if moved by some invisible urgency, Santé bolted down the steps and seized my arm. He spirited me upstairs swiftly, leaving me breathless.

As my feet touched the main landing, I yearned for the familiar embrace of the second-floor master bedroom. Instead, he ushered me into the living room, where his image filled the seventy-five-inch television screen. Inescapable, vast, and naked, Santé appeared in a previously recorded video. Watching the video footage, my gaze fell upon his semi-hard dick swinging from right to left in the background as he approached a bed in the foreground.

On the bed, a woman was also naked. She was a white woman with massive breasts and appeared to be in her forties. She rocked a short layered haircut and had a blue ball gag shoved in her mouth. She seemed to be wearing a dog collar from which a pedant with the initial "K" dangled.

The larger surroundings had a cheap motel vibe all over it. The camera was rigged to catch the woman from the front and get Santé lurking sketchily from behind.

Santé demanded I get on my knees and face the television. "Face down, ass up, shoulders toward the TV." His orders were clear, so I did as instructed.

Once on all fours, he asked, "Do you wanna chance to make things better?" I eagerly said, "Yes Papi."

He asked, "Do you know what you're saying yes to?"

My mind spun with the possibilities, but deep inside, I knew what he wanted, what he had always wanted, the taboo I had denied him for years. I had resolved that I would consent to give Santé anal sex long ago, but no moment ever seemed to hold the ideal conditions.

Needless to say I just never imagined such an offering would be under such stressful circumstances.

In that delicate moment, the looming presence of the living room's grand window flickered into my awareness. My eyes darted right, and there, the beige curtains, felt like a shroud covering our secrets. Safe from public humiliation, a brief comfort washed over me, only to be chased away by a riptide of dread when, over my shoulder, I saw Santé removing his dove gray Tommy Hilfiger underwear.

My nerves went from zero to a hundred, and my anxiety morphed into raw fear right when Santé muttered, "After everything you've put me through, it's time you start proving your value."

He reached for the lubrication bottle and slathered a glob around his rock-hard dick. I fumbled for words to delay the fate that awaited me, but Santé quickly extinguished all doubt of any reprieve.

Before I could speak, he grumbled, "No more playing games, it's time for Papi to fuck that ass."

My heart vaulted to my throat as my eyes returned to the glowing screen. In a moment of unsettling clarity, I understood. The girl in the video had walked the path of anal annihilation first, right where I now teetered. Ass fucking was never my thing. It was one of the reasons I waited so long to have sex. I wanted unobstructed access to my pussy, and now I was milliseconds away from having my asshole reamed.

There I was, hiney-hole high on Santé's cold living room floor, and he was about to take my anal virginity. The man who had forced me to sleep on his concrete basement floor overnight. I wouldn't have believed it myself if it had not happened to me.

With a cool breeze across my ass cheeks and my shoulders on the ground, I craned my neck upward. My eyes ascended to the television screen, and there, in pixels and light, was Santé's image. He was now in the bed with his knees behind the woman wearing a dog collar with a dangling silver initial "K."

Santé's hand was wrestling to remove the ball gag from the mysterious woman's mouth. Once released, her breath was rapid, and her mouth opened.

I heard Santé's voice on the video, "Say the magic words bitch. Nothing happens until I hear those magic words."

The woman said," Please Fuck my ass 'Big Daddy.'"

Santé said, "That's right, I need to know you want this dick." He then put the ball gag back in her mouth.

I was in the exact same position she was as I lay watching her eyes reflect my fear. I had the privilege and torture of watching a preview of what I was about to experience.

"Watch me fuck that bitch up the ass," Santé announced with pride and glee. The charm of his edgy, coarse language had dulled. No longer could I drape his misogyny in softer shades. Santé's naked objectification was almost unbearable."

"Watch this part and learn," he said. In the video, Santé moved behind the woman. He hunched over her ass, she remained in the doggy-style position. Suddenly, she let out a scream. As she did, I felt Santé's dick slap across my ass cheek.

"Don't let her screaming scare you. She loved getting this big dick up her ass, and so will you…eventually." In his words, I found no reassurance or peace. Terror tightened its grip around my voice, rendering me mute.

I had made my choice and given my explicit consent, just as "K" had; there was nothing more to say; my job was to endure and find pleasure where I could.

I felt the pressure of his spongy flesh against my asshole. The pain of the first penis penetrating my ass was most searing. The screams from the television screen swelled, and then, as if entwined by some cruel fate, "K's" cry and mine converged, melding into a single, solitary wail.

After seven minutes of agony and mirroring the video performance, the pain of penetration transformed into a strange sensation of false incontinence and weird stretching. I felt like I possessed an internal accordion.

Santé's long, deep dicking pushed my body to defy the laws of physics. Beyond reasoning, my tiny butthole was accommodating Santé's massive dick. The pain slid to the background, never absent but not as prominent. While the sensations of pleasure lurked in the shadows, awkwardness took center stage.

Slaps across my ass and degrading language followed. I only remember traces of uncomfortable sensations. Santé was in heaven, and I was in purgatory. Not yet able to feel the carnal pleasures suggested by Santé's moans and groans, but not in as much pain as "K" appeared to be on the screen.

Santé increased speed, and the temperature of my asshole warmed. He picked up his pace, and I lurched forward. He pulled me by the hair, "No bitch don't run from the dick. You ain't going nowhere." I was simultaneously turned on and turned off, the confusion of which wreaked havoc on my psyche.

Santé's dick felt like a hot rod. Lubrication allowed entry, but friction and heat were building. "My ass is on fire, Papi," I yelled.

"Don't worry bitch. I got the hose right here."

I could hardly dream he possessed even more dick, but from a hidden well of magic, he brought forth additional inches of his cream-toned meat python and plunged it deeper into my newly devirginized asshole. My eyes swelled to the size of headlights, and my butthole stretched to a-gape.

I screamed, "Oh my God, Papi." My head collapsed onto my hands, where I rested for about three seconds before Santé pulled my hair.

My head jerked back, and although the face of the real, flesh-and-blood Santé eluded my sight, his image filled the tv screen before me. Without warning, my pussy sprung a leak. My hips involuntarily swayed. "That's it bitch," said Santé.

My legs trembled, making it difficult for me to keep my balance. Santé was keenly aware of every nuance of my body's motion and rhythm. Like an experienced jockey, he rode my asshole to the finish line.

Santé pushed my head down onto my hands in front of me. Being fucked hard in my ass, the pain and pleasure was now of equal measure. I felt I was going to jump out of my skin. The intensity and the power were all-consuming. He was hitting deep into the bottom of my gut, and my hole was stretched like a rubber band, desperate to hold it's shape.

Suddenly, I felt a warm sensation, one unfamiliar. "Something's happening, Papi. I don't know what's happening."

Santé quickly retorted, "I'm turning you out—bitch! That's what da fucks' happening."

I yelled, "I don't know, Papi, I just don't know."

Suddenly, I was flushed, my fingers trembled, and an electric sensation involved my entire body. I screamed, "Jesus!"

Santé yelled back, "The name is Santé, bitch." Those were the last words I heard before my body convulsed with pleasure and a small amount of pain previously unexperienced in my lifetime. Something similar, but less intense had happened once before, also with Sante.

I felt my spirit slightly levitate above my body. Tears fell from my eyes, and my mouth was undoubtedly as open as my asshole. A fleeting glance at the grand television screen revealed a disturbing echo. K's movements mirrored my own.

"Look at that shit!" Santé demanded. "Do you see her?" he asked.

Under the unrelenting ass pounding, my voice surrendered but a single utterance, "Yes."

Santé's voice was boastful. "That's the moment she became my ass-whore…now you are too."

Santé jackhammered my anus. I crawled on all fours, no longer sure I could take the whole anal adventure.

Santé yelled, "I said no running bitch. This is what you wanted, right? You love me, right?"

As I fell onto my stomach, still feeling Santé's dick slamming inside me with the force of a multi-car collision, In answer to his compound question, I cried out, "Yes, I love you, Papi."

Santé offered his approval and twisted validation. "Good ass-whore, now that's what I love."

After a wait of almost ten years to hear the sacred word 'love' fall from Santé's mouth, the term was bittersweet. I never envisioned it would manifest amidst such twisted deviance. The master-dominant, Santé, was keenly aware that he had given me a distorted shadow of my long-held desires.

He punctuated his dominance by thrusting another weaponized form of validation upon me, one which rose to a symbolic pacification. I sensed Santé adjusting the axis of his hips. Dazed from his withering domination, I watched, from my lowered perspective, as he aggressively swung his leg over my shoulder to plant his bare foot firmly in my face. "Suck on Papi's big toe, bitch."

Opening my mouth, Santé stuck his foot into my second warm opening. I sucked on his toe like I would have sucked a pacifier. Papi stretched my mouth as he stretched and plowed my ass, stuffing his entire foot into my face. I tucked my teeth, swirled my tongue across his toes, and deep-throated his right foot, triggering my gag reflex. My moaning vibrated through his foot as Santé slammed his humongous dick into my asshole with a fury that echoed into my skeletal structure, leaving my entire body quivering.

Without warning, I was cumming, but unlike in the past, this time, I was squirting. With each downward thrust of Santé's dick deep inside me, I wet Santé's floor with a spray of squirt. Both my pussy and asshole twitched and vibrated. Then, the impossible happened. My asshole gave way and opened more.

Santé was delighted. "That's right bitch. I've been waiting a decade for you to take this dick. Finally—balls deep bitch!" I found myself screaming into his foot, like into the mouth of a megaphone.

I was angry with him and hated how he had treated me, but my brain had been temporarily re-wired by the power of Santé's dick. To my astonishment, I recognized the muffled words screaming into Santé's foot as "I love you, Papi." Santé also comprehended the tangled, mumbled words of submission as well.

His response was tinged with the audacity of arrogance, the power of domination, and the flair of bravado. "I know you do bitch. Daddy's lil ass-whore is in love… I know bitch, I know."

Santé reached back and slapped my ass with the power of a falling gavel and the sound of a thunderclap. The taste of

Santé's toes swirled on my taste buds as my asshole stretched further than I ever thought possible. I was overwhelmed. So as Santé's dick threatened to touch my belly button from the inside, I drifted, not above the skin that holds me, but within it. My thoughts and very existence began to curl inward, weaving through an internal maze I feared might become my permanent home, sub-space.

I have no clue how long Santé bashed at my asshole or how many times his balls slapped mere centimeters from the brim of my anal rosebud.

In my memory's haze, I only know that I glimpsed the kitchen window bathed in the evening's glow as the bittersweet essence of Santé's cum weaved its spell around my tongue for the fifth time that Sunday.

Unlike the previous hours of Santé's sexual marathon, when he demanded I open wide to drink Papi's man milk, I was not placed back on my knees for more ass pounding. After the final cum quenching, he allowed me to collapse onto the floor, sprawled and weakened. I looked at the heels of his feet and up at his ass cheeks as he swaggered away upstairs. I had no idea my respite from his debauchery was only momentary.

CHAPTER
Seventy

A PLACE OF POWERLESSNESS

Santé reemerged ten minutes later, his dick fresh from a shower and a full day's workout. He was now wrapped in a new pair of red Tommy Hilfiger boxer briefs. He drew closer to me, his feet still bare and carrying the wet traces of his shower. I was sore. My asshole was on fire. I lay huddled at the base of the looming television screen above.

The video on the grand screen had long vanished during my anal marathon, leaving only a sea of monochromatic blue. I had dreamed my consenting to Santé's asshole jamboree would redeem me in his eyes and forgive the sins I had cast upon him. However, my dreams were swiftly shattered."

Santé grabbed me by my shoulder and marched me a few feet from the living room. He opened the door leading to the two-car garage.

"Get in here, you two-faced ungrateful BITCH." Santé's words felt like a hand across my face as he yanked me into the garage. I thought hours of being his anal trampoline had curried favor. However, once inside the garage, the faint smell of gasoline and oil filled my nose while fear invaded my heart. Whatever Santé was up to, it didn't feel like forgiveness.

He slammed the garage door closed, adding to the tension. There was only one vehicle in the two-car garage, the tan suburban truck, because Jackie was in possession of the Toyota.

I guessed Santé could see the puzzlement written all over my face as I attempted to familiarize myself with the new environment. His voice was cold as steel, and he said, "Yeah, look around and get used to your new home." His words were as stinging as they were surprising. In fact, I couldn't quite comprehend the meaning and magnitude of his phraseology, given his cavalier attitude.

I debated whether to question Santé or even speak at all. Yet the haunting words, 'Get used to your new home,' echoed ceaselessly in my mind. I had to know what it meant, and I was about to find out, along with just how far Santé would go for revenge."

Assuming I was going somewhere, I walked to the door of the tan suburban. I asked, "My new home? Where are you taking me?"

Santé chuckled. "I'm not taking you anywhere BITCH, this is your new home."

I shook my head, and my speech stammered, "I-I know I'm home, but—"

Santé interjected, "Not this house, you dumb BITCH. This garage is your new home."

"Here?" I asked.

Santé promptly replied, "That's right BITCH. You no longer deserve to set foot in my house unless I invite you. This garage is where you will stay." Without warning, Santé grabbed me by the arm and took me over to a corner. I glanced down and saw what appeared to be an animal cage.

My heart raced, and the pain of adrenaline surged through my body. I could barely contemplate my circumstances. Suddenly, the environment and the situation became surreal. Santé's voice sounded like it was coming across a radio broadcast, not in real-time.

"That is where you will sleep. These are your new living arrangements."

The shock of Santé's announcement shone across my face.

Santé continued, "That's right BITCH. This is your new bed. Actually, it's the old bed of my old four-legged BITCH, but I think it suits you just fine."

Just as I garnered the energy and clarity to speak, I felt myself thrust to my knees. Santé had pushed me. I looked up at Santé, his fingers pointed toward the cage.

"Get your trifling ass in that cage, you dirty scheming BITCH."

This is not happening, I told myself over and over again.

I said it with such intensity internally that I must have inadvertently spoken out loud because Santé's reply was as curt as it was final, "Oh yes, it is happening. This is now your life. In the cage, bitch."

I didn't have time to question whether the cage size would be sufficient for my entire body. I felt a kick to my ass. I knew it was time I knew what was expected of me. Santé had made it very clear.

I looked at the cage and then glanced up at Santé. The cost of my obsession was coming into view. A single tear fell from my face as I crawled into the cage. I barely fit. My back was arched. Despite the large size, it was still a confined space. With a burst of energy, Santé slammed the cage gate, strode to a black shelf, and returned holding the instrument of my fate, a padlock. In a blink, that click sound hit the air. That was it, trapped…, and it felt final as fuck.

Santé bent down, his face appearing large and looming outside of the gate. He spoke slow and clearly with constrained emotion, "I'm going to show you what happens when you cross me, bitch. Get some rest. Now that I've opened both your holes for business, it will soon be time for double penetrations."

I murmured, "Papi, please."

Santé replied, "Aww, my lil ass-whore doesn't have to beg. I appreciate it, but I was already gonna fuck that ass again. It's cool if I invite friends, right. I know you had your grand opening today, but that butthole's still tight. It still has that new car smell."

My body fell limp against the cage.

He said, "Think about it and give me your answer later, me and my homies having fun—taking turns." Santé's face pulled back from the cage. He rose to his feet and strode back into the house.

I was trapped in a nightmare orchestrated by the man of my dreams, Santé Sabatino.

CHAPTER
Seventy-One

THE CAGE OF CLARITY

In Monday's predawn gloom of the garage, I lay naked in a cage where Santé had placed me just a few hours before, awash in a sea of half-lit objects and lost intentions. The air was somber, a cocktail of motor oil and lingering memories, a scent that evoked both homeliness and despair. How chilling it was to feel the air seep into me all night as if the atmosphere was trying to remind me of the frost that had settled between Santé and me.

Before long, footsteps arrived, each echoing like a distant drumbeat. The jangle of Santé's keys resonated and hit my ear with an uneasy dissonance. Thanks to his auto start function, the engine came alive with a roar before Santé entered the garage.

The words I had rehearsed, begging for his forgiveness and my release, caught in my throat, suffocated by the magnitude of my deception, and the exhaust from his Suburban. So my plea remained unsaid, leaving my mouth tinged with the flavor of regret.

Santé strolled into the garage and peered at me in the cage but said nothing. He slid into the driver's seat of his truck, briefly haloed by the soft interior light, like an ephemeral angel disconnected from my grueling reality. His truck windows lowered. His name, "Santé" escaped my lips, a whisper carried on the tide of my hopes, sailing toward his ears.

His cold response, "I'll be back to fuck you some more later," punctured the air with disappointment, landing like the final words of a dismal eulogy.

As he backed out into the early dawn. It was as if the morning mist swallowed not just the car but also the version of Santé I had once known and adored.

The garage door closed, leaving me alone, lost in a vacuum that drew in the unique scents of his departure. His body gel melded with the exhaust fumes, crafting a poignant perfume of our relational decay.

It mattered little whether I saw him as he truly was; to me, my vision of Santé as an Adonis was unshakably real. I clung to every scrap of evidence—no matter how insignificant—that reinforced that ideal.

My relentless need to see him as something greater than he was, to fill the gaps left by my own perceived shortcomings, transformed him from a man into an idol. Rather than allowing him to inspire me toward wholeness, I elevated him to the role of savior.

The irony wasn't lost on me: the very image I had built could only be shattered by the harsh reality of Santé becoming, quite literally, my jailer.

It was a delicate realization, fragile yet forceful as a feather caught in an updraft. To find my path again, I needed to see my reality, raw and unembellished. This epiphany, symbolized by the cage in which I was confined, while somber, held the promise of freedom and the allure of a future unfettered by past illusions. Then, and only then, could I turn toward a future unshackled, leaving behind the illusions that anchored me to Santé Sabatino for so long.

DELIVERANCE IN THE DARK

Sleep refused to come, an elusive creature fluttering just out of reach, taunting me in the darkness. A dark abyss, cold and empty, much like my prospects of escape, had swallowed me whole.

"In God, I live and move and have my being," I found myself whispering. The words trickled from my lips as a drizzle of honey might, sticky and lingering. And much like that drizzle, it seeped through the cracks of my shattered composure.

With watery eyes, I repeated the phrase, each repetition stirring the stagnant air like a gentle breeze, soothing the churning pit of my stomach, if only a little. By the seventy-fifth chant, the jagged edges of my fear were smoothed, worn down by the cadence of my newfound mantra.

Then, cutting through the sensory deprivation like a knife through flesh, the mechanical roar of the garage door opener vibrated through the air. My heart leaped into my throat. Santé wouldn't be home for hours, of that I was certain.

A snake of fear slithered its way back into my consciousness. What if Santé hadn't gone to work? What if he brought people over to fuck his trapped concubine? I felt as if I'd been plunged into icy water. But summoning the last wisps of defiance within me, I turned to my mantra once more, the words now a lifeline. "In God I live and move and have my being."

The cacophony of grinding gears ceased, replaced by the cascade of sunlight that unfurled itself across the garage floor like a golden carpet. And there he was, a man in a crisp blue uniform, clutching a cardboard package, his eyes meeting mine in a moment of disbelief. "What the hell?"

"Please, sir, can you let me out of here?" My voice quivered, tinted with desperation.

"Should I call the police?" His eyes widened, uncertainty flashing across his face.

"Yes, but first, please let me out."

The man hesitated momentarily before his gaze followed my pointing finger to the hook above a cluttered shelf. His fingers clutched a ring of two keys, one of which fit into the padlock securing the cage to the wall, the other key to my handcuffs. And just like that, I was released. Breathing in garage air, still edged with the smell of oil and metal, yet impossibly sweet.

THE DELIVERY MAN MADE THE CALL WHILE I DASHED UP THE staircase, my bare feet thumping against the wood. Each step carried me further away from that stifling cage but not far enough from danger. My fingers dug into Santé's closet, pulling out a Gucci jogging suit and a pair of sneakers that I slipped on in a hurry.

My purse was on the nightstand, conspicuously devoid of cash and no car keys. A quick search through Santé's drawers revealed not one but two of my cell phones. Including the one I thought I had lost. Had he been hoarding them like twisted souvenirs? I grabbed both and stuffed them into my purse, practically leaping down the stairs. My fingers closed around a water bottle in the kitchen. Hydration felt like an afterthought but one I could not afford to ignore.

As I approached the front door, my hand gripping the doorknob, I cast a final glance over my shoulder. The walls that had confined me looked back impassively, indifferent to my capture and my escape. With a shiver, I stepped out, pulling the door shut behind me.

I was free, but for how long?

CHAPTER
Seventy-Three

RACE TO THE BANK

My heels met the cold, unforgiving asphalt with a staccato rhythm, each step echoing through the two-mile journey to the bus station. The air was piercingly dry, each inhale a burst of cold that crystallized in my lungs, mingling with faint whiffs of car exhaust and dormant, frost-covered earth.

My water bottle, long emptied, had been discarded in a trash bin, yet my throat felt as dry as if I'd swallowed flakes of frost. I pulled out both of my cell phones. Apprehension rippled through me as the older one illuminated to reveal a fifty percent charge, but zero bars. The newer one sputtered on at a weak three percent, but offered a hopeful glimmer of connectivity.

Then it hit me like a face slap: my charger was back at Santé's. Regret and urgency twisted in my stomach, each pang a gnawing reminder that time was ticking down. I'd sold my home and was now locked in a race to get to the bank.

Desperate times, desperate measures. My fingers shook as I dialed Patricia. Her voicemail greeted me, "Hey, you've reached Patricia. I'm on my honeymoon. Leave me a message, and I'll call you back eventually."

The words bored into me like shards of ice. Patricia was basking in newlywed bliss while I grappled with disaster, every bad choice snapping back like a taut rubber band.

Shivering, I moved to the next number. "Boss, is that you?" sang the voice on the other end.

"I might not be your boss anymore, Beth, but I love to hear you call me that. I also hope you meant it when you said I could call if I needed help." My voice shivered, desperation seeping through.

"Of course, Victoria, we're friends," she reassured me.

A torrent of tears broke free, each droplet a miniature iceberg sliding down my cheeks. "Good," I managed through sobs. "Because I need a friend right now."

"Where are you?" Beth's voice pierced through my emotional fog.

"I'm entering a bus station in Turnersville, New Jersey. But I could meet you in Center City—Philly. Can you do that?"

"I think so. What time?" Beth asked.

I glanced at the bus schedule, tacked to the terminal wall in a weathered frame. It read 2:35 PM. My eyes scanned the timetable. I could be in Center City by 3:30 PM—until another sickening realization hit me: I couldn't use my debit card or I'd be tracked.

"Oh my God, I'm...I'm trapped," I whispered, panic breaking through.

Beth's tone sharpened. "Wow, Victoria, are you in danger?"

"Yes." The word slipped out like a fragile shard, a frigid admission I could barely stand to say out loud.

THE GROWLING ENGINES OF CARS FILLED THE PARKING LOT, each rumble tensing me in anticipation. The familiar hum of a truck made my heart race wildly, an instinctive fear of seeing Santé there. My pulse quickened, and for a moment, I could've sworn I saw a truck like his slowing down near the station. My hands tightened around my purse, clutching it like a shield until the vehicle passed by, its driver a stranger.

Finally, Beth's gray Mazda rolled into view, its engine purring like salvation. I lunged for the car, my fingers wrapping around the handle as if it were a lifeline. The warmth of Beth's perfume—vanilla with hints of rose—wrapped around me in a way that almost made me cry.

"We need to hug," I blurted, my voice breaking. Beth's arms became my refuge, letting me unleash a wave of tears, momentarily loosening the agony I'd kept buried.

"Where should I take you? Your condo?" Beth's voice was soft, full of genuine concern.

"No...I sold it," I whispered, each syllable tearing at my heart. They weren't just words; they were the epitaph of the life I'd left behind.

Beth's eyes widened, deep compassion shining through. "Oh my God, Vicky."

"I need to go to TD Bank. I need to withdraw everything. Every last dollar," I said, barely able to contain my urgency.

"Should we go to the police?" she asked, her voice filled with the cautious concern of someone who cared deeply.

"Yes, but not right now. First, the bank. Then a motel. I have to wash this nightmare off me," I said, gripping the edge of my seat.

Beth sighed, understanding yet cautious. "I can't leave my son for too long. But I could drop you at the motel, go fetch him, and then come back if you need me to."

I met her gaze, overwhelmed by her kindness. "No, that's too much to ask. Once you drop me at the motel, you don't need to return. I'll figure it out," I assured her.

"By the way, where's your car?" Beth asked, steering through the traffic toward Route 42.

"It's at my ex-boyfriend's place. I couldn't find the keys, and there wasn't time to search. I'll get it back, but only after I'm safe and my money's secure," I said, determination hardening my voice.

As we rolled onto Route 42, I placed my hand gently on Beth's shoulder, the fabric of her blouse anchoring me in the moment. "Thank you, Beth. I can never repay you for this."

"You don't have to," she replied, warmth in her voice. "You were there for me when I needed to see my mom."

I remembered that small act of kindness I'd offered reluctantly, never imagining it would be returned so graciously. Beth's kindness felt like an unexpected light, cutting through the storm my choices had created. Her affirmation, pure and unselfish, became my flickering lighthouse. Her presence seemed to reweave the fraying fabric of my hope, pulling me through the shadows of my distorted life.

CHAPTER
Seventy-Four

DRAINED TRUST

"**Y**ou've got to be kidding me?" I bellowed, my voice splintering the calm atmosphere of the bank. Customers in the privacy cubicles glanced up, and even those in line at the tellers' desks turned their heads, momentarily distracted from the monotony of their errands.

I stared at Mr. Mitchell, my eyes not believing, my ears not trusting. I clenched my teeth so tightly I could taste a hint of salty bitterness from my own gums.

Mr. Mitchell leaned toward me, lowering his voice in an almost paternal way as if trying to rein in my volume by example. He smelled like old spice and decayed dreams. "All of your money has been accounted for. Only six thousand dollars remain."

"How is that possible?" I demanded, my voice taut with incredulity, snapping back to the moment. "I deposited over two hundred thousand just a few days ago, then added another twenty-five thousand from my Wells Fargo account. How could it all be gone?" Both my voice and hands trembled as I awaited his response.

Mr. Mitchell said, "All of your money has been accounted for. It seems you're not considering the two hundred thirty-three thousand dollars removed on Saturday morning."

Confusion ebbed into nausea. My stomach recoiled, performing a sickening series of flips. "What the hell are you talking about?"

His eyes flicked to a spot over my shoulder as if searching for an escape. "Mr. Santé Sabatino is also on this account, is he not?"

Feeling as though the floor had turned to quicksand beneath my heels, I nodded weakly. "Yes."

"He came in Friday evening and wanted to make the withdrawal," Mr. Mitchell continued, hesitating as if weighing how much to divulge. "I was here. I personally told him we couldn't fulfill that large request immediately. We didn't have that much cash on hand. I made special arrangements for him to come back the next day, on Saturday. And he did. That is when he withdrew the two hundred thirty-three thousand dollars."

The room swayed. I eased back into my seat, numbed. My fingers trembled as they gripped the armrest, feeling the cold, impersonal leather against my skin.

I was dumbfounded. "You let him walk out of this bank with two hundred thirty-three thousand dollars of my money and never called or tried to reach me? It's a joint account, so you know at least half of that money was mine!" I desperately tried to make the moral argument, though I secretly doubted I had much of a legal argument. Mr. Mitchell confirmed my suspicion.

He glanced at his computer screen again as though it might offer a different narrative, and then he burst my bubble gently. "I understand this is difficult, Miss Victoria. But Mr. Sabatino's withdrawal was carried out according to the terms of your joint account. Both parties have equal access to the funds, and there's no legal requirement for either to inform the other of large withdrawals."

As he spoke, I felt a throbbing sensation behind my eyes. It was as if the numbers were swirling around me: $206,000, $25,000, $233,000, all mixing into an incomprehensible fog. The back of my throat was parched like I'd swallowed sand.

"We had to make special arrangements for that large amount," Mr. Mitchell added flatly, "since we didn't keep that much cash on hand. When he returned on Saturday, we handed it over." Mr. Mitchell added one last detail," Mr. Sabatino put the money in a black duffel bag and left the bank just before closing."

I stared at the envelope he had given me, the last $6,000 of my once-secure life. It seemed so incongruent now, so meager. I heard the crinkling sound it made when my fingers tightened around it, each small noise a sledgehammer to my fragile composure.

Mr. Mitchell looked at me, his gaze half-sympathetic, half-apologetic. "Would you like me to call our security to escort you out—or your safety, Miss Victoria? Given the circumstances, it might be best."

I shook my head. "No, thank you. That won't be necessary."

He nodded and retreated to his desk, his footsteps receding into the distance like the last echoes of my former life. I looked at Beth, her grip on my hand steadying me in a way I didn't even know I needed.

As I stood up, clutching the envelope, I could feel the dull, numbing ache in the pit of my stomach slowly transform into something else, a burning resolve fueled by my indomitable spirit of survival.

I took a deep breath, each inhalation a wisp of the stale, conditioned air, and stepped out of the bank. The setting sunlight, usually inviting and warm, felt abrasive on my skin. It was too bright, too harsh, yet impossible to look away from. It was as if the world dared me to see it in all its cruel clarity. And for the first time in a long time, I didn't blink, or look away.

CHAPTER
Seventy-Five

HUNT FOR THE RUNAWAY

The hum of that damn factory still vibrated in my bones as I pulled up to the crib after a long day of work. Right away, some shit was off. My garage door was standing wide open like a gaping mouth, ready to be fucked. I shot a quick glance to the side street. There, like an old bat, sat Victoria's 300C. Her car was there, but still, a little bubble of alarm popped in my chest.

I swung my truck into the driveway harder than I should've, my tires screeched. I jumped out before the engine even settled, my boots crunching against the concrete. The garage felt colder than it should've, and there it was. The cage but no Victoria.

"Bitch!" I hit the button, and the garage shut with a dull clunk, a sick feeling crept over me.

"Victoria!" My voice shot through the empty house, echoing off counters and cutting through the quiet. I took the stairs two at a time, my heart thumping. "Victoria, where are you, damn it? You really think you can hide from me?" Each step sent made my stomach a little sicker like I was on some twisted carnival ride.

I charged into the master bedroom. The door I'd shut tight now stood wide open. The room? Empty. The bathroom? No trace. My eyes swept the room—her purse, usually cluttering the nightstand, gone. I jerked open the drawer—both phones, gone. She'd played her move. She'd broken free.

I tore into my daughter's room, sweat and fury breaking out. Sliding a hand under the mattress, I felt the cold metal of Victoria's 300C key fob. After a deep breath, I tucked it back under the mattress.

I ran to the loft, my laptop gave a dim glow. Fingers flying over the keys, I pulled up the shady software connected to her trap phone. The last GPS ping hit the bus station two miles away. My gut twisted, and the sour tang of adrenaline brought a nasty taste to my mouth.

"Damn it," I hissed, urgency burning through me. I bolted downstairs, hitting the night air—the hunt was on!

CHAPTER
Seventy-Six

HAUNTED BY HIS THREAT

Beth's cell phone ruptured the silence of our ride, its ringtone bursting through the car's audio system like a clarion call. I felt a sharp edge of tension cleave the air. The atmosphere grew charged.

"Hello." Beth's voice brimmed with studied politeness as she engaged with the unseen caller.

Through the car's finely tuned speakers, a masculine voice thundered. "Where da fuck is Victoria?" My heart didn't merely jump; it erupted, bursting forth like an uncontained firework, sending shivers cascading through my veins. I shot Beth a panicked glance, frantically shaking my head in terrified desperation.

Beth replied, her voice as fragile as porcelain. "I—I don't know what you're talking about. Who is this?"

"Santé," the voice responded, sharp as a honed knife. "I'm pretty sure you know exactly who I am. But even if you don't, I know exactly who you are. So I'm gonna ask you again…where the fuck is Victoria?"

The air thickened, acquiring the texture of curdled milk as tension soared to unbearable heights. I knew Santé knew my old office number, but how did Santé have Beth's cell number?

"Sir, Miss Robbins no longer works for our company, and I don't know where she is. Now, if you'll excuse me, I have to go." Beth's voice wavered like a flickering candle in the dark.

Santé's last words struck like a poison-tipped arrow. "I didn't call her old job. I called you. So tell her to come home now. She doesn't get to destroy my fucking family and then abandon me. Got it?"

"Got it," Beth replied, her face painted with raw fear, every line painfully vivid. She severed the call with an abrupt tap on the touchscreen, as if she could also sever the tendrils of dread that now entwined us both.

"He sounds dangerous," she whispered, each syllable heavy as molten lead.

Beth spoke of her previous suggestion, which was still hanging in the air. "I know you want to get settled, but should we go to the police first?"

I had pondered that very thought earlier, yet the narrative of my life had become so convoluted it would not easily translate into a few coherent words. To divulge the truth would make me run a gauntlet of shame and ignominy. The eventual visit to the police station was another puzzle for another time.

We finally reached the motel, a humble but shabby oasis in the disorienting desert of my life. I unfolded an envelope of money, counting out a few tens to give to Beth, each bill tinged with the hue of last chances. Beth refused, her eyes brimming like reservoirs in a monsoon. "Not a dime, Victoria. That's all the money you have in the world. Get on your feet and keep in touch."

We embraced, crossing some ineffable boundary. The roles of boss and employee dissolved into a kinship as strong as blood. When we finally broke apart, I sensed a shard of Beth's essence lingering in the space between us. She watched me as I checked in at the motel's office and waved as I held up my room's key card.

Unlocking the door to Room 37, I felt Beth's gaze upon me, a lighthouse beacon through the murk of uncertainty. Only when I had safely crossed that threshold did she finally drive away, leaving me to rest and unpack the pressing decisions that loomed ahead.

CHAPTER
Seventy-Seven

NOT BEVERLY HILLS

"Well, this is not the Beverly Hills Hotel," I muttered, my voice barely rising above a groan. The instant I set foot in Room 37 of the Beasley Motel, I knew I was galaxies away from the lush comforts I used to enjoy when I was away from home.

Then I remembered I didn't even have a home.

The aged heater rattled as though gasping for its last breath while I shook a storm of dust from the thin, pitiful comforter. The bed creaked in protest as I settled onto its edge, the springs grumbling like ancient bones.

The walls, ablaze in a hue of fire engine red, seemed to pulsate with a life of their own, injecting the room with an almost palpable kink. Underfoot, the carpet was an inky black sea that clung to my shoes with a static embrace as if reluctant to let go. My nostrils flared involuntarily, assailed by the scent of stale cigarettes mingled with a trace of mildew.

I delved into my purse and retrieved my two cell phones. Remembering that only the new one had service, I powered it up. "Two percent. Great," I sighed, mentally kicking myself for forgetting to ask Beth for a charger. But I had already burdened her enough. I had to focus on what lay ahead.

Fumbling through my recent calls, I found Patricia's name and redialed her. My heart fluttered with each ring, an erratic drumroll in my chest. She answered on the third ring.

"Hello." Hearing Pat's voice, my heart warmed.

"Hey Pat, please don't hang up. I need your help."

"What's wrong?" Pat asked, sounding genuinely concerned.

I fidgeted on the dingy motel bed. "Everything," I said, the word filled with many implications.

"Are you with Santé?"

"Not anymore, and I won't be again." My watery eyes surveilled the motel room's drab, grim surroundings.

There was a pause. I could hear Patricia drawing in a cleansing breath.

"Where are you?" she asked.

"I'm in New Jersey."

"Where are you?" I returned the question.

"We were on our honeymoon, in Puerto Rico, but we're back in Philly now," she replied.

I felt my heart skip a beat, and my breath fell short. "Yeah, I heard your voicemail earlier."

"Where in New Jersey, Vicky?" Pat asked.

"Just outside of Sicklerville. It's a place called the Beasley Motel. I can text you the address."

"Do you mind if Jagger comes with me?"

I let out a sigh. "I do not mind if your husband joins you. He's your husband now. Congratulations, by the way."

"Thank you," she said, her voice imbued with a subtle warmth that cut through the digital static. Then she said, "For the record, I wouldn't have hung up on you."

"I'm so embarrassed. I've really messed up my life, Pat." My voice broke.

"But now that you're ready to put it back together again, I'll help you."

I texted Pat with the address, and she confirmed receipt. Our coordinates were set.

"According to the GPS, we're forty-five minutes away," she said.

"Perfect," I replied. "That gives me just enough time to take a shower and wash away some of the dirt and misery."

Just then, my cell phone died, its screen flickering into darkness. One tear escaped, carrying with it a fragile bud of hope, daring to bloom in the barren landscape of my fear. Forty-five minutes to shed some of the grime and fear clinging to me, and maybe, finally, to find solid ground.

CHAPTER
Seventy-Eight

ARMED WITH FEAR

The motel room was bathed in a lurid red glow as if lit by the inner chambers of a heart. Patricia's arms enveloped me in a warm embrace. The scent of her jasmine perfume infused the air, a welcomed contrast to the ambient funk of the motel room.

Jagger kept his distance, hovering near the back of the room. His eyes, were somber and seemingly trying to unravel the mystery contained within my devastated demeanor.

"Victoria, are you safe?" Jagger inquired, a vein of anxious sincerity threading through his voice.

"Yes, I am now." I said before recounting my horrific experience with Santé, each word reliving a love gone wrong, an imagined paradise turned to a disastrous descent. After a ten-minute dissertation on the dread and degradation I had suffered, I veered away from the gravity of my predicament and shifted gears. For the second time, I congratulated Pat and Jagger on their recent wedding.

Patricia's eyes shimmered like polished sapphires as she thanked me, Jagger mirroring her sentiment. Then Pat's eyes locked on mine as she generously offered her home. "You could stay with us, you know."

"I can't, Pat," I said, skirting the fine line between intrusion and graciousness. "You two just got married. Plus, Santé knows you. He'd probably start looking for me there."

"How are you going to manage financially?" Patricia pressed, her concern palpable.

I exhaled an uncomfortable vulnerability, before saying, "I'm not sure yet. I told you about the sale of my condo. The part I didn't tell you is the joint account he convinced me to open was drained, too. I could only get a few thousand dollars out of it. He walked away with two hundred thirty-three thousand dollars. Honey, I'm broke."

Jagger's eyes fell, absorbed by the jet-black carpet that swallowed the room's meager light. Patricia's mouth opened in a wordless gasp, her face a canvas of dismay. "Vicky, you need to talk to someone. A domestic violence counselor, perhaps. Then maybe a shelter."

I shook my head as I contemplated Patricia's advice.

Exiting the room briefly, Jagger returned, his demeanor laden with newfound gravity. "Victoria, I may have judged you unfairly. I didn't know how dangerous Santé was." Jagger's words were a riddle that I could not quite understand, a fact that I passed off due to my exhaustion and emotional state.

With a cautious hand, Jagger presented a blue and silver Glock. I felt a visceral tightening as if my stomach had clenched into a fist. The gun, starkly real and cold, represented a terrorizing duality of safety and peril. "You should keep this nearby," Jagger warned.

Though I hesitated, Patricia's eyes locked onto mine, a silent urging. "As a precaution, Vicky," she whispered.

With a reluctant nod, I pocketed the gun, its weight an unsettling blend of reassurance and dread. "I hope to God I don't have to use this," I said.

As they gathered their belongings, Patricia's voice wove a comforting plan for future communications.

"I'll be in touch as soon as I get a new phone charger," I said. "I left in such a rush, I forgot to grab one."

Jagger excused himself again. I turned to Patricia, my voice tinged with regret. "I thought Santé was the one, Pat. He became my everything." I paused, my eyes drifting to Patricia, then flicking briefly to Jagger as he returned with a charger in his hand.

His expression turned muted as he looked away, visibly uncomfortable. Jagger placed the charger on the motel bed and I thanked him.

Overwhelmed by all that had unfolded I continued my thought, "Loving Santé was like staring into the sun—blinding and all-consuming. And now? I don't know who I am anymore."

Patricia enveloped me in an embrace that spoke louder than any words. "You haven't lost yourself, Victoria. You're standing at the doorway of a new beginning."

I hugged them both, and one final time, my heart fluttered with conflicting emotions. As they disappeared into their car and I bolted the motel door behind me, I was alone but connected, isolated, and yet fortified.

I removed the gun from my pocket and placed it cautiously in the nightstand drawer, its metallic presence ironic next to an unread Bible. Briefly, I pondered the idea of flipping through its pages. I desired to read ACTS 17:28 and more after, but then I dismissed the instinct with a wry chuckle.

Instead, I plugged in my phone, its screen igniting in a fleeting moment of assurance. As I lay on the motel bed, its sheets were a mix of alien comfort, and an unease that wrapped around me. I was trapped between the haunting past and a dark unknown—teetering on the edge, with only the sound of my heartbeat in the room's eerie silence.

CHAPTER
Seventy-Nine

OUR HOUSE, HIS MESS

As I steered my Blue Toyota onto Pond Drive, the memories hit like a wave, my old neighbor's silent witnesses to my hopes and dreams—life with Santé and our kids.

A U-Haul full of dreams for a fresh start. I'd twisted his arm to get him outta that Philly dump, all for our family. But coming back to the house he threw me out of? It made me feel bitter and damn alone.

I shook off the thoughts. No point going down memory lane—not when he'd been cheating on me left, right, and center. I'd made my own mistake once, and he hung that over my head whenever he could.

I forced myself back to the here and now. I was here to get my kids' clothes. I'd asked Santé to drop them off at my dad's, but he never showed, of course. That's why I had to come back to my former home.

After all I'd been through with Santé, I thought I was ready for anything. But seeing four cops by my garage door and two more in the driveway? That threw me for a loop.

Before I could ask questions, I figured they'd want proof I lived here. I did, just not on paper. Changed my address to my dad's, so I realized my ID wouldn't match. I opened the glove compartment, my fingers brushed the cold metal of my Beretta 92. I pushed the gun back and grabbed my vehicle registration. My Pond Drive address was right there, and so was my name, clear as day: Jackie Sabatino.

THE TENSION WAS SO DAMN THICK STANDING ON THE EDGE OF my garage with Officer Ortiz and his crew. They couldn't be more clear: open the garage door, or they would. Words like "obstruction of official investigation" and "obstruction of justice" buzzed around me like flies. I punched in the code, and as the garage door rose, the officers rushed in.

A shout broke through the air, "There's a cage!"

I was dumbfounded, I turned to Officer Ortiz. "Can you say that in Spanish? Maybe I'm just not getting it in English." I'm fluent in both, but this was my last-ditch attempt to make sense of the chaos.

Officer Ortiz's words were no different in Spanish. Someone—a woman—was supposedly being held captive here. By Santé, they thought. Officer Ortiz's question left me more in shock. "Do I know anything about the woman being held captive?"

I knew Santé was crazy and had a cruel, vindictive side; I also knew he was kinky as hell, but women in cages? I told Officer Ortiz I knew as much as they knew—Nothing.

"Do you mind if we enter the rest of the house?" one of the officers asked. When I questioned them about a warrant, they insisted probable cause was enough. They were just being polite by asking. What a joke, polite? 32 Pond Drive was still half my house, no matter what Santé claimed. But I didn't want to see it wrecked, so I let them in.

My nerves were a shattered mess. I ran to my Toyota and dialed Santé. He picked up, same old tone, annoyed.

"What is it, Jackie?"

I could hardly find the words. "What kind of trouble are you in? Should I be worried?"

"Stop talking in circles," he snapped. "Where are you?"

"I'm home, Santé. Our home."

"You don't have a home. You must mean your father's house?" Santé's Spanish accent flared.

I opened my passenger-side car door and sat down. "No, not my parents' home. I'm at OUR house—the one you seem to think is only yours."

"That house is mine," he insisted. "I bought it. The mortgage is in my name."

"Let's not forget, I was your wife when this house was bought. As you'll find out in divorce court, half of it is mine."

Santé cut in, "I don't have time for your bitter, soon-to-be ex-wife, *bullshit!*"

"Make time Santé, the cops tearing through OUR house," I shot back. The way the cops moved around had my nerves all twisted up, but I tried to hide it.

"Wait, what? Do they have a warrant?" Santé asked.

"No, but they have probable cause. Something about you having a bitch hook to a cage in the garage. Just get here and sort it out. I'm done."

He paused and arrogantly said, "I have something else to handle. I'll deal with the police later."

I couldn't believe my ears. "Santé really? More important than cops in our house? Where are you?"

"You don't get to question me—not anymore, Jackie." He hung up.

Shaking with feelings of fear, and rage, I called our cell carrier. I had to know where he was. "I need to speak to a supervisor. It's urgent," I insisted."

"A guy named Mr. Harley got on the line. "I need to find one of the phones on our family plan," I told him. "My son lost his phone, and I need to track it. The number ends in 2366."

"Mr. Harley paused, probably checking the system. 'Looks like that phone's near a motel. Want me to text you the location?'"

"Yes, text it. I want to use GPS to get there."

From the driveway, I looked at my house and wanted to burst into tears, but I had cried enough over Santé. I was a strong woman—I had to be—I had kids who depended on me.

A moment later, my phone buzzed with the text from Mr. Harley. Once I confirmed receipt, we ended the call.

A motel. Really, Santé? More bitches? As if our lives weren't already unraveling at the seams. "You're going to get busted this time," I mumbled, my thoughts a swirling storm I couldn't contain any longer.

I dumped my original plan to get the kids' clothes. Ignition on, I swung my Toyota out of the driveway, tires screeching as I headed straight for that motel with one thought. *Santé, whatever you're caught up in, it ends now.*

CHAPTER

Eighty

ROOM 37

M an, I just hung up on Jackie, Not givin' a fuck'bout what she gotta say right now, and fuck the police too. They just better not tear up my crib, I know that much.

It was time to get on with my mission. Findin' Victoria. The trackin' app on that zombie phone was working again. It stopped working for a minute, but then it led me right to that dump: the Beasley Motel.

This tech shit ain't perfect. It told me Victoria was in the motel, but ain't no red X markin' which room she was in. That was for me to figure out.

Cars filled the parking lot. It looked like two messy crews tryin' to hang. Both of 'em blastin' beats. I felt like those bass notes were hitting me in the chest.

I opened that spy app and hit the option to read Vicky's texts. And there it was, a message from Vicky to her infamous friend, Patricia, revealing she was in Room 37—Jackpot!

What are the odds? I was in front of Room 35.

I checked myself in the rearview. "A'ight," I said to the dude in the mirror with the amber eyes. "Let's get this."

My boots on the gravel sounded like applause, cheering me on, and I felt it, man. I was about to burst into Room 37, and that bitch on the other side of that door had better be ready 'cause Santé Sabatino wasn't playin' no more games.

CHAPTER
Eighty-One

FROM DREAM TO NIGHTMARE

Jolted awake by a series of thunderous bangs, my heart leaped into my throat. I grappled with my surroundings for a disorienting moment: the strange motel room awash in the red peeling wallpaper, the pungent mix of mildew and stale cigarettes, all momentarily alien and oppressive.

Santé's silhouette loomed darkly through the frosted, milky glass, an ominous outline forecasting his intended chaos. The door convulsed under the thunderous assault of Santé's fists, sending quivers through the air and jolting me to my core.

The distant murmur of music from car speakers easily penetrated the paper-thin walls. As did the occasional distorted laughter and muffled conversation from the other motel rooms. Both punctuated the reality of lives rolling on, oblivious to my impending storm.

Bang, bang, bang!

My heart ricocheted in my chest like a stray bullet. I bolted to the nightstand, snatching the drawer open with a metallic rasp that cut through the room's ambient noise.

My fingers clenched around the cold, stony grip of the Glock Jagger had pressed into my hands hours before. Its frigid touch steadied my trembling hands, infusing me with a grim sense of purpose.

"Victoria, it's time you stop playing games and come home." There was no longer any doubt that the man on the other side of the door to Room 37 was Santé Sabatino. He bellowed through the wooden barrier, "You know deep down we're not over. We'll get through this." His voice was a volatile blend of sweetness and menace.

A charged silence filled the space before he added, "Remember nine years ago? What did I tell you? It's never goodbye, it's see you later. Well, damn it, later is now, so. Open. This. Goddamn. Door!"

His boot slammed into the door, once, twice, thrice, each impact a mini-explosion that rattled the flimsy frame and echoed in my bones. My knuckles whitened around the gun, but I fought to maintain my composure.

I reached for one of the pillows atop the bed, placed it beside me, and slid the gun under the pillow, every movement a fusion of adrenaline and cold calculation.

I inhaled sharply, air scraping against my lungs like sandpaper, and then moved to unlock the door. When it swung open, our eyes locked in an electric jolt of mutual defiance and unresolved history.

Retreating, I returned to the bed, feeling the yielding caress of the carpet against my feet, a small, absurd comfort in a room otherwise fraught with tension. I sat down, pulling the crisp blue sheet over my lap as a makeshift barrier between us. Under the guise of casual movement, my hand shifted the pillow closer, bringing the hidden firearm within easy reach.

"This isn't working anymore, Santé," I announced, each syllable sharpened with the accumulated bitterness and regrets of a love gone horribly astray.

He slammed the door behind himself and replied defiantly, "Fuck dat. I say what works, and you do what da hell I tell you!."

He pointed at me, then crooked his finger and demanded, "Let's go."

This was it. It was time to take a stand. All the years of subservience and pleasing Santé had come down to this one stark moment. Respectfully setting a boundary, my voice quivered, "I can't go back there, Papi."

Santé's face grew flushed. He took a few steps closer to me, my hand inched toward the pillow beside me. "Oh, you will come back home, back to the garage, after you make my dinner.

Santé slowly and deliberately moved his head to the right. "I'm already planning a party with some friends joining…You're gonna make me some money."

In a flash of newfound boldness I didn't even know I possessed, I threw caution to the wind and challenged him directly. "Money? You've already stolen all of my money outta the bank."

Santé reared back as if I had struck him with some invisible force. He moved his body side to side like some strange stretching exercise. "Your money is my money damn it. You wanted us to be married, right? That's why you tore up my marriage, right?"

My voice broke, laced with raw sincerity and a desperate plea for understanding, "No, Papi, I made a mistake. I wanted you to love me."

Santé rubbed his hand across his face before slightly bending his knees and sticking his hands straight out. He yelled, "Shut. The. Fuck. Up… fuck man."

Santé straightened. "You did all of this for my love? Huh?" His head tilted at the question mark of his pause.

I raised my face, and through eyes green like the sea, I glazed upon Santé with sincere emotion and vulnerability and affirmed, "Yes, Papi, I did."

When Santé's head dipped in a slow nod of acknowledgment, I let my fingers slip away from the cold metal under the pillow. For a fleeting heartbeat, I entertained the notion of a more compassionate ending marked by shared understanding. Yet, in keeping with every prior experience with Santé, such moments of optimism were doomed to fizzle.

Santé contorted his face, annoyance chiseled into his scowl. "Here you go with that love shit. Okay, fuck it. You want it, here it is." He pointed at me. "I *LOVE* the. way. you. *suck. my. dick!*" Santé took two steps back. "How about that?" With palms open and shoulders lifted in a shrug, he postured as if he'd given me some valuable treasure rather than the contemptuous slur he'd spat out.

My heart felt as if it were imploding, a balloon punctured by an unforgiving truth, sending shards of emotional shrapnel through my veins. My eyes prickled with imminent tears, each one a small ocean of grief, each droplet wobbling at the edge against the levy of my eyelids.

Santé's rant gained momentum. "I love the way you deepthroat my dick. I would say I love your tight pussy, but I only like that. It is tight but way too small. Your intersex pussy could never please a dick as big as mine."

My body jerked involuntarily as though struck by an invisible blade, the emotional shockwave too seismic to conceal.

Santé's words functioned like a surgeon's scalpel, slicing cleanly through to my innermost core. "But wait, you want more love. Here you go. I love your tight asshole. I especially love the way you scream when I shove my big dick all the way up that asshole… balls deep."

My fingers stealthily snaked under the pillow, lightly skimming the cold contours of the hidden gun. The emotional agony, initially confined to the chambers of my heart, now surged through my system like an electric current. The naked truth stared back at me, impossible to dodge or deflect. To Santé, I was but an object for his sexual expeditions. A sex toy, not a breathing, feeling person.

It was as if a blindfold had been suddenly yanked off. The man I had elevated to the realms of the divine was exposed to be nothing more than an empty facade. The grandeur I believed he held was merely a reflection of my own desires… my own creation. Consumed by a flood of embarrassment, it dawned on me: my love, though deep and true, had been rooted in a self-inflicted misperception.

Worse still, my love for Santé became a tool he used ruthlessly to fuel his endless sexual appetites and curiosities. My value had been reduced to a mere function, making his dick feel good and nothing more.

I was torn between labeling him as wicked or simply childish. What was undeniably clear was my own naiveté. As the epiphany broke through, even amidst the lingering scent of love, a newfound emptiness began to gnaw at me, a compelling cue that it was time to disentangle and evolve. But was it too late?

The air around Santé crackled with impatience as if his tolerance had reached its tipping point. He gestured for me to join him urgently, as though my newfound clarity threatened to rupture his control. Perhaps he detected the first light of my self-awareness and wanted to quash it, restoring me to obedient docility.

What was indelibly clear was this: I stood at an unambiguous fork in the road. Santé took another step toward the bed, his words brimming with vulgarity, "When we get back, I'm a fuck you up the ass and prepare you for my friends to fuck that ass too."

An irreversible certainty took root in my core. There was no scenario in which I would go with him. Santé approached, his proximity more palpable, sidling up beside me at the rim of the bed. "Now get da fuck up." His fingers flicked my shoulder dismissively. Sweat began to bead on my increasingly nervous fingers.

Right at that moment, the pulsing beat of music from cars parked just outside the motel breached the walls and wormed its way beneath the door. A tune all too familiar to both of us began to play loudly.

Santé's body rocked to and fro in time with the music, his voice stern. "I said get. Da. Hell. Up." But the invading melody seemed to hijack his focus. "Yo, you know what that is? That's my shit!" He launched into a brash, off-key chorus of, "*Ooh na—NAH—ooh na-naaa—NEVA LET GO—ayyy!*" Perilously close, his leg grazing mine in an intimate dance just a hair's breadth from me and the edge of the bed.

After slogging through the most agonizing and unbearable thirty seconds of "Never Let You Go," I hollered over the discord of Santé's off-key singing and the booming soundtrack, "Papi, I love you, please don't make me hurt you."

The subtext of my words hit home, and Santé's singing ceased on the spot. He jerked his head back as if slapped. "Hurt me? You gonna hurt me, bitch?" The question came again, this time as a full-throated yell, "You gonna hurt me… bitch?"

Santé's right hand slid behind him, skimming his tailbone as he pulled his gun from its concealed spot in his waistband. In a split second of pure reflex, I somersaulted off the side of the bed furthest from him, my fingers finding their way to Jagger's hidden Glock under the pillow. With adrenaline-fueled precision, I flicked off the safety and fired a single shot.

Lifting myself from the floor and peering tentatively over the bed, I witnessed Santé's eyes swell with surprise. The jolt from my bullet caused his fingers to unfurl, releasing his weapon. Grasping his right pectoral muscle in evident pain, he plummeted to the floor. My eyes overflowed with a sudden rush of tears, and I let out a guttural scream, "Noooo! Why'd you make me do that?"

Dropping my weapon, I sprang from behind the bed and darted to where Santé lay. His panting was harsh, his eyes glazed with a surprise that rendered him speechless. "I'm sorry, Papi. Please forgive me!" I howled, my words filled with bitter remorse as I enveloped him in a hug laden with all the affection I'd ever held for him. "Hang on, Papi, I'm going to get you help."

CHAPTER
Eighty-Two

NEVER LET YOU GO…

I ripped open the motel door, and there she was: Jackie Sabatino, Santé's wife. I was coming face-to-face with Jackie for the first time. She was tiny but imposing, and her presence was magnetic. Her brown doe-like eyes locked onto my green peepers. Jackie let her words steep in a rich Puerto Rican cadence, with slightly broken English "So, is you the bitch, been after my husband all these years?"

Her searing question struck me. I didn't think she knew anything about me beyond that damning episode when she discovered those compromising emails between Santé and me years previously. The digital paper trail that had severed us briefly, paving the twisted path toward their tortured marriage.

Stationed by the door, my voice faltered. "I—I have to go."

Jackie's response was swift and cutting, laced with sardonic flair, "Oh, running off to find my husband? No need, Puta, his truck's already out front."

Jackie's eyes darted past me into the room, zeroing in on the floor. An icy prickle crawled up my spine. I knew exactly where her eyes had settled. "¡Ay, Dios mío. Santé!" she screamed, muscling her way into the room to hover over Santé, sprawled on the floor.

Jackie sank next to her husband, his moans filling the air like a mournful soundtrack. Her voice was no longer kind but rather contemptuous. "You fuckin fool, was all this shit worth it?"

From my stance at the doorway, I called out, with frantic concern, "I'ma go get him some help. I'll be right back."

Jackie's eyes flared as she yelled over her shoulder. "No. Don't you fuckin' move."

Driven by a rising panic, I insisted, "You don't understand. I have to get him some help now."

Jackie's eyes swept the dark carpet, locking onto the forbidden: Santé's gun. And it was close. When Jackie's eyes flickered back to mine, the silence was electric, a searing tension cut only by the faint, lingering smell of burnt gunpowder in the air. It clung to my nostrils, sharpening every word left unsaid. The race had ignited. Standing at a distance, I burst into motion, lunging for Santé's gun just as Jackie did.

As I saw her hand inch closer, I realized she would beat me to his gun. I shifted trajectory mid-leap, propelling myself toward the bed in a series of rapid strides. I dove over the mattress and hit the floor, landing on the opposite side.

Scrambling, I reclaimed my gun and peered cautiously across the bed's surface for Jackie.

My eyes met the barrel of Santé's gun, glaring at me like the single eye of some predatory beast. In the electric tension of that moment, I could feel how little my life must have meant to her. One false move or perceived provocation would end my life in the most gruesome way imaginable.

Though I clutched my own weapon, my finger was far from the trigger, and I hadn't squared Jackie into my sights. On the other hand, she had me in her crosshairs, and my choices had dwindled to one: surrender. I lifted my hands. My gun resting gently between my thumb and palm, an unspoken truce, an offering of my surrender.

Jackie's eyes flickered. She knew she was in control. "I'd be justified to pull this trigger right now, Mama." Her words sent ripples through my body, jolting me into a rapid montage of all the sacrifices and compromises. My disregarded morals and goals. All in service to a married man entwined in a chaotic circus. Santé's life would have spiraled out of control even without my complicit role.

Jackie then disarmed me in a way her gun never could. "But I'm not gonna shoot you, Puta. I don't need the bad karma. Believe it or not, that's why I never confronted you for all those years." My face tightened, every muscle wrestling with a puzzle I couldn't solve.

Jackie scrutinized my expression, catching my surprise. "You can't be serious? Did you think I didn't know about the two of you? That's the arrogance of you side bitches." I could only respond by shaking my head. Jackie said, "Let me make this clear to you. If I didn't have so much to lose and I didn't have self-control, you would have been the one sprawled out on a carpet a long time ago."

Casting a worried glance at Santé, I saw his movements becoming sluggish. "We need to get him medical assistance," I argued. Jackie spoke as if I hadn't uttered a word, continuing, "I chose not to shoot you so I won't have to deal with the karma that you've got coming."

Her words, "The karma that you've got coming," chilled me to my core, sending a ripple of goosebumps across my arms. As if she had read my face, Jackie said, "That's right girl, you're going to learn what it means to take another woman's husband."

Gambling with my life, I couldn't hold back any longer. "I didn't just 'take' him, Jackie. I loved him, genuinely loved him!"

Jackie's sneering reply was instant, "So in love with him that you shot him, huh?"

My desperation rose. "Jackie, please, let's not waste more time. He needs help now!"

Jackie paused and then looked almost wistful. "You probably did love him, we all love his good side, and by good side, I mean his dick!. That big pretty dick almost makes you forget about the rest, doesn't it?" I sucked my teeth, exasperated.

Jackie added, "Sometimes it's hard not to love that sexy jackass."

My pleas grew more urgent. "Well, don't let that sexy jackass die then. Call for help!"

Jackie's wavering hand seemed like a ticking time bomb. Her voice took on a sarcastic edge. "So that mess back at my house, I guess you finally saw the other side of Santé, huh?

Did big dick daddy make you do things you never thought you would? Or maybe he got violent? That would be a bit soon. He didn't get violent with me until we lived together for almost three years."

Her words were like knives, cutting into my soul, but trying to stop her was a lost cause. I just swallowed hard and hoped for the best.

Jackie said, "Your concern for him is sweet, but you should know he's gonna blame you for fucking up his family. It's all your fault. He never takes responsibility for his actions. That's just not his thing. Trust me, I know."

Jackie chuckled. "The funny part about this is that you didn't have to break up my marriage. I had enough. The deviant sex, the hot and cold running whores. Kay was probably the biggest threat to my marriage. But none of you side bitches ever knew just how callous and selfish he could be. Y'all spent so much time wanting to be me. Y'all never really knew him at all."

Jackie lowered herself closer to the floor, and at the same time, she lowered the volume of her voice. "You know what? I had already planned to leave him. That's what's funny. You could have had him, legitimately. So many broken lives, all because you just had to win, right?"

My wet eyes meandered to Santé. The weight of the tears pressing against my weakened eyelids caused droplets of shame, regret, and naïveté to fall from my eyes silently.

Jackie saw my weeping and responded in a monotone flatness, "I'm not moved by the fact that you loved my husband. I am moved by your arrogant belief that winning him would make him better for you than he was for me. I loved him more than any of you. I gave him a family."

Jackie slowly rose to her feet, keeping me in her aim. "And now, because we share the same pain, I will tell you the secret that he never could. Santé was never going to love you like you loved him. Because Santé Sabatino only loves himself. And now, because of your love for him, you're going to go to jail."

Staring down the barrel of Santé's gun, Jackie's words echoed in my head several times as I watched her use her free hand to reach into her pocket and call 911. The sound of Jackie's telephone call with the police seemed to exchange places with the sounds in the background. Jackie's voice faded while the distant song in the background seemingly grew louder. "Never Let You Go," which had been repeating on a loop from Jackie's running car, played as my tears fell. *"Ooh na-na... ooh na-na—NEVA LET GO."*

EPILOGUE
Part One

On January 13, 2021, the courtroom was wound tight, every sound striking hard in the silence. The air carried the essence of polished wood and worn leather, as if centuries of judgment hung in each breath. Every subtle footstep, whisper, paper shifting—sounded louder than it should, pressing on my nerves as the verdict drew near.

I clung to the bench beneath me, willing its firmness to steady the knot of dread and faint hope twisting inside me. As the clock struck 9:00 A.M., the final moments crept toward me, deliberate and unstoppable.

The years since my arrest replayed in sharp fragments: being escorted out of the dingy motel by police, the wail of the ambulance carrying Santé, and the cold grip of handcuffs snapping around my wrists. The harsh flash of the mug shot camera, the suffocating quiet of a jail cell—each detail felt etched into my mind.

Patricia's financial lifeline was both a gift and a debt, tangling me in a web of obligation. Living on bail under her roof, I could never quite read Jagger. He was there, but distantly, his silence hinting at the guilt he might have felt for the trouble his gun had brought me.

Our conversations were brief and uncomfortable, as though we spoke different languages. I watched him and Patricia together—she let him get away with a lot—and I secretly wondered if their relationship ran on hidden terms. But with my life coming apart at the seams, it felt almost absurd to analyze theirs.

Santé, once a magnetic presence—a salsa step I couldn't resist—had faded into a barely recognizable tune. Hearing his testimony a few days earlier had left me reeling.

I never imagined someone could rewrite my actions and intentions so completely, turning me into the villain. But Santé did exactly that within minutes of taking the stand.

I watched in disgust as he posed up there, trying to look meek and mild. The prosecutor asked, "Did Miss Robbins take advantage of the fact that you are younger than she?"

Santé sighed heavily, then replied, "Yes. She came on to me when we met and never let up, even after I told her I had a girl. She stalked me for over a decade."

There was a slight pause before the prosecutor's next question, "How did she seduce you?"

Santé said, "She introduced me to sexual things that confused me, freaky things my girlfriend didn't do."

I remember watching Santé recreate my life and our relationship into some unrecognizable, upside-down parody.

"Could you share some of those sexual things, please?" Asked the prosecutor.

Santé spoke up quickly, "She sucked this dick like crasy—I mean, ahh, let's call it… oral sex."

The prosecutor said "I see."

Without further questioning Santé added "She promised me anal sex, too, and told me she liked being handcuffed."

I heard whispers from the court's gallery as my face warmed.

Standing at the lectern, the prosecutor asked, "Did any of those things—sexual offers happen?"

"Yes. Lots of dick suc—uh, … oral action happended over the years. She would call me out of my relationship even after I got married and offered me… oral sex. She asked me to leave my marriage hundreds of times with promises of BDSM sex too."

The prosecutor said, "For the purpose of some simplicity, let's call it kinky sex. Did you engage in kinky sex with Miss Robbins?"

Santé replied, "Unfortunately, yes, especially in 2018."

The courtroom was eerily quiet when the prosecutor asked, "What happened in 2018?"

Santé shifted in his seat and then said, "Victoria stalked my wife and found that she had become weak in our marriage and was cheating on me. Victoria took pictures of my wife cheating and sent them to me anonymously. When I told her, she encouraged me to break up with my wife."

Santé paused for what could only be described as a dramatic effect. My stomach churned as he sprinkled elements of truth into his freaky fairytale, "So I fell for the trap; I left my wife and moved Victoria into my house. As soon as she got in the door, she wanted to have sex in each room of my house. I was a weak man and fell under her spell, so I did. When we got back to my room, she pulled out a pair of silver handcuffs, and that's when things really got freaky."

The prosecutor asked, "Freaky, how?"

Santé leaned close to the microphone in front of him, "That's when she told me to handcuff her to my bed and do her... from *behind*."

An audible gasp rang out in the courtroom. I'll never forget the look of horror and disgust from several of the female jurors. While a few of the male jurors leered at me with curious eyes.

The prosecutor asked, "Did you do what she wanted?"

Santé replied, "Yes. I felt I had to, in a way. I had gone so far, I couldn't turn back."

The prosecutor's voice lowered. "Were you ashamed at what she groomed you to do?"

I looked at my lawyer just as she finally objected, only to be overruled.

The prosecutor repeated the offensive question, "Were you ashamed at what she groomed you to do?"

Santé glanced at me and said, "Yes. Especially later when she wanted me to put her in my old dog's cage. Who does that? I should have known she was crazy."

Another objection from my attorney followed, and another lousy ruling against me, allowing Santé's lies to keep rolling along.

The prosecutor asked, "According to your police interview, she asked you to lock her in your former dog's cage, to play a kinky sexual dominance game?

Santé replied "Yeah she did… freaky."

The prosecutor the asked, "But why did you leave her there all day while you were at work?"

Santé looked down and replied, "Because while she was locked to the cage, she told me her secrets."

"What secrets?" The prosecutor asked.

Santé's gaze lifted; he said, "Victoria told me she was the one who sent the pictures of my wife cheating anonymously, all while telling me to leave her."

The courtroom's observers grumbled; the judge gaveled, "Quiet in the courtroom. Continue Mr. Sabatino."

Santé didn't hesitate. "But that wasn't the biggest bomb."

The prosecutor asked, "And what was the biggest bomb?"

Santé looked directly at me, pointed, and said, "Victoria told me she was born a man."

Gasps, louder than before, spread like wildfire. Male jurors who had once looked at me with curiosity now wore expressions of visible disgust. The courtroom buzzed with whispers and shock. My attorney objected, trying to correct the technical record on the difference between transsexual and intersex, but the objection was overruled.

The judge's gavel struck hard. 'Quiet in the courtroom!' But I knew, deep down, that no medical explanation would have made a difference. That moment was exactly why I had hidden in the shadows my entire life. It was also why I held on to the breadcrumbs of attention Santé once offered.

In and outside the courtroom, transphobia and ignorance of intersex realities mixed with society's shallow grasp of gender remained an impenetrable curse.

Society held the simplistic biology knowledge of a third-grade classroom, in which sex and gender were always one and the same, determined solely by what lay visibly between your legs. But I lived in the real, more complicated world of science and reality, alone, often lonely and vulnerable to attack.

Santé capped his testimony with more lies, telling the jury that he left me locked to the cage because he needed time to calm down. He returned intent on unhandcuffing me and asking me to leave his home, but I had run away with money from his dresser.

Santé's lies reached their devastating conclusion when he said he and I spoke on the phone, and I told him where I was so we could talk things out face to face.

Santé went on to say that when he arrived at the motel, he told me he could never be in a relationship with someone who used to be a man and was returning to his wife. I got mad and shot him.

Although I wanted to tell my story and refute his ridiculous claims, my lawyer told me I had the right against self-incrimination. She also said that because I had time to go to the police and didn't, proving self-defense would take a lot of work.

Lastly, despite the fact that I was a woman, she warned that some jurors might weaponize any hint of masculinity in my voice or demeanor on the stand. All I could do was hope that that day's cross-examination of Santé would keep me free.

EPILOGUE
Part Two

S uddenly, the moment of truth had arrived and brought me back to my senses. My heart beat so hard I thought it was trying to leave the courtroom without me.

The silence tightened as Judge Braxton entered, her presence seeming to draw every eye and breath to her. "All rise," the bailiff called in a voice that seemed steeped in generations of law and order. The door sighed open, and she entered a formidable and impartial figure. Her robe absorbed the collective focus as she ascended the bench. She sat, and we followed.

The courtroom held its breath, tension thick enough to cut with a knife. My hands grew clammy, nerves tingling with anticipation, a metallic tang lingering on my tongue.

Judge Braxton's voice cut through the silence. "Please bring the jury in?"

As the jury filed in, my heart hammered against my ribs. I stole a glance around the courtroom and spotted familiar faces amidst the sea of strangers. Patricia's worried expression etched lines of concern on her face as she clutched Jagger's hand tightly. Beth stood stoically, her eyes red from unshed tears. And there, in the back, a flicker of disbelief crossed my mind as I thought I saw Robyn, my former employer.

A moment of inexplicable detachment washed over me before Judge Braxton's voice brought me back to reality. "After careful consideration of the evidence and arguments made, has the jury reached a verdict?"

The foreperson stood, her voice steady. "Yes, Your Honor, we have."

"Okay." Judge Braxton nodded, her gaze unwavering. "On the count of third-degree aggravated assault with a deadly weapon, what is the jury's verdict?"

"Not guilty," the foreperson's voice echoed through the room, offering a fleeting moment of relief.

"And on the count of fourth-degree aggravated assault with a deadly weapon, has the jury reached a verdict?"

"We have, Your Honor," the foreperson confirmed. "On the charge of fourth-degree aggravated assault with a deadly weapon, the jury finds the defendant guilty."

The room erupted in gasps, and Santé's bitter words pierced through, "Gotcha, bitch!"

Judge Braxton banged her gavel. "Quiet! Disruptions will not be tolerated."

The floor seemed to drop from beneath me. I gripped the desk for stability. Despite the good news on the first charge, the single word 'guilty' for the other charge echoed in my ears. It was the culmination of the landslide of my life's ruin.

With restored calm, Judge Braxton addressed what would come next, "Sentencing will be determined at nine AM on February 18, 2021. As for custody…"

Jill's voice quivered with desperate eloquence, "Your Honor, Miss Robbins has complied with all court obligations…"

The prosecutor's words fell like final nails in my coffin, "Your Honor, in light of the guilty verdict, the defendant should be remanded."

Judge Braxton's voice was unemotional yet decisive. "The defendant will be remanded into custody pending sentencing."

Armed guards took their places behind me, signaling my transfer into the machinery of the prison system. Disillusionment and humiliation washed over me.

A nearly invisible door that had blended into the wood paneling with quiet deception opened. As my eyes tingled, I was led toward the imposing hole in the wall.

Behind me, I heard distant echoes—Santé's mocking taunts, the sound of Beth's and Patricia's tears, and a murmur of Bible verses from a voice I couldn't quite place.

But there was no turning back. I had stepped through what felt like the Doors of Doom—a human recycling mechanism, designed to discard defendants from society with the sterile efficiency of an assembly line. The doorway's plainness hid the devastation it marked, a final threshold indifferent to the lives it swallowed on the other side.

EPILOGUE
Part Three

S eeing Patricia's face through the barrier of visitation glass stirred something between comfort and sorrow. She searched her mind for words that could lift my spirits, and I found myself grappling for any language at all. After just fifteen days inside the prison walls, I was psychologically drained.

"Don't worry about the ten thousand dollars," Patricia said. She and Jagger had worked out a way to settle the debt without me lifting a finger. A tiny seed of relief took root in the wasteland of my heart. Speaking felt like lifting a hundred-pound weight, but I managed a, "..thank you."

Sensing my internal battle, Patricia shifted gears. "You know, it turns out Jackie and I have a mutual friend." My eyes, which had hung low, rose to meet hers as she continued, "Jackie's been talking. A lot."

A large part of me didn't care about Santé or Jackie anymore. But a quieter part was curious—not because I longed for Santé, but because I needed to know if I was the only one left tangled in the wreckage of their lives.

My face had forgotten how to form a smile. Yet, as Patricia spilled the tea on everything that had happened—both while I was out on bail and during my time behind bars. A strange sensation tingled in my cheeks. I hadn't smiled in so long, it actually hurt.

Patricia told me how Jackie wasted no time reuniting with Santé, reassured that I was sidelined by a no-contact order, a condition of my bail. For a moment, it looked like they'd have their happily-ever-after, with me as the villain, legally banned from coming near them. From Jackie's perspective, they could reign over their world without any more hiccups.

But real life is messier than any fairy tale. It turns out Santé couldn't play the devoted king for long, not even for his Queen Jackie. He was caught fucking not one, but two women at the same time. Apparently, he was ass-banging a white woman and the African-American woman who was licking his ass happened to be a prostitute. Their so-called 'matrimonial bliss' suddenly didn't look so blissful anymore. This time, Jackie officially filed for divorce.

As I maneuvered through my own legal entanglements, Patricia's gossip served as a strange reminder: life outside continued its chaotic dance, as unpredictable and complex as ever. People could point fingers, but in the end, we all have our stories—threads of chaos and order, weaving together in the flawed symphony of being human.

EPILOGUE
Part Four

The tension in the courtroom was almost unbearable, thick as fog, and twice as suffocating. Sitting in my drab prison uniform, the coarse fabric scratched against my skin. My once luxurious, long, curly hair was now confined to a series of symmetrical cornrows.

We all rose as Judge Lynda Braxton took her seat, the crowd's murmur hushing almost instantly. Everyone returned to their seated position.

"Court is in order. We are reconvened in the matter of the State of New Jersey versus Victoria Robbins, case number NJ-CC-2019-03087-1. Before I proceed with the sentencing, I will allow statements to be made to the court. Does the prosecution wish to make a statement?", the judge inquired.

Prosecutor Josh Starwood stood, his eyes locked forward. "Yes, Your Honor. The defendant's actions have had a devastating impact on the victim and the community at large. We urge the court to impose the maximum sentence allowed under the law for the charge of fourth-degree assault with a deadly weapon."

The prosecutor's words hit like a freight train, leaving no room for interpretation. He wanted me to be crushed under the weight of the law, and he ensured everyone knew it.

Judge Braxton nodded. "Thank you. Does the victim or the victim's family wish to make a statement at this time?"

Santé approached the microphone. "Hey, Your Honor, look, my life's been turned upside-down, you know? Victoria, she came into my world, charmed me, jumped my bones, and then, boom! She shoots me. You see this arm? I can't even dribble a basketball no more, and I used to be good, real good."

I could feel my nails digging into my palms. Santé's victim act was convincing but annoying as hell. I knew the truth of who he was and what he had done. I also knew his small shoulder wound would never stop his basketball obsession. Just when I thought he couldn't be more insincere, he talked about his family.

"And it ain't just about me," Santé continued. "My family's been through hell 'cause of her. My marriage? Ruined. So, I hope nobody here is talking about mercy. Come on, she made her bed. She knew what she was doing. Your Honor, she deserves the maximum, nothing less. Thank you, your Honor."

As Santé sat down, a part of me crumbled. I questioned myself. *Had I really ruined his life? Or was this just another one of his manipulative games?*

Jackie was next. "Look, I get it, aight? Victoria and my ex-husband, Santé, teamed up to ruin what I once called my marriage. But the last couple of years have opened my eyes. Ain't no saints in this mess, Your Honor. I made my mistakes, and my ex, the 'victim,' is as much a villain as he is anybody's victim."

Her words, oddly comforting, seemed to echo my own thoughts. I was not alone in seeing Santé for what he was. I listened carefully.

"I get what 'mitigating circumstances' means now," Jackie continued. "Victoria, she wouldn't have even thought of pulling that trigger if Santé hadn't been messing with her head all those years, all while betraying me. I can't believe I'm saying this, but I am. I'm asking you, Your Honor, to show her some mercy. Hold her accountable, *sí*, but don't destroy her life over this. Gracias, Your Honor."

Jackie's statement ended, and I felt a pang of something I hadn't felt in a long time—hope.

Jill nudged me gently. "Miss Victoria Robbins wishes to speak for herself."

Gathering every last shred of my courage, I stood and spoke loudly without the benefit of a microphone.

"I never understood how quickly one's life could devolve into madness." I took a breath then continued, "If I could take back the night of January 7, 2019, I would. Or better yet, if I hadn't involved myself with Santé and certainly not intruded in his marriage, that would have been even better.

"I'm sorry that I shot Santé, but I sincerely believed my life was in jeopardy. I know my claim of self-defense was rejected by this court, but I hope the court will consider why I behaved the way I did and Santé's role in his shooting.

"I apologize to Jackie for disrespecting her and her marriage. That was my first mistake, which ultimately led to the chaos of that horrible night. I am remorseful and ask the court to consider that in your sentencing."

Judge Braxton said, "Thank you. Miss Robbins. I've listened to all of the relevant parties, and I'm ready to move forward." I held my breath briefly as Judge Braxton began her sentencing.

"Okay, will the defendant remain standing," Judge Braxton ordered, her eyes meeting mine for just a second—cold and calculating.

My defense attorney, Jill Stinger, stood up beside me. My legs felt like they were made of straw, barely holding me up.

Judge Braxton glanced in my general direction and spoke at full volume. "You have been found guilty of fourth-degree aggravated assault with a deadly weapon by a jury of your peers. However, this sentence reflects the court's finding that your actions, however reckless, showed neither premeditation nor malice."

Judge Braxton took a sip of water, and the silence loomed. She returned to her speech, frequently looking down at her notes, suggesting she was guided by prepared notes.

"This sentence does reflect that you did not call the police once you left Mr. Sabatino's residence. Additionally, you voluntarily opened the door to Mr. Sabatino before you shot him. Although I do not find Mr. Sabatino's version of events entirely credible, and I find his effort to slut shame and misgender you repugnant, you are not without blame."

Judge Braxton then pushed her yellow legal pad aside, leaned forward, and locked eyes with me as she continued.

"Based on the circumstances of this case and considering the defendant's lack of prior convictions, the court has taken into account specific mitigating factors such as the defendant's fear and claims of previous false imprisonment. In light of these factors, the court sentences the defendant to sixty months in the state penitentiary for the fourth-degree assault with a deadly weapon charge.

"The defendant shall, under certain conditions, be eligible for parole after serving thirty-five of the sixty months. It is the hope of this court that this sentence serves as a deterrent and allows the defendant the opportunity for rehabilitation."

"Judge Braxton continued, "Now that I have rendered the sentence, I will say a few important things. This is an unfortunate case, even beyond Mr. Sabatino's intentional use of biased stereotypes and scapegoating." By your own admission, Miss Robbins, you set the stage for this tragedy.

For some reason, Miss Robbins, you seemed not to know what a beautiful, talented woman you were and how many men would be lucky to have your love. Maybe it was your gender complexity that made you believe Santé Sabatino was your only path to love."

"Judge Braxton folded her hands and continued, "I'm not precisely sure why, but it seems to me, somewhere along the way, you entered into war for Santé Sabatino's love. You won symbolic battles along the way to your ultimate victory. But I hope you now understand that the cost of your victory was too high."

My heart tightened, and my ears rang as the truth of her words struck my soul.

Judge Braxton continued, "You helped unravel a marriage, compromising the very stability children depend on. And, more crucially, you brought yourself and your victim to the edge of ruin. Miss Robbins—whether or not you meant for things to unfold as they did—it's fitting: you have earned the name *Pyrrhic Victoria*."

Judge Braxton took a cleansing breath before continuing. As my mind swirled, trying to process the impact of the judge's decision, I watched as she pointed at me briefly, then in a tone less judgemental, she added, "It is also my hope that you, Miss Robbins, will learn which battles to take up in life and which wars are simply not worth winning. To help you with that, I suggest you study Pyrrhus of Epirus, specifically the Pyrrhic War."

As Judge Braxton rocked back in her seat, I remembered the story of the Pyrrhic War from high school. And to my surprise, I saw the personal parallel.

Judge Braxton looked around the courtroom and said, "A brief history lesson for all present, but especially for you, Miss Robbins."

She narrowed her focus on my face and said, "The Pyrrhic War was a conflict between Rome and Epirus around 275 BCE, marked by Pyrrhus's costly victories. The timeless lesson of the Pyrrhic War cautions us against battles where the military or personal toll outweighs the gains of a so-called victory.

Life's victories should not come at the expense of your emotional well-being or relationships or have costly long-term consequences. We should measure success not just by immediate achievements but by the enduring harmony and fulfillment a victory brings to our lives."

Judge Braxton's parting words focused my attention as sharp as a razor's edge.

"Miss Robbins…"

I nodded, offering a sign of my undivided attention. Judge Braxton said, "May you one day be wise enough that you never be accurately referred to as 'Pyrrhic Victoria' again."

A millisecond later, the gavel fell, its sound echoing through the courtroom, sealing my fate.

Judge Braxton's automated cadence returned. "The defendant shall hereby be remanded to the custody of the state's correctional department to begin serving her sentence immediately. This court is hereby adjourned."

Officers surrounded me. I could hear both mournful sounds and Santé's loud taunts, but only as distant background noise, seemingly squeezed as if through a funnel.

My lawyer, Jill, touched my hand and told me she would meet with me soon, and that she would be working on an appeal. My body was numb as I was led away, but my mind was racing.

Of the twenty million thoughts I had buzzing through my mind simultaneously, one emerged above all the others. As I was escorted out of the courtroom, the judge's words echoed in my mind. I knew with the certainty of sunset, the judge was right…I was *Pyrrhic Victoria*—a victor who had lost everything.

EPILOGUE
Part Five

In God, I live and move and have my being. That Bible verse had been my anchor for years, but it became my rock after reading Robyn's letter the day before. The former Chairlady of Nybor Productions had sent me a letter that was short and sweet; it read:

Dear Victoria,

I would be much more devastated by your unfortunate descent if I wasn't confident that you shall rise higher than your current vision can imagine. Apparently, you did not receive my letter, the ten thousand dollars, or the gift box upon your departure from the company. No worries, all that and more will be here for you when you return to society. You are not alone, and your fight is not over. I'm unsure of your religious beliefs, but if you agree, please read ACTS 17:28. I will be in touch sooner than later.

Love,
Robyn

The irony was profound. The truth was, I wasn't very religious, but my spiritual path led me to that Bible verse years ago. So, to have the woman I admired the most recommend that same Bible passage, I viewed it as a sign.

For the next six days, I kept to myself, limiting interactions with other inmates and staff, and prayed: In God, I live and move and have my being.

On the seventh day, I was chanting the verse for the third time when I was called to Warden Greystone's office.

He asked me who I knew in high places. Before I could form an answer, he said he had received a call from the governor's office. A full pardon was being issued for me. The paperwork would be finalized by the day's end.

I held my breath, waiting for a punchline that never came.

The words weren't sarcasm. They were grace and a second chance. I don't recall what I said to the Warden in response or the few staff I spoke to sparingly on my way back to my prison cell.

But I will never forget the embrace of Patricia, Beth, and Robyn as I emerged from the prison gates. Gratitude and tears overflowed as I hugged Patricia first, then Beth and Robyn last. Almost telepathically, Robyn and I recited ACTS 17:28 together; "In God, I live and move and have my being."

After the third recitation, Robyn spoke. "There are some powerful people who want to meet you, people with whom I worked to highlight Santé's false imprisonment and torture of you prior to your offense. They helped me secure your freedom. But first, we'll find a place for you to live and rediscover your purpose."

Patricia said, "You can stay with Jagger and me as long as you need."

Overwhelmed, I thanked them, then said, "I don't know how I'll ever repay you all."

Patricia chuckled. "Well, I hear you have ten thousand dollars."

I laughed. "So I've heard. The repayment plan is in effect."

Patricia responded, "Just kidding, girl. I know you've got me."

Standing feet from the prison gates, a cool breeze gently blew. Robyn moved her hair from her face, pulled a blue box from her purse, and handed it to me. "It's time to open this."

I struggled to process the blessings unfolding around me. I resisted the temptation to ask if I could wait to open the box. Instead, I inhaled sharply and lifted the box lid.

My eyes widened at the sight of a shimmering diamond necklace. Several large heart-shaped, ice-blue diamonds gleamed with a fierce brilliance that set the air ablaze with light.

I gasped with delight and gratitude. "Oh, Robyn, for me?"

Robyn replied, "Yes. I had this necklace custom-made to remind you—it's okay to love again someday, but remember, your heart belongs to you first and always."

The sensations of pins and needles enveloped my body as the power of her words permeated my soul. Robyn then placed the precious gems around my neck as I smiled with glee.

Beth remarked, "I wish I had bought you a gift, It couldn't be anything like Robyn's gift, though."

I assured her, "No regrets, Beth. Your friendship is my gift."

Robyn nodded. "That's right. No regrets. You move forward from here." I turned my head slightly in an attempt to look back at the prison, but Robyn stopped me. "No, don't look back. Only forward."

I said, "I understand. I just wanted to say goodbye."

With a knowing smile, Robyn placed her hand on my shoulder. "I ask only three things of you."

Without knowing what she was requesting, I said, "Anything."

Robyn locked eyes with mine and said, "Promise me you'll never take on a battle that doesn't honor you and isn't worth winning."

In hushed reverence, I said, "I promise."

Robyn brushed my cheek as she asked, "Promise me you will always protect your heart."

My fingertips lightly grazed my new sparkling diamond necklace as I declared, "I promise."

Robyn's warm smile affirmed her belief in me. Then she made her final request, "Lastly, walk forward to my Rolls Royce and let me say goodbye for you."

I clutched Robyn's hand and replied, "I can do that."

Robyn released my hand as Patricia, Beth and I locked arms. Together, we took steps toward Robyn's black Rolls Royce.

Above us, the low-hanging orange-yellow sun cast a warm, heavenly glow on our faces, while the diamonds around my neck sparkled, mirroring an identical hue.

The sparse stratus clouds resembling bubbles of fire and hope, floated lazily in the sky. Behind me, I heard Robyn's voice say, "Goodbye...goodbye—*Pyrrhic Victoria*."

ACKNOWLEDGMENTS

"No weapon formed against me shall prosper," and "In God I live and move and have my being." These two Bible verses carried me through, allowing me to continue breathing, rebuild my life, and write this book while persevering through one of the most intentionally destructive attacks on my life.

To Conor Meenan, Esq., you were the first legal professional I met shortly after my trauma, and yours was the first hand I shook upon achieving legal and moral victory. Thank you for listening to me, and for your patience and skill in getting to the truth—a quality so often lacking in today's world of expediency and tactics. In the story of my life, you will always be my hero.

Daddy, happy 90th birthday. May you feel the depth of my love and appreciation for the incalculable contributions you have made to my life. I acknowledge and declare: I am forever a daddy's girl. I love you.

Mommy, I love you. I cherish the love and lessons you've given me, which have shaped who I am today. I see you more in my mirror each day, and I am grateful. Thank you for everything.

I wish to thank and acknowledge my editor, Maryssa Gordon of Pocket Editing. As a writer with dyslexia, a good editor is not just a luxury but a necessity, and Maryssa is wonderful.

Special gratitude to the team at CapriAGE, who translated my vision for the cover into a striking and memorable design. Your work has been an incredible blessing, and I look forward to collaborating on more creative projects in the future.

To my brother, Rome, you were my bridge over troubled waters and the voice of reason in a cacophony of chaos. You were my angel as I faced my Judas. I am supremely humbled and grateful for you. Thank you.

Not all the people who shaped my journey did so in obvious or consistent ways. To S.S., the man who broke me out of my shell and ultimately changed my life: for the moments you offered love—and/or the moments I experienced as love—I thank you. For the selfishness, the psychological yo-yo, and the damage caused by your "player" ways, I forgive you.

To the small but mighty list of supporters and loved ones who stood by me, offered love, and attested to my character when it mattered most—Aunt Sis, Big Brother Gino, Juliet, Coty, Janita, Special K (Karen), Monique, and my perpetual birthday gift, Dallas—I extend my deepest appreciation, gratitude, acknowledgment, and love.

—Jade Green

ABOUT THE AUTHOR

JADE GREEN SPENT TWENTY YEARS writing, producing and directing independent films and television with emphasis on erotica. In Pyrrhic Victoria, her debut novel she constructs a powerful erotic, and psychological journey of unique modern characters. Jade brings provocative & creative stories to life in vivid and compelling ways.

Follow Jade:

BONUS MATERIAL
FROM
Sticky Novels

Sneak Peek At The Second Novel Of,
The: Love, Lust and Liberation series
Santé's Secrets (Censored edition)

The following is chapter one of the censored edition
of Santé's Secrets

If you prefer the Sneak Peek of the uncensored edition of Santé's Secrets it can be found at the end of the uncensored edition of Pyrrhic Victoria available in bookstores or available directly through Sticky-Novels.Com

SANTÉ'S SECRETS (UNCENSORED EDITION)

Sneak Peek

CHAPTER

One

SANTÉ'S KINGDOM

"There's nothing ever so wrong with me that a good blow job can't fix. That's what I wanted to type, staring at the endless questions on that damn medical form. Why had scheduling a simple doctor's appointment started to feel like solving a riddle?

I leaned back in my black leather chair, the cool, smooth surface pressing against my skin, and glanced around my kingdom. My dining room's dove-gray walls and polished sandalwood floors still gleamed as though I'd just bought the place yesterday, not three years ago.

The soft light in my kitchen hit just right, giving everything a clean, organized look that anyone would envy. Who says a divorced guy can't keep a tidy home?

1

Sure, the basketball in the corner gave off a bachelor vibe, but the rest? Spotless stainless steel appliances, a gleaming gray-and-white backsplash. Nobody would guess that, in over a year, no woman had stayed in my house longer than it took for me to empty my balls. Well, maybe forty-eight hours, if she let me fuck her up her ass for most of her stay.

The point is, my home wasn't just a place—it was a symbol. A shrine to my independence, a testament to the fact that I didn't need anyone to make my life work.

I'm not like most modern guys, the type of guy afraid to be a man. I make no apologies for having a dick and according to my bitches, a pretty big one. My name is Santé Sabatino, Latino lover, dominator, and master to many.

But on the Saturday afternoon of May 1, 2021, I was just a dude trying to set a fucking doctor's appointment using my laptop because the phone app was for shit.

The dull ache in my shoulder made every click of the keyboard echo in my head like a basketball smackin' the court, even though the ball just lay there silent in the corner.

After the fifth error message, I gave up. Fuck technology; I'd call later. Leaning back, I massaged my shoulder, the pain spreading like wildfire. Maybe it was from the pickup game last night. Or had I overdone it in the pool?

Then, a darker memory hit me. A flash of green eyes, a gunshot—Victoria. My hand drifted to the scar she'd left, a mark etched into my skin and my soul.

I shook off the memory and wandered toward the sliding glass doors leading to my backyard. Watching the sprinklers hiss and spray across the lawn, the scene moved in slow motion. Fluid. Forgiving. Maybe it's because I'm a Pisces, but water has always called to me. Something primal, a real turn-on.

Water wasn't just water to me. It was a force that erased mistakes, washed away flaws, and left nothing but purity in its wake. Every time water touched my skin, it felt like I was getting a fresh start, cleansing me from the deeds of my darker moments. A baptism for sins I'd refused to name, and for lust I couldn't tame.

The rhythm of water hitting the earth reminded me that no matter how dirty things got, there was always a way to get clean. To be restored. Lost in the display of dancing droplets, time seemed to stretch and bend.

The hiss of the sprinklers slowed time, but then, reality snapped back. The mail. *Shit!* Collecting mail was one of those things my ex-wife Jackie used to do. Now, I ran my house myself, which meant stuff like going to the mailbox was my job.

Grumbling, I made my way to the laundry room. Living alone meant doing everything myself, even the little things Jackie used to handle. I enjoyed the sound of my dick slapping against my thighs as I moved—ultimate freedom. My house was my domain. No rules. No interruptions. Just me.

For a brief second, I toyed with the idea of strolling to the curb free-balling; then, I had second thoughts.

I thought my suburban neighbors might not appreciate the Big Dick Papi experience. This was Turnersville, New Jersey, after all, not Philly, my urban birthplace, where a bold display might be appreciated—or, if not, at least respected.

So, I grabbed a pair of blue ball shorts instead. I chuckled, my dick print was still visible, even though I wasn't even semi-hard; what can I say? I'm Santé Sabatino—dick-blest.

I thought; *If anyone had a problem with me—or that reality... fuck 'em, literally—fuck 'em.*

Taking a deep breath, I swung open the front door and stepped outside, the sun hitting my skin like a welcome dare. Whatever waited out there, I was ready to conquer.

TWO STEPS OUTSIDE OF 32 POND DRIVE, THE DOVE-GRAY SIDing of my house caught the last light of the peach-toned sun. No matter how many times I looked at it, pride swelled in my chest. This was mine—earned, owned, and thriving.

My worn tan Suburban sat in the driveway like a battle-scarred champion. That truck had seen more pussy in the back seats than the average gynecologist's office. It was also the ride that hauled groceries for my kids when we had nothing else, and it was still kicking.

Not bad for a Puerto Rican kid from North Philly who folks thought was dumb and wouldn't make it past 25 outside of a prison cell. Now, I was living the dream—my dream. The house, the truck, the single life. Divorce was the best thing that ever happened to me.

Let's face it, I was a catch. Thirty-two, handsome as hell, good job, nice house, and a good paying job.

I had it better than most men on my block. I had my kids every other weekend and a bigger pussy parade than guys in their twenties could dream of.

I didn't even bother to smash most of the smuts I hooked up with at my house. I usually just pulled out my dick on some side street or an alley, slid on a condom, and fucked the freak of the moment until she was more foolish than she was when she hopped in my truck. Then I'd leave her in a ball of dust, with my truck's exhaust fumes up her nose and the bitter-sweet aftertaste of my cum dancing on her tongue.

No invitations to my crib were left; instead, most of the random sluts were left with throbbing pussies and one of my many disposable cell phone numbers. Little did they know I changed those app-based phone digits more often than they changed the winning Powerball lottery numbers. Nawh, my house—was mainly for me and my peace of mind.

I walked down the concrete path toward my driveway, the sun warming my skin and fueling my confidence. I was the man. No doubt about it.

That's when the sprinklers kicked on with a sharp click and hiss, spraying me in the chest with cold, stinging jets. I flinched at the icy water beads rolling down my skin, half-an-noyed, half-awake from the jolt.

I made a mental note: *Fix the damn sprinkler system. Cheap hoses weren't cutting it anymore.*

Then, a sharp yelp turned my head. Across my property line, a woman danced around the sudden spray of water. She had light auburn curls that caught the sunlight, denim shorts that skimmed over long, lean legs and a blue v-neck shirt just barely holding back some huge titties. The cleavage was barely closed hanging on by the mercy of one overworked button.

I caught myself staring at that button, half-wondering if it would survive the raucous titty bouncing.

Shaking it off, I sprinted to shut off the spigot by my house. From the corner of my eye, I caught her dodging the sprays with surprising grace and rhythm. Her laughter mixed with the hiss of the sprinklers. The water slowed to a stop, the hose deflated, and I walked back toward her, the lawn still glistening from its unintended shower.

She stood on the edge of the lawn and her walkway's border, her golden skin catching the light just right. I tilted my head slightly, letting the sun hit my eyes. Women always noticed my eyes—amber and seafoam green with flecks of red. When sunlight hit my eyes pussies tended to get wet. I knew it, and I used it.

"Damn, really sorry about that," I said, letting my chest glisten in the fading sunlight. "Overzealous sprinklers, you know?"

She smirked. "Well, that's one way to get a girl's attention."

My eyebrows arched in mock surprise. "Oh? It worked?"

She laughed and replied, "Sorta." During a pause, I noticed her white teeth as she smiled. The attractive stranger asked, "So, you're in 32?"

It took me a few seconds to realize she was talking about my address.

Once I caught on, I said, "That's right. And you're occupying 30 now?"

She nodded and replied, "Yeah, just made settlement on the place recently. Still have a lot of unpacking to do."

We had drifted to the middle of the lawn, stopping just at the edge of our property lines. That's when I got a better look at the beauty before me. Kissed by the sunlight, her skin was warm and golden—smooth as silk. The curves of her face highlighted her high cheekbones, giving her an elegant look but still somewhat down-to-earth.

Her eyes weren't as sexy as mine, but, man—with those big, almond-shaped, cherry-brown beauties, I was sure she'd been breaking hearts for a while.

She had those perfectly arched eyebrows, and her nose was delicate. Her moving lips were full and naturally rosy. The upper lip curved gently, while the lower lip was round and inviting. I thought: *The perfect place to tap the head of my dick.*

I grinned as she spoke about some shit I didn't really care about. But I did appreciate her down-to-earth beauty. She had the package: her eyes, her smile, and everything about her was just magnetic.

After a moment, I realized she seemed to be waiting for a response. Since I had no damn clue what she had been rattling on about, I couldn't reply even if I had wanted, so I hijacked the conversation.

"Well, if you ever think of welcoming your neighbor with a cake," I said with a playful wink, "I'm big on vanilla icing and Medalla Light beer."

The sexy stranger's eyebrows quirked in amusement, and she said; "Not exactly an answer to my question, but intriguing." She put her hand on her hip and asked, "Wait, isn't the older neighbor usually supposed to welcome the newbie?"

"Well, I never play by the rules," I answered with a smirk.

I could tell she was taking a moment to consider both my words and my swagger before announcing, "My name's Amanda, by the way."

I suggested, "Amanda... Too formal for cake-sharing neighbors. How about Manda?"

Amanda tilted her head, her cherry-walnut peepers sparked with amusement. "Manda, huh? I suppose I can live with that," she said before asking, "And what should I call you?"

"Santé... you can call me—Santé," I replied.

"Okay, Santé, nice to meet you," Amanda said before turning to leave.

From her flushed, rosy cheeks, I could tell what I said next caught her off guard. "By the way, next time? It's your turn to get us wet."

As Amanda laughed slyly, I noticed she looked a lot like one of my favorite singers, Mariah Carey. Her laughter had a warm, rich tone. She sashayed toward her new home, her voice fading as she said, "I hope you'll be ready for the splash zone."

Chuckling, I kept watching Amanda walk away. *I'm always ready for the wet action,* my inner voice replied. 'Manda' had a Phat ass, just as I liked. From years of donating dick to both the needy and the greedy, my experience gave me confidence that Manda's ass cheeks would spread easily as soon as she bent over, providing a perfect view as I fucked her from behind.

Suddenly, I remembered why I had come outside—the mail. I marched down the driveway to the curb and reached into the mailbox. My mind was half on the mail and half on Manda. I grabbed the envelopes and kept sneaking glances next door. Amanda was slipping into her house with a smooth, feminine motion that made my dick twitch.

Heading back to my front door, I considered how my new neighbor might add some fun to my life. Those thoughts stayed with me as I stepped back inside my kingdom, the sunlight drying the last water droplets playing on my bare skin.

ALSO BY
Jade Green

The Lust, Love, & Liberation Collection:
Pyrrhic Victoria (Now Available)
Santés Secrets (Coming 2025)
Victoria Rediscovered (Expected 2025)
Karmic Consequences (To Be Announced)
Victoria's Victory (To Be Announced)

The Sisters Series (In Development)
For author updates, censored or uncensored book versions,
or book development news, visit:

StickyNovels.Com

SIGN UP FOR

STICKY NOVELS

NEWSLETTER!

Be the first to learn about Jade Green's latest novels, projects in developments, book discussions, Interviews and exclusive content.

StickyNovels.Com